TALES OF AMBERGROVE

# WHEEL OF FATE

## DRAGONWOLF TRILOGY BOOK THREE

## H. T. MARTINEAU

authorHOUSE

*AuthorHouse™*
*1663 Liberty Drive*
*Bloomington, IN 47403*
*www.authorhouse.com*
*Phone: 833-262-8899*

*This is a work of fiction. All of the characters, names, incidents, organizations, and dialogue in this novel are either the products of the author's imagination or are used fictitiously.*

*Published by AuthorHouse 05/20/2022*

*ISBN: 978-1-6655-6041-2 (sc)*
*ISBN: 978-1-6655-6042-9 (hc)*
*ISBN: 978-1-6655-6040-5 (e)*

*Library of Congress Control Number: 2022909514*

*Print information available on the last page.*

*This book is printed on acid-free paper.*

This book was planned out years ago,
and somehow only a close circle knew the ending.
This is for anyone who has difficulty keeping secrets.

Whew.

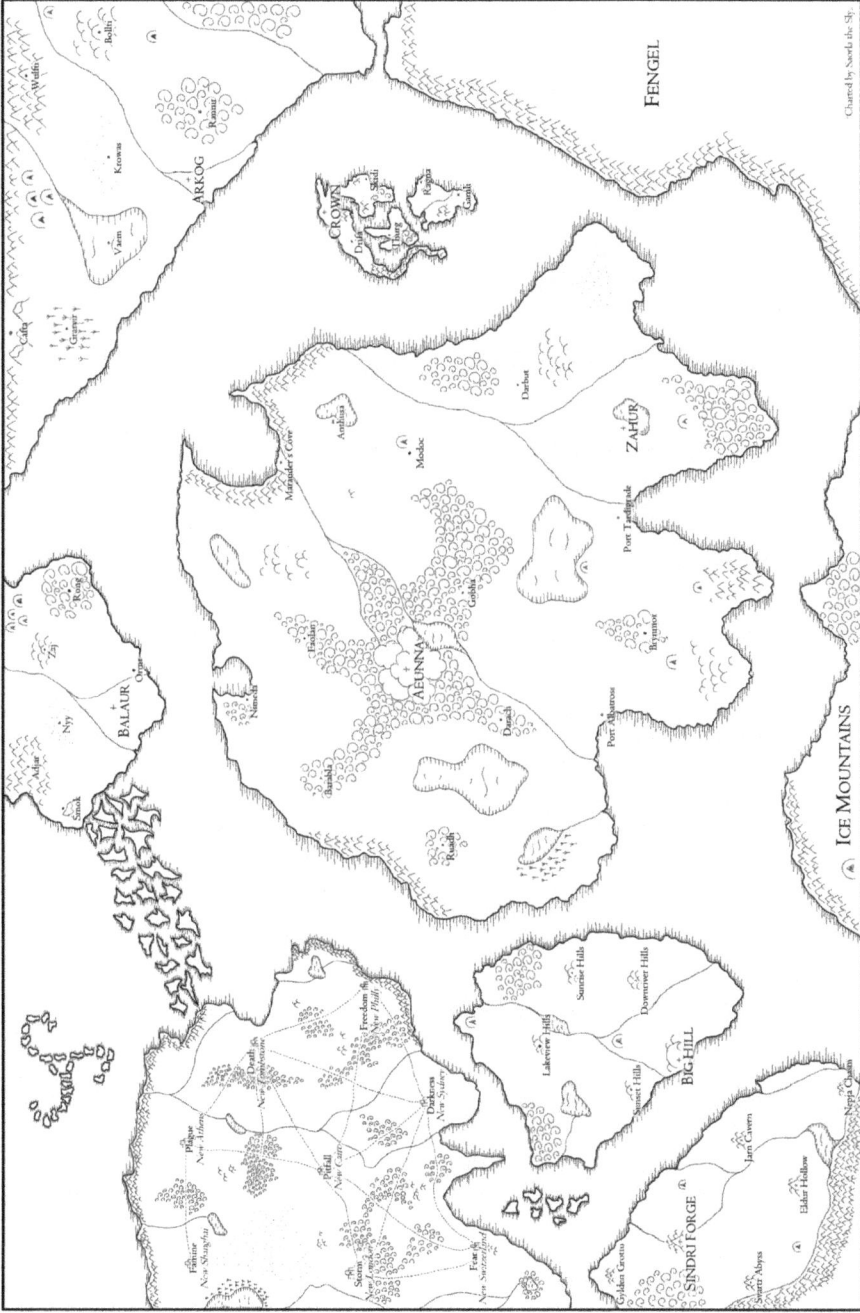

LEGEND  + CAPITOL  • VILLAGE  ⬡ TREES  ⬡ AEUNNA TREES  ⬡ WATER  ⏶ MOUNTAINS  ⏝ HILLS  ⟋ RIVERS  Ⓐ CAVES  ⟍ SWAMP  ⬭ VOLCANO  DESERT

ⓐ ICE MOUNTAINS

# CONTENTS

# CHAPTER ONE

# WHEN THE HAMMER FALLS

Mist had begun to settle on the battlefield as two warriors faced each other. Gurku, the larger of the two, was shaking in his boots. Ambergrove in his time was a world where his people were often unmatched. Standing head and shoulders taller than even the tallest of forest dwarves, Gurku was considered small still—as far as giants were concerned. He was certainly a brawny man, and some of his human fellows who talked of earth compared him to something called a Neanderthal or an Andre.

One thing he knew for sure, as he stood and stared at the enemy before him, was that hill giants were supposed to be tough. Fearless. Especially with the Earthers' unparalleled guns for weapons, Gurku shouldn't be afraid of anything. But those grey eyes staring back at him were filled with the smoke that only came with dragon fire. Looking at the fire-haired woman, he would have thought her capable of transforming into a dragon and burning him to a crisp. He'd heard stories of the southern raiders, but nothing compared to the real thing.

Gurku barely had time to bring his rifle up to parry or to roll out of the way before she came at him again. She was human-sized, meaty and strong. Her hair was collected neatly into a bun in an iron cage. She wore purple and blue chainmail like that of the sea elves, and it was rumored that she had defeated the sea elves' champion when she was only sixteen. He believed it.

The fiercest thing about her wasn't the rumor of her deeds or her stern appearance. It wasn't even the way her eyes burned when she swung her weapon at him. It was *how* she swung her weapon. The giant hammer she wielded seemed to be too large for someone of her size to bear. She didn't have the burly strength a man might—even a human man. It was sheer, impossible rage that allowed her to swing hard and true. She let out a battle shout with every swing, and every swing became harder to evade. She moved with such fervor her hair burst free of its cage and whipped wildly about as she swung.

"This is for Kip!" she screamed, whipping the hammer upward into Gurku's jaw with enough force to shatter the bone and send him to the ground, stunned.

He blinked away stars, and he saw her hammer coming down toward his face before he saw no more.

❖

Mara panted and rested Kip's hammer on the ground. She wiped the spattered mud and filth off her face and collected the fallen bun cage, wrapping and binding her hair neatly in it as she surveyed the area around her. A human, two goblins, and now a giant lay still on the battlefield. *Four more of Gaele's people who will not spread her dream further than this land*, she thought bitterly, looking down at the ringed hand that held Kip's hammer.

It had been three months since her grandmother, the self-proclaimed Great Harbinger, had ordered her men to kill Kip with just a simple clap of her hands. Mara's eighteenth birthday came and went, and she learned that birthdays were not something celebrated in Ambergrove—the last birthday celebration, when Kip had orchestrated a lovely dinner and found a way for her to play DUNGEONS & DRAGONS, was all due to the gnome's love for her.

She had grown to love Kip, too, so strongly that just weeks before he died they had talked about becoming lifemates. His death left a bad taste in her mouth. *Someone has to die for a Ranger trial to be completed.* That's what she was told. But they hadn't completed it. If anything, they seemed to have gotten further from completing it as the months wore on. When Mara had seen that the leader of the scourge in Chaosland—known to the rest of the world as the forbidden lands—was none other than her grandmother, she was sure in that moment that she was going to lose her uncle Teddy. Teddy, like Gaele, was a full-blooded forest dwarf. Unlike Gaele, Teddy had raised

Mara's father, Toren, to be a good man—until he left Ambergrove for a life on Earth with Mara's mother.

Gaele's hatred for her brother surely should have won out, but no. Mara ran those words over and over in her mind. *I, too, have little men who would do anything to protect me.* She was evil, plain and simple. It would have given Gaele great satisfaction to order the death of her brother, but that wasn't the goal of that whole meeting. The goal was to break Mara to awaken her chaos. Kip had moved ever so slightly to place himself between Mara and Gaele when the old woman had threatened her. He was the one who tried to protect her, so he had been killed. What a curse love had been.

*I've got news for you, Gaele,* she thought, *I'm destroying your chaos. I am. And I will continue to destroy your chaos until there's none of it left. You've taken him, but you won't take me.*

As Mara spat at the ground in defiance, her uncle's angry, horrified cursing met her ears.

⸙

Mara and her companions had set up a temporary camp at the southern peninsula of Chaosland near a small stream. While they had spent months raiding supply lines back when Kip was with them, lately they had just been picking away at the patrols that came looking for the southern raiders, and they were careful to stay out of the forest nearby. There were too many painful memories there—though that was probably why it attracted so many of Gaele's followers.

About six months back, Mara's companions had been tortured in that forest. Teddy had a few missing fingers to show for it, but he had learned how to hold things well enough. He'd bounced back. Mara's other companion, Finn, had not done the same. The haggard man now standing next to Teddy with his arms crossed was blue-skinned with long, green hair. He wore the blue and purple chainmail of the sea elves and often wore a thick, dark headband to cover his ears. He looked like a regular sea elf at first glance—and he was actually their prince, no less—but there was a reason those ears were covered.

The past months in Chaosland had been hardest on Finn in many ways, and he was even less tolerant than Teddy about how Mara had been acting.

Teddy, Mara had learned, had the typical appearance of a forest dwarf. He was tall, like a tree, and his body was naturally in the tones of the forest. The russet hair and grey eyes of his family had passed to Mara. The green had not. His deep frown was still clearly visible behind his bushy, red beard.

"This is unacceptable, Mara," her uncle snapped. The green man rubbed his bald scalp in frustration and glowered at her.

"Oh, yeah? What part?" Mara asked as she plopped down by the water's edge to clean the hammer. When she stood and swung the hammer around her to dry it, Finn stood in her path, and his blue skin was almost purple.

*"Every part,"* he said severely.

"I get it. Don't kill the bad guys. Won't do it again," she replied, rolling her eyes as she set Kip's hammer down on the beach.

Teddy strode toward her and grabbed her by the arms. His eyes blazed. "No," he snapped. "We're done with this." He tilted his head toward Finn and commanded, "Pack up the camp. We're heading back to Questhaven. Now." He glared at Mara. "And you are not leaving the island again until I say so. I've had enough."

Perhaps guessing she would bolt, he stood while Finn loaded up the dinghy—this one he called *Cronecrusher* after Gaele's followers had burned *Earthbiter* and they got a new one—and when the elf was done, Teddy hauled Mara onto it and didn't let go of her until they were too far away from land for her to swim back.

❖

They arrived at the camp late the following night, and Finn blew his signal horn when Questhaven came into view. Ashroot, their bearkin friend, would come out to meet them, likely with one or two horse-sized wolves with her—not including Mara's dragonwolf, Keena.

Mara had been seething from the moment her uncle had grabbed her, and as soon as they neared the island, she jumped out of the dinghy with Kip's hammer and strode across the beach, through the camp, and into the forest, passing everyone who was lined up to greet them. When Teddy caught up with Ashroot and the wolves, he dipped his head in apology.

"That bad, is it?" Ashroot squeaked.

The toddler-sized bear was full-grown for her kind, and the way her russet fur bristled at the sight of Mara striding past her and away only served to make her look smaller. Teddy nodded gravely, and he and Finn began wordlessly unloading the dinghy.

*Why is Mama so angry?* Keena whimpered as she followed Finn to the water's edge.

Forest dwarves had the ability to speak to animals—at least those who wished to be heard. Ashroot, as a bear herself, could also understand Keena's words, but Finn did not. He'd gotten used to the others translating for him as time wore on. Keena stepped forward to allow Teddy to load her little saddlebags up with supplies, and he almost had to crane upward to look at her.

Keena was a rare creature—a dragonwolf in terra cotta red with a wolf's body that would one day be the size of a small dragon's. Her leathery dragon skin was reddish black, and she had curved horns, large wings, and a fluffy wolf tail that ended in a small dragon spade. When Teddy had met her, when Mara had brought her to the ship as a gift from the goddess Aeun—a fitting joke for the future Dragonwolf of Aeunna to be gifted a living dragonwolf—the wolf was the size of a normal puppy. A normal puppy grows a lot in a year, but for Keena, that meant she was now the size of an adult horse. When Teddy had last seen her, she was more akin to a pony.

"You've grown, haven't you, little one?" Teddy replied brightly. He gave the dragonwolf a pat on the neck. "She'll be okay, Keena. We'll be sure of that."

Keena bobbed her head, and then she turned and trotted across the beach to the main tent of the camp. Without the need for cargo of their own, the giant wolf yearlings trotted behind her. The yearlings were the offspring of the island's fiercest creatures—an elephant-sized wolf named Fang and his mate, Moon, who had her own struggles when Keena first came to Questhaven.

The Questhaven camp consisted of six tents. The main tent was centrally located, large and spacious, with the galley table from their ship,

*Harrgalti*, in the center. The other tents were smaller, more spread out, and were each home to one of Mara's group. There were also training areas for weapons and a cooking area for Ashroot. Teddy followed the bearkin as she and Finn crossed the beach to their camp.

"How long has it been?" Finn was asking her. "It seems like she was half that size the last I saw her."

"She was," Ashroot replied quietly. "It's been almost two months since you've been back here. That's a long time for a pup."

"That's a long time for anyone," Teddy said.

Ashroot nodded. "You were gone longer the last time you went to that evil place. But ... she told Keena she'd never leave her again," the bearkin said quietly.

"We all deal with these things in different ways." Teddy rested a hand on Ashroot's head. "This is a first for her, and Keena will understand in time."

"It will definitely help to shake some sense into Mara," Finn muttered. He turned to the others, and they stopped. "Who's going to do it?"

✦

Mara sat and let her feet dangle over the edge of the cliff as she watched the water swirling in the spring beneath her. When her vision began to blur, she sighed and stood, walking down to the edge of the water. She rested Kip's hammer against a boulder before stepping into the pool fully clothed—including her chainmail. She reached through her neckline to a secret shirt pocket Ashroot had sewn for her, slipped a worn polaroid out of it, and held up the photo.

It matched perfectly with its surroundings. The boulder, the water rippling against the bank, the willows ringing the pool. Only now, twinkling brown eyes looked back at her, and a pleasant smile stretched behind a coal-black beard. She looked happy next to him, grinning as they both reached out to take the photo together.

As she lay the picture down on the bank, safe from the water, she looked down at the wooden ring around her finger, carved from the strong, shielding wood of a sgiath tree. A promise broken. She clenched her fists, suddenly filled with rage, and screamed her frustration. She strode out of the spring—quite a feat now that her chainmail weighed her down—grabbed Kip's hammer, and began striking at the trees with it.

"How. Could. You. Let. This. Happen?" she cried, emphasizing each word with a swing of the hammer.

She paused and panted from the effort, turning back to look at the spring—at the boulder where he had sat as he professed his love for her. *Curse that boulder*, she thought bitterly, turning the hammer to the stone. She gasped with the effort and was blinded by tears as she took out her anger on the only thing around her that could take it.

Suddenly, she felt a sharp pain in her left cheek. Wincing, she touched her cheek and pulled her hand back to see her fingers stained with blood. Unthinking, she wiped her cheek, and her hand caught a small piece of something in her hair. She pulled it out of her hair and leered at it.

"No. No, no, *no*," she whimpered.

She held the shard in her hand, not reacting when it dug into her palm as she raised Kip's hammer to inspect it. A small chunk was missing from the head. She sighed miserably and groaned before dropping the hammer to the ground next to her, clutching the missing piece to her chest, and breaking into sobs.

✣

Keena trotted through the forest and sniffed at the undergrowth as she walked. She liked the smell of the little critters that scurried on the forest floor, and as she sniffed a tree, her tail began to wag.

*Fluffy-tailed friend*, she said. She shook her head, stopped wagging her tail, and whimpered. *No time for you. Mama needs help.*

She made herself keep walking until she made it to the giant wolves' den. Now yearlings, lanky as they were, Keena and the giant wolf pups were nearly the size of Moon, but they still minded her as if they were half her size. When Keena saw Moon lounging just outside her den while her pups wrestled, she bowed her head in respect before even acknowledging the pups.

There was a yelp as all but one of the pups quit playing and someone's ear got yanked. Moon snarled sharply, and they all stopped to look at their mother. She raised her head and nodded to Keena, and the dragonwolf was immediately tackled. Claw yipped and nipped playfully at a wing and Star plopped down and showed Keena her belly. Keena hunkered down and wagged her tail before a few thundering thuds signaled the appearance of the largest creature on the island.

*What is it you have come for, Keena?*

Fang stepped out of his den and plodded over to his mate. Keena's friends all laid down and quieted in respect of their father. Keena did the same, tucking her wings in to make herself smaller.

*Wise wolf-father, I have come for your help,* Keena answered quietly.

Fang stepped forward and sat regally in front of her. *What is it?* he asked.

She sat up straight as she replied, *Mama came back today, and . . . she wasn't very nice.*

*How so?* Moon asked, sitting up next to her mate.

*Kip, the smaller one, stopped moving and left on a boat a few moons ago, and she has been sad since then,* Keena explained. *Now, she just doesn't care about anything, and the others are getting upset with her. Everyone is upset and I don't know what to do,* she whimpered.

*What do you think we can do?* Moon asked gently. *They are of your pack and their ways are strange to us.*

Keena huffed and shook her head again. *When I was a new pup on this island, and even just this morning, you taught me things I needed to know. You have been here to help me as I've grown and, to me, you are wise and strong.*

Fang tilted his head inquiringly.

*My pack said that someone needs to talk to Mama about what has happened and what makes her sad. I thought that since you taught me things that maybe . . .*

Moon looked kindly at Keena and finished for her, *You'd like us to talk to her about the loss of her mate so we can teach* her *too.*

Keena nodded.

Moon looked at Fang and they shared a moment in that look that Keena didn't really understand. Then Fang growled quietly and replied, *Okay, fine.*

Moon smiled and pressed her head under Fang's chin. *Let's go ahead and go see her, my mate,* she said. As she stood, she surveyed her pups and added, *Stay here and play while we are gone. I do not want you getting into trouble on the island while we talk to the wolf-friend.*

She beckoned to Fang, and they plodded off into the forest. When

Keena turned back to her friends, she was able to see for a split second that the pups had stood before she was tackled into a big doggy pile.

❖

*Your mate would be disappointed in you,* Moon growled. The giant wolf loomed over Mara where she sat at the edge of the spring and leered at her disapprovingly.

Mara blinked, shocked out of her state. "What did you just say?" she asked, horrified.

*You know very well, young dwarf.*

"Well, what—"

Moon lunged and silenced Mara with a ferocious growl and snap of her teeth before beginning to circle Mara slowly. *Do you really think that this version of you is one that he would have wanted?* Mara opened her mouth to speak, but Moon growled and added, *No, gesture with your head only.*

Mara paused and sighed before slowly shaking her head. In all the time she had known Kip, she had never let herself become so consumed by rage. And she'd chipped his hammer. She ran a hand along the weapon in her lap as the wolf continued.

*You feel pain, yes. Your whole pack does. But you cannot be consumed by it. You are a pup no longer. When you are not a pup, you have to learn to put your pain second to the others who need you. Continue to be what he wanted you to be. Yes?*

Mara opened her mouth to speak, and Moon growled. Mara stammered. Moon huffed and commanded, *Fine. Speak!*

"It's just that ... well, I wasn't able to do anything! It just happened! He was in that situation because of me and there was nothing I could do to save him! You have no idea the guilt and pain I'm feeling right now, Moon!" Mara shouted.

*I don't?* Moon asked quietly. *When you met me, my lifeblood was soaking into the forest floor. My pups were being dragged away in cages. Don't you think I wanted to help them?*

Mara blanched. "Moon, I—"

*Of course, I did!* the wolf growled. *But I couldn't! We were out in the forest without Fang that night because I wanted to take them out. I brought my pups into that danger, and I was nearly killed while they were being put into cages. I couldn't do anything for them at all.*

Mara stood and rested a hand gently on Moon's shoulder, over one of her many scars from that night.

*You're not the first person to feel pain, Mara,* the wolf added quietly. *And you are not the only person to feel the crushing weight of this loss. While you are letting it consume you, your pack is coping on their own—and taking care of you—without the opportunity to truly deal with the loss themselves.*

Mara felt a sharp pang of guilt. When she opened her mouth to speak, she heard a rustle from the edge of the forest and turned to see the hulking figure of Fang emerge from the trees.

*You have a task to complete, dwarf,* the wolf told Mara as he approached. *You have come all this way to complete it, and your pack has been through so much. You have lost your mate, but your pack is still here, and you still have a task to complete. If you do not learn to deal with this and keep on living, you will cause the deaths of more that you love, and you will fail your quest. If you fail . . . what would his death mean then?*

Mara stared at him, unblinking, before looking down at the hammer in her hands. "Nothing."

Fang made a quick gesture, like a sharp nod, and then he crossed the clearing in three steps to nuzzle his mate. He looked out over the pool and returned his gaze to Mara. *Did your mate tell you about this place?* he asked.

"He just said that he found it when we first came here," Mara replied, shaking her head.

*That he did, but he came here a few times afterward to talk to the water and pretend that he was talking to you, and when he was here, I told him what makes it so special,* Fang said.

"But how did *you* tell him? Gnomes can't talk to other creatures."

Fang bared his teeth in a wolf's grin.

❖

*Kip paced along the edge of the spring, holding a small, wooden ring in his hands. The crossbow bolts in his hip quiver clattered as he walked, so he paused, unstrapped the quiver, and chucked it into the forest. A growl erupted from the spot, and Fang emerged, continuing to growl.*

"Hey there, Fang," Kip said awkwardly, slipping the ring into his pocket. "I hope those aren't angry growls, because I really wouldn't know the difference."

"They're grumpy growls," Teddy said as he came into the clearing behind Fang.

"Oh, okay. Wait, what did I do?" Kip asked, throwing his hands in the air.

Fang turned and growled at Teddy, who nodded as he listened before turning back to Kip. "This is a sacred place to Fang and his pack—and any other sensible creatures in the area," he explained.

He bent down and picked up the quiver, tossing it to Kip, who looked sheepishly up at Fang. Teddy motioned to Kip, and they both sat on the boulder by the spring as he continued, "Some animals can sense flowing water, did you know?"

Kip shook his head and glanced back at Fang, who still leered at the gnome.

"Well, they can," Teddy said. "There's ample water sources all over this island, and there's so much life here that grows because of this water supply. Fang can sense that here is the source of all the water on the island. He and other animals have traced it back to here . . . but they don't know where it comes from. It's like a gift from Daeda, the god of animals."

Kip turned toward the spring and his eyes trailed up to where the water inexplicably flowed from the cliff face. He'd just assumed it had an underground source, but now he stroked his dark beard and pondered. He heard Fang's furthering growls, so he turned back to listen as Teddy translated.

"This spring is the most sacred place on this island. The animals treat it as a place of new life and blessing. He says—" Teddy paused and looked from the wolf to Kip.

"What?" Kip asked.

Teddy rested a hand on Kip's shoulder and smiled. "He says if you are ready to make Mara your lifemate, this is the place to ask her. Your future would be blessed, and your new life would be unified in the water from the island that soaks into everything."

Kip pulled the ring out of his pocket and handed it to Teddy, looking at the ground as he did. The dwarf inspected it and nodded before handing it back.

"That looks just about finished, son," Teddy said.

"It is," Kip replied. "Now I'm just waiting for the right time to bring her here . . . and the right things to say." He thumbed the ring absently.

"You'll find both. I'm certain of that." Teddy said. "Your bond is strong." Fang bowed his head in a nod and then growled softly at Teddy. "Time for us old boys to head out," Teddy translated. "Just speak from the heart, and you can't go wrong."

Teddy stood and patted Kip on the shoulder once more before heading back into the forest with Fang. Kip kissed the ring in his hand, watched the water flowing into the spring, and smiled.

✢

*The spring has never brought us anything wrong,* Fang said quietly. *Your mate cared for you deeply, and you need to treasure the life brought to you here at the spring instead of mourning what was lost. Use this pain you feel to make things better. Complete your task. Keep the rest of your pack alive. Cherish the life you have until it changes again.*

*You cannot change what happened,* Moon added. *You cannot go back and save him, and your rage will consume you without hurting your enemy at all. He's gone. You need to decide what life you're going to live, and it's your choice to be a person he would be proud of . . . or keep being someone he would be ashamed of.*

With that, the wolves left Mara alone in the clearing. She looked at the water, at where it flowed from the earth itself, and she kissed the ring on her finger. Then she sniffled and strode over to where Kip's hammer lay discarded on the ground, picked it up, and whispered, "You have not fallen for nothing. You were mine, and I was yours. I'll always be yours. I will defeat her, but I'll do it the right way. The way you would have wanted me to. Without this."

She took a deep breath, and then she stretched a hand out over the spring and let the hammer fall into the water and sink. As she turned and headed back to the camp, a wisp of glowing green flowed out from the water source and enveloped the weapon. By the time Mara reached the edge of the trees, the hammer was gone.

# CHAPTER TWO

# ONWARD

When Mara entered the Questhaven camp, she was not surprised to see all her companions in deep conversation around the table in the main tent. When Ashroot saw her, the bearkin nudged the men and pointed. They both turned, and Teddy curtly pointed toward the seat beside Ashroot. Nervously, Mara sat.

They sat in silence for a moment before Mara cleared her throat awkwardly and asked, "Where's Keena?"

"She ran off into the forest after you left, because she couldn't understand why you didn't care to see her," Teddy snapped. Mara looked up to the forest and made to stand, but Teddy grabbed her wrist and hauled her back down. "No," he commanded. "Not until we know you aren't just going to make things worse."

"Mara, we have all been through a lot," Finn said, just as forcefully but a little more kindly. He sighed and slowly removed the headband he wore to cover his ears.

Ashroot gasped. Mara had seen Finn's ears right when they had been maimed, but he had kept them carefully covered since. Ashroot had heard what had happened to the sea elf, but it was the first time she had seen the clumsily rounded ears textured by the jaggedness of the cuts and by the scarring from Mara's attempt to cauterize the wounds and keep her friend alive.

Finn cleared his throat. "This is who I am now, Mara. No matter what you say to try to fix it, this has changed who I am forever. Kip helped me when I was at my darkest. When I was consumed by my fear of guns, he told me a story about fear and what the pain and nightmare can do to people. He helped me to cope with this loss, just like you did. Then he was killed by someone with a gun—someone we couldn't see—my fear out in the darkness. When I turned and saw him lying there, I wished it had been me instead of him."

Mara gasped and opened her mouth, to speak, but Teddy kicked her hard under the table.

"I would have given anything to save him from my own nightmares," Finn continued quietly, "but I couldn't. And you couldn't. All you can do now is hold onto what he did for you—for all of us—and face what scares you with a cool head."

"We have kept a light going through every night since we lost Kip, because he told Finn that a light in the dark can keep nightmares at bay. We have been doing everything we can to make this easier for you, Mara, but he wasn't just yours. He was Finn and Ash's friend. Keena's friend." Teddy's voice cracked. "He was like my son."

"I know, Teddy," Mara said quietly.

"Do you?" Teddy snapped. "Because all of us have been shouldering our grief to help you, letting you go off and be reckless because we hoped you would work it out of your system, and worrying that you were going to get yourself killed. Then what? How will you get justice for Kip if you're dead? Will you doom all of Ambergrove to the darkness of chaos because you can't learn to handle this?"

Mara shook her head slowly. He had no way of knowing Fang and Moon had just read her the same riot act.

*"Then what?"* her uncle shouted. "Gaele said that killing Kip would awaken the chaos in you. You have been unrecognizable since then, Mara. So, what are we supposed to do?"

She looked across the table with watery eyes and whispered, "I've learned my lesson, Teddy. Okay?" She glanced around at her companions' shocked faces. "I'm sorry for the burden I put on you all. I talked to Moon and Fang, too, and I understand now what I've done. I'm not acting like the person Kip saw me to be. I'm going to change that. I need to go find Keena, but tomorrow, we'll come up with a plan to face Gaele the right way. Together."

"Well ... good then," Teddy said haltingly, the wind fully out of his sails.

The men nodded at her, and Ashroot smiled. Teddy gestured for Mara to go ahead and go, and as she disappeared from view, Finn said, "Well, I guess you were right, Ash. We should have gone with the wolves."

He stood and cast his carefully written notes into the campfire, and Ashroot grinned toothily.

✤

Mara found Keena by the waterfall near the center of the island playing with the giant wolf pups. *I guess they're not really pups anymore,* Mara thought, looking at the horse-sized wolves tromping around. They would always be pups to her.

The great nemesis of the pups at this time was a stick. Well, a small branch. They seemed to be playing a game of their own invention, each tumbling to the ground and skidding into trees as they tried to be the one to get the stick. Keena snatched the stick and launched herself over the waterfall. Some of the pups skidded to a stop and others crashed into their siblings and tumbled over into the pool below.

Howl spat and sputtered as he burst out of the water below and swam to the edge. *No fair,* he groaned. *The rest of us can't fly!*

Keena laughed, causing a small puff of heat to come out of her mouth and toast the stick. She dropped the charred stick next to Howl and flitted to the ground beside him. *You can fly. You just get wet when you do,* she told her friend.

Wolf and dragonwolf got into a play-wrestle stance and pranced around each other while the other wolves watched. Mara chuckled and stepped forward to reveal herself to them. Keena tackled Howl triumphantly and looked up to see Mara smiling apprehensively at her.

Keena stepped off of Howl, and then tucked her ears down and hid her tail between her legs as she asked, *Are you still mad, Mama?*

Mara rushed over to Keena and wrapped her arms around the dragonwolf's neck. "Not at you, my girl. Never at you," she said. She began to sob, wondering how there were even any tears left. She clutched onto

15

Keena's fur and willed her pup to love her despite her behavior. "I just lost myself for a little bit there, and I'm so sorry you had to deal with that from your mama. I promise I will never do that to you again. I am so, so happy to see you after all this time, and I hope you're happy to see me."

Howl rolled his eyes dramatically and licked Keena's nose before leaving the clearing with his siblings.

*Of course, I'm happy to see you, Mama! I was just sad*, Keena told her, ignoring Howl's attitude.

"I know you were sad. We're all sad, and that's okay."

*Not about Kip*, Keena said, shaking her head.

Mara pulled back to look at the dragonwolf. "Not Kip? Then what?"

Keena shifted uneasily. *When I was little, you told me you wouldn't leave me here when you left ever again, as long as I was good. I've been good . . . but you left me anyway.*

The color drained from Mara's face. She'd done exactly what Gaele said she was going to do. What was all of this if it wasn't chaos? She had to do better. She *would* do better. There was nowhere to go but onward.

❖

Ashroot sighed as she sat down at the galley table in the main tent of the camp. Relieved to have the meal cleaned up and everything prepared for the next day, it was finally time for her to sit and read her daily diary entry from Maggie Sanderson. Ashroot had savored this diary in the months she'd been at Questhaven. Mara had brought it back after her and the men's first sojourn into the forbidden lands—what they now called Chaosland.

She couldn't ask her friends to risk their necks to return to the Sanderson house in search of another diary, though she would miss Maggie's stories. Yet, when she read the last entry in the book, she realized it must be the last one anyway.

> *November 1, 1889 (?)*
> *Margaret,*
>     *Today is a fateful day. We are being led away from the darkness that has taken over New Switzerland. Mistress Aoife MacThaimis has introduced us to a pagan way that may be our salvation. Today is the*

first day of the Druids' new year, according to Aoife. Many of us in New Switzerland are embracing her people's idea of rebirth on this day to begin building new lives for ourselves.

John Martin and his men have built us a ship. Those of us who have decided to go will be boarding the ship this morning and heading to the fabled land of Aoife's family. She says there are forest men and humans who live simple lives in peace on a continent she just refers to as "the mainland." We will be accepted there just as we are.

She says the people there are a little backward, according to our standards, but they will introduce us to a better way of life, away from the violence and greed that has been set upon Lesser Earth. She says that sometimes if you can't go forward, go back and let that show you the way forward. We'll join these backward people and embrace a sort of life those on Earth gave up centuries ago. Maybe that will lead us forward to a better life.

There's only one way to find out. I have hope for us. I want to leave this journal here to let others in New Switzerland read my story. Perhaps it will lead them forward as well. Anyway, I hear the bells in the streets. They're calling us. It's time to go, Margaret. Today, an adventure begins.

Ashroot smiled. *Someone led Maggie and her family to the forest dwarves and the human settlements nearby. A better life. Hang on.* She read back through the entry. "Sometimes you have to go back and let it show you the way forward," she whispered. *That's it!*

❖

The following morning, Ashroot woke early to make mountain man breakfast, with a little sausage gravy to sweeten the pot, and the aroma shortly pulled everyone from their beds.

As the last of them, Teddy, sat down at the table and spooned some mountain man and gravy onto his plate, he took a big whiff and said, "This smells like a trap of some kind."

He looked suspiciously at Ashroot, and Finn did the same. Ashroot squeaked, "No! No, it isn't! I just ... I have a plan, and I wanted to make sure you were in the right way to listen."

Mara sat upright, scooting her bowl over for Keena to eat instead. "Tell us, Ash," she said.

Ashroot trotted over to where a Chaosland map lay rolled up with some supplies, and Teddy and Finn moved the large pot of food to make room for it on the table. She stretched the map out and sighed, preparing herself. "What was the original plan for stopping the Great Harbinger before we knew who it was?"

"We were just going to find them and fight them. That was basically the extent of it," Mara said before spooning some food into her mouth straight from the pot.

"Kill them," Finn corrected, gesturing to Mara with his own spoon. "We had to kill everyone to get to the Great Harbinger, so the original plan to stop the Great Harbinger was to kill them."

"Just the original plan?" Teddy said bitterly.

Mara gasped. "Teddy!"

"Okay, let's not get into that just now," Finn reasoned. "Let's just go with 'stop' the Great Harbinger."

"Okay!" Ashroot continued quickly as Mara glared at Teddy. "So, we need to just find her and stop her. How did we find her before? Mara?"

Mara's eyes snapped away from her uncle as she answered, "We investigated the entire island and fell into a trap, and they just said where she would be." *They just told Kip where she would be,* Mara added silently.

"Yes, yes. Exactly. And where is the only place you have ever seen her?"

They looked at each other, and Finn answered slowly, "Uh ... just outside Death." He swallowed.

"What are you suggesting, Ashroot?" Teddy asked sternly.

"Well, uh ... If that was the only place she's been seen, maybe that's where she'll be. Or, at least, maybe there you can find someone else who can give you information," Ashroot explained quietly.

Teddy's brows furrowed as he took a bite of his breakfast. Finn stabbed at his with his fork. After a moment, Mara said, "Well, I mean, it is the only possible lead we have at this point. It wouldn't hurt anything to just start there and see."

"It could hurt," Finn said quietly. "Just going back to where Kip ..."

"We'll be prepared. Back to sensible fighting with the crossbows and the ... chainmail," Teddy grumbled. He'd happily gone back to wearing his leather armor after losing the chainmail along with a few of his fingers. "That should be enough. And we'll go in the daytime."

Finn nodded and so did Mara.

"Good!" Ashroot rolled up the map and began collecting the breakfast items from the table. When she snatched at Teddy's plate, he held onto it and asked, "Hey! Ashroot, what do you think you're doing now?"

"W-well," she began, embarrassed. "You usually immediately head off for Gylden Grotto whenever you make plans like that, so I figured you were about to gather your things and get *Harrgalti* back out to sea."

"She's not wrong," Mara said, taking her own plate, which Keena had already licked clean, and placing it on a stack in the center of the table.

Teddy looked at Finn, who shrugged. Teddy groaned and mumbled something under his breath, said "Fine!" and shoveled a few more mouthfuls in quickly before adding something that sounded like "Let's go" and stomping off toward his tent.

Shortly afterward, Teddy, Mara, and Keena boarded *Harrgalti* and Fang pushed the ship out onto the water. Keena was excited to see Hodd again, since he was nice and gave her treats, but Mara wasn't so sure that the grotto could hold the dragonwolf's larger frame. Still, Mara wasn't about to leave her, and Keena wouldn't be left.

They hadn't been back to the grotto since their previous trip to Death, so Teddy had a stack of letters for Freya. When they sat below deck for lunch and he offhandedly mentioned this to Mara, she grabbed the nearest utensil—a ladle—and popped him on the top of the head with it just as his dear wife would have done.

"It has been more than three *months*, Teddy!" she shrieked. "She has been sitting at home for *months* wondering if you're alive. You'd better send those letters out as soon as we dock, put some sort of gift in there, and tell them it's for Express Mail with a claimed value of items to prevent a loving marriage from imploding due to idiocy!"

"What's express mail?"

*"Never mind!"*

Mara threw the ladle behind her and stomped back up to the deck leaving Teddy bewildered. Keena, who had squeezed herself in down there, retrieved the ladle and dropped it on the table in front of Teddy, wagging her tail.

✦

Their ship was recognized as soon as it came into view, so by the time they stepped onto the dock Hodd was there to greet them. Hodd was the leader of the Gylden Grotto settlement of mining dwarves, more akin to the types of dwarves Mara read about as a child—those who lived in tunnels in the mountains. Hodd was the epitome of her former image of dwarves—short, stout, muscular, and thick-bearded.

"Dragonwolves! Brother! It is good to see you well!" he boomed, giving Mara and Teddy each a pat on the shoulder and slipping what looked like a small steak into Keena's mouth. "Does the Great Harbinger still live?" he asked Mara.

"She does," Mara replied.

"*She?*" Hodd asked incredulously. "Well, well. Let me guess—giant?"

"Sister," Teddy replied. "Mine."

"*What?* One of our forest kin is the Great Harbinger?" an onlooker shouted.

A few others began to look at Teddy in disgust or fear. "HEY!" Hodd boomed. "Just because one of our forest kin is the leader of darkness does not mean anything about any other dwarf. Tederen and Mara are still our brethren, and they will be treated as such!" It was an order, and the crowd dispersed.

"Thank you, Hodd," Teddy said quietly.

"It's nothing." Hodd waved a hand dismissively before shaking his head and adding, "I must say, Teddy, I thought you must have perished."

"Oh? Why is that?"

"Because if you hadn't, I would have expected you to be right back here with a letter to tell your lady so."

"AHA!" Mara shouted triumphantly, jabbing a finger in her uncle's face.

20

"Yes, they're here," Teddy replied quickly, pulling the letters out and handing them to the messenger dwarf Hodd already had there waiting.

"She hasn't sent any new ones," Hodd continued. "Probably because she didn't want to send them before you confirmed that you were alive."

"Yeah, probably," Teddy grumbled.

Hodd glanced at Teddy's properly chastised expression and quickly said, "Well, now! What else brings you to us this time?"

"We need to replenish our supplies," Mara told him. "Teddy needs a new chainmail shirt, we could use some more quilted shirts and chainmail repair pieces, and we need more crossbows and bolts."

"The whole lot then!" Hodd said merrily. He called two women over to them and gave them directions before sending them off through the grotto. "Since it's the lot you've had before, I'll have some of my people gather them for you. You deserve some rest and food. Dear Mara, since you aren't being rushed off this time, would you like an escort through the grotto?"

"Oh, I definitely would!" Mara cried. "You know, Teddy told me I'd have plenty of time to explore next time about four 'next times' ago."

Hodd laughed as Teddy made a face, and then he raised a hand and called a young dwarf man over to them. The young man had bright red hair cropped short and a long red beard adorned with beaded braids. Clearly a laborer, his dark, muscled arms and stern face were covered in soot. He stood about as high as Mara's chin.

"Yes, sir?" the man asked as he arrived.

Hodd lay a hand on the man's shoulder and turned to Mara. "Mara, this is Kotr." Mara waved. Hodd turned to Kotr. "Kotr, this is—"

"I know who she is," Kotr interjected with a smile.

"Uh, right. Of course, you do," Hodd stammered. "Kotr, I want you to take Mara on a tour of the grotto. Show her how we live. Once you've seen everything, bring her back to the tavern for a meal."

"Yes, sir." Kotr turned to Mara as Hodd and Teddy walked away together toward Hodd's hall. "Come with me."

The best reference Mara had to describe the grotto was the anthill mold her sixth-grade class saw on a science museum field trip. Someone had made a cast of the inner workings of an anthill and the thing had been on display as a sort of three-dimensional exhibit.

Gylden Grotto had many tunnels and pockets made into buildings or stalls, and each were in levels. The tunneled rooms networked up toward the peak of the mountain and also a great distance below to little suburbs for living spaces and miscellaneous shops.

In addition to the armorer and weaponsmith she'd seen, there were grocers and tinkerers, jewelers and tailors. She had to tour just the pathways this go around because there surely wouldn't be time to browse every shop and she would certainly not be able to choose.

She drowned out Kotr's prattling on as much as she could. She thought he would tell her more about who the mining dwarves were as a people, but the guy sure did like to drone on about himself. "Here's the jeweler. You know, I have a lot of jewels. The people around here envy me. Mining dwarves like jewels, and I have more than everyone here. A lot more."

*Okay, buddy,* Mara thought. *The mountain is echoing with the sound of you tooting your own horn.* She looked up and found him staring at her. "Sorry, what?" she asked.

"You got a man in your life?" he repeated.

"Ye— well ... no," she replied.

"And what does that mean?"

"I did, but he died," she said quietly. She caressed the wooden ring on her finger. "He was the gnome who came with us before."

To her surprise, Kotr doubled over and burst into raucous laughter.

"What's so funny?" she snapped.

"A gnome!" he gasped. "He was a gnome. No wonder he died! Gnomes are so weak a falling twig could have put him out of his misery!"

Too shocked to say anything else, Mara stammered, "W-well there are many different kinds of strength. He was stronger than you think."

"Yeah, well, I didn't spend a lot of time learning my numbers, but nothing and nothing is still nothing. A strong gnome! Ha! Probably died by filling his own bottoms at the first sight of danger. Strong!"

Kotr continued to cackle, and a fire burned in Mara. This unpleasant, unhelpful, and seemingly *useless* man thinks it's okay to just laugh and laugh and insult Kip? *Probably died filling his own bottoms?* Mara heard the gunshot in her head and saw Kip crumple. Listened to Kotr laughing. *Enough of this.* She balled up her fist, leaned back, and punched Kotr in the mouth as hard as she could.

Kotr staggered back and dabbed at his bloodied lip before taking a wild swing at Mara, who ducked. Someone tried to pull Mara out of the way and Kotr hit him instead, and a brawl began. It was ended quickly when Hodd appeared and blew a horn to get their attention. Mara halted mid-swing, though she still held on to Kotr's shirt.

"Who started this?" Hodd demanded.

A burly man pointed at Mara and another man smacked him upside the head.

Hodd guffawed. "The Dragonwolf of Aeunna! Of course!" He came to stand in front of her and a defiant Kotr. Assessing Kotr's bloody lip and puffy eye, he added, "Unfortunately, I can't have you further damaging my nephew. My dear sister would never let me hear the end of it if I did."

"Maybe that would teach him to keep his mouth shut," Mara grumbled.

"What's that?" Teddy asked, squeezing through the crowd to stand behind Hodd.

"You heard me," she said. "He asked for it explicitly. He said, 'Please, dear lady, I would love for you to pop me one in the mouth to teach me not to comment on things that don't concern me.' I was just obeying his wishes, Teddy."

A few of the brawlers laughed. Teddy looked at Kotr and asked, "Was that the way of it?" His voice was tightly controlled.

Kotr scoffed. "I simply said that if her gnomish sweetheart died in the forbidden lands, it was only because he was a cowardly, little boy who—"

Teddy and Mara had both pulled their fists back, but Hodd's made contact first. Hard. Kotr dropped like a bag of feed. Teddy and Mara looked at Hodd in surprise, but the mining dwarf just said, "You don't speak ill of the dead. You just don't. Not the loved dead." He shook his head. "I am sorry for your loss, Dragonwolf. I could see when we met briefly that he had a stout heart."

"Thank you, Hodd," she said quietly.

"I think this calls for a drink!" someone hollered.

"Aye!" someone replied. "To the tavern!"

Teddy and Mara shared a tender glance before following the herd to the tavern, leaving Kotr out cold in the street.

✦

The next morning, Teddy and Mara packed their things early and headed back to *Harrgalti*. Once Kotr was out of the picture, the evening had been grand. Mara ate some delicious meats while the dwarves around her partied and asked her to tell them stories of her adventures. Apparently, she wasn't the only one who'd been wanting to pop Kotr in the mouth. Although Hodd's sister was in Svartr Abyss, they had all been too worried to harm their leader's nephew—no matter how much they wanted to—so Mara's punch suited all of Gylden Grotto. She made many new friends before the night was over.

Before long, they had boarded *Harrgalti* and were speeding away toward Questhaven. When Teddy and Mara picked up Finn and Ashroot at Questhaven, although Ashroot went with them to watch the ship, they didn't spend a lot of time packing and saying goodbye to the wolves, because they planned to return this time. In short order, Mara and the men were once again on their way north toward Death.

✦

*But why, Mama?* Keena asked. *You said—*

"I know what I said, honey." Mara patted Keena's neck as she stood on the deck of *Harrgalti* at the upper rim of Chaosland. "We aren't going to leave you behind again, but someone needs to stay here with Ash, and we need to be sneaky."

Teddy and Finn gathered their supplies below deck while Mara broke the news to her pup, but Ashroot stood beside Mara.

"We'll have a good time, Keena," Ashroot added. "Just you see."

Keena whined. *Oh. Well . . . okay.*

"That's my girl!" Mara said, hugging Keena around the neck before turning and leading Teddy and Finn to shore and away from the ship.

They hardly spoke as they walked the path toward Death. None of them said it, but they were remembering their last journey this way and what it had meant.

# CHAPTER THREE

# PITFALL

In a small cave nestled between two large boulders near the edge of Death, the goblins' guards sat bound and gagged with Teddy standing guard. The pudgy goblin sat alone on the far side of the cave, also bound and gagged, with Finn standing over him. In the center, the goblin woman stood defiantly in front of Mara as Mara knelt and reached for her gag.

"Now, I'm going to take this off of you. Like we told your guards, no one can hear you out here. There is no use screaming, and it will all be smoother if you don't. Okay?" Mara looked at the goblin sternly.

The goblin woman spat and cursed under her breath as the gag was removed, glaring at Mara but otherwise making no noise.

"There. That's easier, isn't it? What's your name, fine lady?" Mara asked.

The woman straightened herself as much as she could while bound, and she flicked her head so her acid green hair fell neatly to her side. "Elizabeth."

"Okay, good. Alright, Lizzie—"

"Elizabeth," the goblin repeated.

"Alright, Elizabeth. I can tell you're of the upper class here in Death. You're sophisticated. You must know people. We just need you to tell us if you know where the Great Harbinger is, or if you know anyone who might know where she is."

"Just because I'm a female doesn't mean I'll give you whatever you want," Elizabeth spat.

"No one is saying that," Mara replied. "If we thought that, I would have had the big man come talk to you. No, I think you can be reasoned with. You're an aristocrat. You aren't part of this dark game."

"An aristocrat?" Elizabeth raised her brows. Unlike most goblins Mara had seen, there were no rings in them. "My blood runs purer than anyone's you have met in this world, human. My family is one of the richest in all of Death. A human from Earth once compared us to royalty."

Mara paused and looked at the woman for a moment before replying, "Okay, but having a lot of money doesn't mean you're happy. Being able to be yourself and do what you want to do means you are." Elizabeth sputtered in disbelief. "What is it that you like to do?" Mara finished.

"I like to learn about Earth," Elizabeth said, as if it were the noblest of hobbies.

Mara fought the urge to laugh. "Well, how about this? I'll tell you one thing you want to know about Earth, and you tell me one thing I want to know about the Great Harbinger."

Elizabeth pondered for a moment. "You tell me five things."

"One."

"Four."

"One."

"Come on, that isn't fair. Three things."

"One. Just one. Take it or leave it. I know lots of things," Mara said simply.

"Fine." Elizabeth sighed and rolled her eyes. "But I get to ask first."

"That's fair," Mara replied, sitting back in a cross-legged position in front of the goblin.

Elizabeth was silent. She looked around her, and she closed her eyes and squeezed them tight in concentration. Finally, she asked, "What is the secret to success on Earth? What makes someone the best?"

Mara shook her head. She figured the goblin would take the opportunity to learn something important. But this? *Typical.* She bit back the laugh as she replied, "Well, there are two things that go hand-in-hand. The first is actually money. The richer you are, the more successful you are—but that still doesn't mean you're happier."

Elizabeth's lip curled into a wide grin as she listened, but she glared at Mara after her last comment. "So you say," the goblin grumbled.

"Now," Mara ordered, "tell me where the Great Harbinger is, and I'll tell you the other thing you need to be successful."

Elizabeth groaned and bit her lip. Then she said, "You will never find the Great Harbinger in a coastal city besides Death, and she has not been to Death since she killed your friend and got her new captain some months ago. Now … tell me what the other thing is."

"But you didn't tell me where she is. I don't know anything I didn't already know," Mara protested.

"Neither do I," Elizabeth jabbed.

Mara glared at her. "The other thing you need to be successful is fame."

"Fame?"

"Yes. Everyone has to know who you are and how much money you have. There's no point in trying to be successful unless everyone knows you are."

Elizabeth nodded thoughtfully, then leaned in and whispered, "Something you don't know. Robert over there has met the new captain and is friendly with the Great Harbinger. You push the right buttons and he'll tell you what you want to know."

"Thank you, Elizabeth," Mara whispered back. She looked up at Finn and called, "We're ready for that one."

Finn brought the pudgy goblin over to the center of the cave and grabbed Elizabeth to take her back to where Robert had been.

"Don't mess up my dress any more than you already have," Elizabeth snapped.

"Yes, that is what's important right now," Finn muttered.

Mara smirked and walked over to Teddy.

"Yes, lass?"

"You need to be the one to question this guy. His name is Robert, and he can tell us where to go." She relayed what Elizabeth told her and quickly took Teddy's place as he strode to where Robert stood.

With his captors all at the rear of the cave, the goblin was attempting to escape when Teddy met him, so Teddy bodily pushed the goblin to the ground, ripped the gag off, and loomed over him. "Robert, I hear you're a man who knows things and won't need too much coaxing from me to spill your secrets," he growled.

"You heard wrong!" the goblin squeaked as he scrambled to sit back up. Teddy leaned in so his face was inches from Robert's. "Did I?"

"Y-yes?"

Teddy turned away from the goblin and began to circle him slowly. "You know, you don't sound so confident there, Robert. Maybe we should just leave you in this cave for a few days without food. See if that changes your mind."

The goblin whimpered. "Now, now, look. Let's not get too hasty, huh? Eh? I don't know much, but I can tell you what I do know. I can do that. You don't need to leave me in here." His lip trembled.

"Okay, then. Tell me what you do know about the Great Harbinger." Teddy stopped in front of Robert and crossed his arms.

"O-okay. Okay. I heard ... I heard that ... she's in Pitfall," he said finally. "At least, her new captain is there. If she's not there, her new captain can definitely tell you where she'll be. The captain will know. Eh?" Robert nodded hopefully at Teddy.

"Pitfall? How will we know this captain?" Teddy asked gruffly.

The goblin glanced at Mara and squeaked, "The captain will be in the center of the city at the barracks or near them. You'll know a captain when you see them, right? What more can I say? You'll have trouble getting in there though, looking like you do."

Teddy scratched his beard and glanced at Mara and back to the goblin. "Yes. Yes, we will, won't we? Looking like *this* anyway."

⊕

They hauled their captives up close to the road and removed the gags. Whenever someone came by, the captives would be able to hear the people on the road and call for help. The guards were hidden in the bushes for modesty, as Teddy had sized them up and decided their uniforms would come in handy for the task ahead.

Before leaving, Teddy leaned down to look at Robert, grasping the front of his fancy shirt and shaking him. "Now, if you tell anyone where we're going—anyone at all—when we're done there, I'll come back for you. And

I'll make sure you have a long existence of imprisonment and starvation. Clear?"

Teddy jabbed a finger into Robert's belly. The goblin squeaked and nodded profusely. Teddy let him go, and he, Finn, and Mara headed off into the forest. When they were a safe distance away, following the road to Pitfall but not actually taking the road in case someone else was, Finn asked Teddy about the uniforms.

"They're for you and Mara," Teddy said.

"Wait, what?" Mara asked.

"That goblin said that we'd find the captain in the center of Pitfall, in the barracks, and those uniforms would fit you two as disguises," he replied.

"But, what about you?" Finn asked.

Teddy scratched the back of his neck. "We can talk about that when we get closer to there. It's a long walk to Pitfall. We can only hope that we pass a patrol and can commandeer a wagon."

"Hang on." Mara stopped and stuck a hand out to halt the men. "We can't just walk to Pitfall now."

"I mean, it's in the center of Chaosland. It doesn't make sense to go back to the ship first," Finn offered.

"No, it doesn't," Mara replied, "but Keena and Ash need to know where we are. And are we just going to walk all the way across this wretched land to get back to *Harrgalti* when we're done? We need the ship close, and they need to know what's going on."

"Agreed," Teddy said. "But we will waste precious time going there and back now."

Silence.

"Well ... we don't need to," Finn began. "We just need *someone* to go that far."

Mara snapped her fingers. "Right! When we were ... captured ... I got an owl to tell Keena where we were and to bring her back to us so she could help. If we can get another bird to help us, they can tell Keena and Ash where we are and where we'll be," she said excitedly.

They followed the road toward Pitfall until dusk before making camp and searching for a messenger. After a few hours passed without luck, Mara and Teddy calling into the forest while Finn searched the map for a good pickup point, a completely black horned owl floated down to rest on a branch near Mara.

*Why do you call for us, dwarves?* the owl asked.

Mara tipped her head to the owl. "Thank you for answering our call," she replied respectfully.

Teddy stepped over to stand by Mara, tipping his head in turn before adding, "We are in need of someone to help us deliver a message to our kin at the tip of this land, so they may find us after we've gone where we're going."

*You have tried long to get one of us to assist you in the many moons you have been here. Nothing has changed. We are afraid of the woman who roosts above all these people. We cannot help.* The owl turned on the branch and spread her wings.

"We understand your fear. We are not asking for your help with her. The only danger in this task is the journey, and Ashroot could pay you well in food when you get to her," Mara pressed.

*Ash . . . root?* She swiveled her head around to look at them. *A bearkin came to this dark land with you?*

"Yes, she did. She is our dear friend, and she is helping us with our quest despite her fears," Teddy replied.

The owl twitched her head around again and ruffled her feathers before replying, *Then I will tell her your message.*

"Thank you for gracing us with your assistance, friend," Teddy said with a small smile.

*I help the bearkin,* the owl said coldly.

"Fair enough." Mara turned around to where Finn stood, quite lost, holding their map. "Did you find a good place for them to meet us?" she asked.

"Uh, yes. Um ..." he stammered. He pointed at the owl. "Can it understand me if I tell it, or do I need to just tell you and you can tell it?"

Mara chuckled. The owl bristled, so Mara said, "Finn, *she* can understand everything you're saying. You can just tell all of us."

"She. She can." Finn bobbed his head awkwardly. "S-sorry about that, miss owl. I didn't mean any offense. I just figured—OW!"

The owl screeched and flitted down from her branch to rest on Finn's shoulder, digging her claws into the skin through the chinks in the chainmail and pecking at his neck for good measure.

"She wants you to get on with it!" Teddy told the sea elf, stifling a grin.

"Okay, okay!" Finn said hastily. He gingerly moved to hold the map out for them all to see, careful to not knock the owl off his shoulder. She dug her claws in further as he pointed at the map, and he winced. "Ashroot can sail the ship along the coast at a safe distance, following the current. If she runs into an area that is too much for her, Keena can help keep her on course if Ashroot just gets a belt from below deck and loops it around the wheel."

Mara nodded. "Okay, that makes sense. But where are they going? Pitfall is in the exact middle. It's silly for us to backtrack to where the ship is now, but it's not better to travel the same distance and speed somewhere else."

"Aye," said Teddy.

"Right. That's where I come in. In all the time we have been on these roads, has there ever been anyone guarding the bridges or rivers?" Finn asked. The dwarves shook their heads. "No, so that's where we'll go. If we go just outside Pitfall to the river here," he pointed on the map, "then we can make a simple, serviceable raft to follow the river to this cove here."

"That would shave over a week off our journey, at least," Teddy agreed.

"Well done, Finn," Mara said. She turned to the owl. "Could you please fly to the northeastern edge of this land, near the Dragon's Teeth? There, you will find a ship with a bearkin and a dragonwolf aboard. Tell them that we are safe, and we are going to Pitfall. They should sail the ship together, as Finn has suggested, down to this cove." She pointed on the map. "When we're done, we'll meet them there. Could you tell them that, please?"

*I will,* the owl replied, spreading her wings and flying off in the direction of the ship.

❖

The following morning, they happened to pass two riders on the road. Since secrecy was less of an object now that the Great Harbinger knew who they all were, there was no reason to just kill the riders. Teddy jumped out into the road and shouted at the horses, making them rear up and dump their riders on the ground. Before the riders knew what was happening, they had been hit by Finn and Mara with the butts of their crossbows. When the soldiers woke up some time later, Mara and the men would be long gone.

Due to his size, for most of the journey, Teddy rode one horse, and Mara and Finn rode the other together. Finn complained about this at length as the journey wore on. He and Mara traded places each time they stopped to rest. There weren't extra stirrups, so the one riding in the back had to hold onto the driver to keep from falling off.

"This is so undignified," Finn muttered one of the times he was riding in the back. "I bet this fancy captain doesn't have to ride doubles with anyone."

"Well, this is Gaele's captain. I'd say being handpicked by my sister to be captain entitles you to all manner of luxury," Teddy grumbled.

"What? You mean this isn't luxurious?" Mara leaned dramatically backward, pressing against Finn and requiring him to grab her shirt tightly to keep from falling off.

Mara laughed and leaned forward so he could right himself.

"I do wonder what the captain is. Maybe a giant. We should prepare for a fight," Teddy said, ignoring Finn and Mara's exchange.

"That's likely," Finn agreed.

"Oh, definitely. A giant would definitely not have to ride doubles. At least unless she rode a draft horse," Mara quipped.

Teddy glared into the distance as the bickering resumed.

❖

"I know, Keena, but we can't just go out there and hope to run into them. I don't know what we could actually do," Ashroot explained.

She and Keena sat on the deck of *Harrgalti*. Ashroot had decided when it was just the two of them there was no reason to try to squeeze Keena below deck to eat, so they just settled themselves in the middle of the deck instead. Keena spread out her wings and huffed as she took a bite of her breakfast.

*But what if they're in danger?* Keena asked.

"We can't do anything to help them if they are."

*I could,* Keena replied defiantly.

"Okay, maybe you could. Maybe. But you're supposed to stick with me while your mama is away," Ashroot reminded the dragonwolf, using the sternest tone she could manage.

Keena huffed again and finished her meal in silence. They were both so consumed by their own worries that they didn't notice when a large bird flitted down to the deck.

*Now, I have been flying all night to get a message to you. The least you could do is acknowledge me,* the owl said testily.

Keena stood, and her hackles rose, but before she could snarl, Ashroot stepped in front of her and held out a hand. "No, Keena. This is a friend," she told the dragonwolf.

*Friend?* Keena whined. She sat and thumped her tail, thankfully hitting the deck with the flat part of the spade and not chopping the wood with the blade.

"Thank you, friend-owl, for flying all this way. Please, what is your message?" Ashroot asked respectfully.

The owl twitched before bobbing her head approvingly. She relayed Mara's message and added, *Your friends said that you would pay me in food for my troubles.*

Ashroot blinked. It was so much to take in. Their friends were going to another city, one they actually had to go into, and they would confront a captain. And she and Keena were just supposed to take the ship to a new meeting point and wait? "Uh ... yes. Just a moment."

Ashroot scurried below deck and fileted a couple fish, cutting the meat into small, owl-sized pieces. She placed the food on a cloth and looped a string around it to tie it together with a slip knot and a loop for the owl to hold.

When she returned to the deck, she held out the pouch for the owl to clasp in her talons. She demonstrated how the slip knot would work—the owl would be able to clasp a small knot in her beak and pull to release the food—and the owl wordlessly took her prize and rose back into the air.

"You're welcome, then," Ashroot grumbled. She shook her head and glanced around for Keena. The dragonwolf stood at the helm and pawed at the wheel. Ashroot shook her head. "Okay, Keena, let's head out to sea."

❖

Finn and the forest dwarves crossed Chaosland at an even pace, and before long, they had made it to the river bridge near Pitfall. Once they'd crossed the bridge, they made camp, searched the area, and Teddy revealed how they would be getting in.

"If you two wear these uniforms and each take a horse, you can tie me up behind you and take me in as your prisoner. With a high-level prisoner like that, we'll surely be waved on right to the barracks and this new captain."

"But what if they just take you from us?" Finn asked.

"According to Elizabeth, she and Robert are important, rich people, and Robert knows this captain," Mara said. "Since we'll be dressed as his guards, all we have to do is insist that he sent us to personally deliver Teddy to this captain and we can't leave until this has been done."

There was a pause as Mara and Finn thought it through.

"Well, I can't poke any holes in this plan," Finn said. "Let's do it."

They donned their uniforms, traded because Finn's was a little small and Mara's was a little large, and prepared to leave. Thankfully, the dark headband Finn typically wore didn't look out of place. They would need to leave their own clothes tucked away at their camp, and Mara would need to leave her axe—since it clearly identified her as the Dragonwolf—but they could reasonably argue that any other weapons they carried were just confiscated from Teddy when he was captured. So, after straightening their uniforms and tying Teddy loosely to Mara's saddle horn, they rode their stolen horses onto the road and into Pitfall.

The city was much larger than any of the others they had seen. Taking root right in the center of Chaosland, it had to be a hub of some kind. Pitfall was like Fear in a lot of ways. Sidewalks and streetlamps lined the cobblestone streets, many houses seemed to be half-timbered and buildings seemed to be Western-inspired. There were factories and tall buildings as close to skyscrapers as they could be. What was different was the people. Not just that there *were* people in a bustling city instead of an abandoned wasteland, but the people themselves were different.

There were no guards on the main road into the city, which surprised Mara, and she thanked Aeun for the blessing. As they walked down the cobblestone streets, the soldiers they saw on foot milling about the city didn't pay them any mind either. Citizens, however, stopped and stared. Kids nudged each other and pointed at Teddy in awe, and he put on quite a little show of being a barbarian as he was dragged into the heart of the city.

Some citizens looked like gunslingers and some wore various uniforms. Some wore Old Western garb and some wore more modern clothes. Mara thought she spotted a well-worn band T-shirt on a child who ran in front of their little procession with his friends before he was promptly scolded by his mother. Others wore fancy clothes more like Elizabeth had worn—aristocrats.

Those Mara recognized to be factory workers shuffled past on their way to or from work. All were clad in navy jumpsuits akin to Rosie the Riveter's, some wore kerchiefs to tie their hair—though they were plain rather than polka-dotted—and all bore steely gazes. Those just heading into the factory wore old, faded, soot-stained suits, and those leaving the factory were covered in soot and grime on suit and skin.

More shocking were the other grime-covered people lining the streets and tucked into the alleys, who wore rags barely held together, revealing how their skin clung to the bone. Their eyes were sunken in and sad. Mara slowed her horse as she passed them, twisting to reach for one of her saddle bags. A thin rope struck her hand and she looked to see Teddy shake his head slightly.

*Of course. Soldiers here wouldn't pity the homeless. They're part of the society that allows homelessness.* She pulled her hand away from the saddle bag and gave an emaciated woman one final glance before urging her horse forward.

"What's this then?" came a harsh, commanding voice.

An exceptionally tall giant strode down the street toward them. He wore the typical garb of a soldier and held his rifle like a man with every intention of using it.

"P-prisoner," Mara stammered.

The giant peered behind her to size up Teddy. "You having trouble with him, girl?"

"We have things well in hand, sir," Finn replied.

The giant glanced at Finn before glaring back at Mara. "You have orders?" he snapped.

"Not on paper," Mara said hastily. "Our master sent us without delay, and we were unable to properly prepare."

"We are to take this prisoner to the captain here," Finn added.

"Get going then," the giant commanded, pointing down the road behind him. "No dawdling around these parts."

The giant stepped to one side to allow them to continue down the street, and they plodded along in the direction of the barracks.

❀

The barracks had a distinct look, and there was a sign outside with the Great Harbinger's bindrune symbol carved above the name. A lone human guard stood at the gate and raised a rifle when they approached.

"State your business!" she commanded.

"We are here to bring this prisoner to the Great Harbinger's new captain. Our master bid us to deliver him to the captain only," Mara said importantly. The guard shifted some but did not lower her rifle.

"You must forgive this one," Finn said. "Trying too hard to impress the boss if you ask me. Our boss *claims* to be on quite good terms with this captain, and it's our hides if we don't deliver the prisoner directly to the captain. Could you inform the captain that we've arrived?"

The guard relaxed and nodded at Finn, lowering her rifle as she did. "I know what you mean. Unfortunately, the captain isn't here right now. She's just gone down to the park. She likes to have an evening walk there. Says it reminds her of home or something. Ya want my opinion, she's a little too green to be the captain, but what do I know?" The guard pointed as she gave directions. "Take the next left down this road. When you get to High

38

Street, turn right. Keep going until you see the trees. She'll be around there somewhere."

"We appreciate your assistance in this matter," Mara said importantly, keeping in character.

"Yes, thank you," Finn said. He opened a small money pouch they had found with the uniforms and tossed the woman a few coins. "Have a pint on us," he said, winking at her.

She smiled and waved them off as they headed down the road and followed her directions.

The park was vast, but it was relatively empty. Lovers sat on park benches, an old man fished in the pond, and park rangers patrolled the area. Mara and Finn dismounted and left the horses at a hitching rail near the entrance. Finn took hold of Teddy's rope and made a show of restraining him as they walked. They carried their weapons like confiscated items just to make sure they were prepared for battle without question.

They asked a patrolling ranger where to find the captain, and he told them that there was a secluded grove just past the fountain where she always stayed. As they walked toward the grove, Mara counted her blessings. With the captain all alone, surely they would be able to at least capture her without anyone else seeing. They passed the fountain and saw a wall of willow trees with branches trimmed back to make an archway entrance. Mara smiled as they slowly stepped into the grove.

The captain sat alone on a bench with her back to them. She wore a duster and large hat like Gaele had, and she was talking. Teddy and Finn looked around in alarm but saw no one. Finn cut Teddy free. Mara was fixated on the captain. Her voice pulled at Mara, but what she said pulled more.

"So, you see, Dad, Sara would really not be able to hack it here. It took me until today to find out there was no nail polish, but you know she wouldn't have gone a day without it. Gramma says that I'm a natural here, and I think I'm doing really well. I—"

A great clatter made the captain pause. Mara had dropped her armload of weapons, shocked and unable to process just what she was feeling or if it was even real. The captain grabbed her rifle and stood in alarm, turning to look for the source of the sound. Her eyes met Mara's and Mara cried out—in surprise, but mostly in absolute anguish.

# CHAPTER FOUR

# THE BONDS OF FRIENDSHIP

A shroot pulled her slingshot back, tilted it upward, and fired it high into the sky. There was a clatter and a great whoosh as Keena launched herself up off the deck of *Harrgalti* and into the air after it. The dragonwolf snapped at the fish as it soared through the air, narrowly missed it, and careened down toward the water as the fish fell.

Keena snatched the fish in her jaws just as it hit the water. She skidded across the surface as she tried to flap back upward at the last moment, but it was no use. She skipped across the water like a stone and then submerged with a great splash. She burst out of the water a few moments later before shaking herself off in the sky and landing back on the deck of *Harrgalti* with a thud.

"Good job, Keena!" the bearkin told her. "You got it before the water this time." Keena shook herself off, as canines do, and Ashroot added, "Well ... mostly."

*I caught it before the water. What happened after doesn't count,* Keena told her. She chomped on her prize briefly before swallowing it.

"No, of course not."

Ashroot grinned and looked across the water toward the nearby coast. They'd made short work of the trip from the Dragon's Teeth down to the rendezvous point, but now a more harrowing task lay ahead—waiting. She frowned. So much could go wrong with this plan, and it was agonizing trying to find ways to entertain themselves to keep from worrying. Keena could only eat so many fish.

Suddenly Keena began to growl. She stood on all fours and her hackles rose. *Someone is coming,* she warned.

Ashroot felt a chill run through her. "What do you mean?" she squeaked.

*I'll go see,* Keena growled, spreading her wings.

"No!" Ashroot cried. She ran in front of Keena and reached out her arms. "No," she said more steadily. "Keena, we have to stay together here. You can't go out by yourself."

*I can handle my—*

"Maybe *you* can, but *I* can't, Keena. You need to stay here with me," Ashroot pleaded. "That's what your mama said," she added, hoping that she was firm enough.

Keena glared into the distance toward the north where a small ship was just coming into view, tucked along the shore. The sail came into full view first. It was bloodred with the bindrune identifying followers of the Great Harbinger emblazoned like a dark stain across it. Keena growled.

"Stay here, Keena," Ashroot commanded.

She scurried below deck in search of supplies. Cloth strips from the storeroom, animal fat from the galley, and the bow she was given when she first left her home. She was grateful to have only used it for training, and more grateful still to have had the presence of mind to bring it along with her on this journey.

She returned to the deck with her supplies and found Keena sitting obediently but growling passionately at the offending ship.

"Keena, come here now," she said. With a huff, Keena obeyed. Ashroot began wrapping the arrows and dipping the cloth in the fat as she instructed the dragonwolf. "Keena, we need to stay together on this ship, okay? Once they get close enough to us that you think you can shoot your fire at them without leaving the ship, you do it. Until then, I want you to light my arrows for me, and I will shoot them. Okay?"

Keena nodded.

Ashroot finished her work as quickly as she could, strung her bow, and stood. In the time it had taken her to prepare, the ship had closed in. She could now see all the crew aboard the ship clearly—the crew and their rifles.

She ducked her head below the bulwark and panted. *Those are the weapons that frighten Finn. Those are the weapons the chaospeople use to wreak such havoc. And now I have to defeat them or lose Keena, and* Harrgalti, *and myself.*

She took a deep breath and nocked an arrow. "Keena, just a little bit of fire here at the tip, okay? Be ready for the next." Keena dipped her head. Ashroot stood. "Now!"

The enemy crew held their weapons, but they were not prepared for a fight. Keena lit the arrow and Ashroot loosed, and it soared through the sail and into the mast. As the crew scrambled and armed themselves, and one of them shouted orders, Ashroot loosed as many arrows as she could. She heard the shouting as the fire caught in the wood of the deck and met with something that made it explode.

She ducked and ordered Keena to duck as swearing and angry soldiers fired their weapons at *Harrgalti*. She heard Keena yelp and felt a twinge of pain in her own ear, and then the shooting stopped. There was more shouting and explosions from the enemy ship. Ashroot peeked over the bulwark to see them panicking, trying to put out the fires with whatever they could. None of them held their weapons.

"Now, Keena! Show them fire!" Ashroot commanded.

Keena growled and launched herself into the sky, soaring high above the other ship and taking a deep breath. She roared, and a great burst of fire exploded from her mouth. She turned her head to cast her flame from bow to stern, and the whole ship was quickly ablaze.

Ashroot rose and hooted, and then a horrid smell made its way to her on the wind, and she leaned over the side of *Harrgalti* to empty her stomach of its contents.

❖

Ashroot was pleased and surprised when they assessed the damage after their first ever ship-to-ship battle. Bullets had pelted the ship, so there were little dings to mark their struggle, but Keena had walked away with only a small wound where a bullet had grazed her tail and barely dug into the strong dragonhide.

Ashroot, on the other hand, had a clean hole through her right ear. She'd cleaned it easily enough and bandaged it, but no matter how well it healed, she would always have a hole through her ear. As she leaned up against a resting Keena and took her watch through the night, she grinned.

She shouldn't be happy. This had been her first battle since they had faced the kraken so long ago. It was her first battle as a leader. It was Keena's first real battle—though her second time going after the chaospeople with fire. She shouldn't be happy to have taken part in the killing of people, but as she touched her ear and felt the sting, she *was* happy. She, a bearkin, had stood on her own in battle and fought for herself and for Keena. She'd successfully won a battle by fighting for herself, making good decisions, and guiding Keena. She'd spent so many years being afraid to act, afraid to fight, afraid of the pain. She looked over at the dark landmass in the distance. She still didn't want to go to Chaosland, but she could feel in her heart that she was less afraid, and she knew that she would not be the same.

She worried for Mara, and Finn, and Teddy, out in that treacherous land, but she no longer worried for herself. She smiled and gazed up at the stars.

Kara's eyes widened and darted from Mara to Teddy to Finn. When Kara looked back at Mara, Mara could see that her little sister was afraid.

"Hey, Kara. It's okay," Mara said, holding her hands out and taking a few steps forward.

To her surprise, Kara stepped back, lifted her rifle, and pointed it at her. "Stay back!" Kara commanded shakily.

"Kara!" Mara gasped. "It's me. It's your sister." She took a few more steps forward. Finn cried out in surprise. Teddy swore. Mara watched as her little sister stared down the barrel of the gun. "Kara, no!" Mara shouted.

But Kara didn't fire at Mara. She raised the gun and fired up in the air. Then she pressed the rifle against Mara like a staff and shoved her down with it. As she made to run, Teddy stepped between Kara and the exit. Finn ran to Mara and helped her stand.

"You alright, Mara?" he asked. She nodded. "We'll have the whole barracks in here soon," he warned. "We need to get out of here."

"You're not going this way, lass," Teddy said firmly, holding his hands up in front of him, close enough to grab the barrel and twist it before Kara could shoot him.

Kara wrenched the gun away from him and swung wildly around to face Mara. Then she charged desperately toward her sister. Not willing to do anything that might hurt Kara, Mara strode past her real weapons and grabbed a large branch and held it up in a defense position just in time to block the rifle.

"Kara, what's gotten into you? I'm your sister. Your family!" Mara cried.

Kara pushed back with her rifle and shrieked, "No, you're not. You're not my family!"

"Kara!" Mara cried, lowering her stick in shock. "How could you say that? I missed you so much since coming here. I didn't leave you on purpose. Surely you know that. You're my little Kare Bear." She brought her stick up to block another swing.

Kara's eyes blazed as she shrieked, "Don't call me that! I know what you do to family here. I can't let my guard down or you'll kill me. You or him!"

Kara jerked her rifle in Teddy's direction, and Mara grabbed the barrel, wrenched it out of Kara's hands, and threw it. Then she threw her stick down. "I don't want to fight you!" she shouted. "I don't understand what's wrong!" The more she talked, the louder her voice became, and she couldn't fight it as it began to crack with emotion and tears began to fall. "When I learned how we came here, I hoped upon hope that I would see you here one day! All I wanted in the world was my baby sister! I figured I would come home to Aeunna when my trial was done and find you there, but I never expected this! What *happened* to you, Kara? W-why are you here? W-why are you doing this?"

"Gramma told me you would try to twist things around," Kara replied shakily. "Dad said I would come to family when I got here, and I didn't come to you. I came to her."

"*Gaele?*" Teddy shouted. "You came to *Gaele?*"

"Haeyla, you mean. She cast out her former life. You. Of course, you would discount that," Kara snapped.

"W-w-what?" Teddy stammered.

"Yes! My true family. And I will never do to her what you did to her. She told me how bad you are! You tried to kill her! You corrupted Mara and made her bad!" Kara shouted, twisting to face Teddy and pointing at him accusatorily.

"What?" Mara gasped.

Kara ignored her, taking a step toward Teddy. "You are a monster, and you tried to destroy Gramma, like you're destroying Mara! But Gramma took me in. She gave me a home and shelter and safety. Safety from *you!*" she screeched. "You will not take me!"

Kara pulled a long dagger out of a sheath at her hip. The blade was twisted and triangular. Mara had heard of those before on a bladesmithing television show. On Earth, there was little chance to survive a blade like that. Here, there would be no chance.

"Kara, no!" Mara shouted, lunging across the clearing and grabbing her sister's arm. "Don't you see?" she sobbed. "We're not trying to hurt you, Kara, because we're not the bad guys. We love you. I love you. Come back to me, Kara."

"Let go of me," Kara grunted, trying to wrench her arm way.

"*No!* Stop this, Kara!" Mara pleaded. "No matter what she said to you, you *know* me. Who bundled you in blankies when you were sick, huh? Who hugged you all through thunderstorms? Who got detention for hitting that boy, Davis, when he bullied you on the bus? Who kissed your boo-boos—real and imaginary? Who has always been there for you your entire life?"

Kara tried to pull her arm free again and shouted, "No, you LEFT! You left me, Mara! I needed you, and you were gone. You've been gone so long I don't even know you anymore!"

Kara grabbed Mara's wrist with her other hand, trying to force her to let go. Looking down at Mara's wrist, she froze. She glanced up at Mara in utter confusion and then back down to Mara's wrist. Her fingers pinched the small, faded bracelet she had given Mara the last time they'd seen each other. She looked back up at Mara.

"You see?" Mara said softly. "I'll always be here for you."

Kara looked around her and back to the bracelet. Suddenly, her brows furrowed. "No!" she yelled. She clenched her fist around the bracelet and yanked.

The threads, now so worn and fragile, snapped easily. "No!" Mara cried.

In her surprise, she let go of Kara's arm. Kara darted away into the trees and out into the main park. Finn rushed after her, but Teddy held him back. They could hear stomping footsteps approaching. Reinforcements had arrived.

"No, Finn!" Teddy said. "We're going to have to fight our way out of here. There's no chance of catching her now."

Mara felt hands shaking her, but she just stared out at the cluster of trees where Kara had disappeared. She felt pain on her cheek, and she turned to look at Finn, who pressed her crossbow into her hands. Teddy and Finn grabbed their own weapons and turned to face the archway just as they heard a shout.

"Here! I found them! To me!"

Teddy fired his crossbow and the whistleblower fell. They backed into the grove and pressed themselves through the wall of trees on the other side. Teddy whistled sharply as they backed away and heard more soldiers filing into the grove.

For a moment, Finn froze. He heard Teddy shouting something to Mara and then the old dwarf's voice broke through his thoughts. "Are you good, son?" Teddy asked. "Are you here? I need one of you to be here."

Finn looked at Mara. Her face was red where he'd slapped her to shock her to the present—to wake her up to battle—but it wasn't in her eyes. *She's not here*, Finn thought. *She's far away from this park, wherever her sister has gone.* He shook his head and clasped the pendant around his neck, pressing the wooden bullet into his palm until his head cleared. "I'm here," he said quietly.

"Good, because they're coming!"

As if it were a proclamation, two soldiers burst through the grove wall, and Teddy swiped his sword across the nearest one's belly. Finn drew back one of his dirks and ran the other soldier clean through as he passed through the hedge.

Teddy tipped his head to indicate it was time to run, and both men reached out to grab one of Mara's arms. She clutched her crossbow, but she didn't seem to take in her surroundings. They heard rustling behind them and a gunshot. A bullet nicked Teddy in the arm, and he swore. They ducked down in some bushes and turned back to their attackers.

"Mara! I understand you're hurt, but you need to fight now!" Teddy shouted, loading her crossbow and pressing it into her hands. "Ready Finn?"

As he set the bolt into his crossbow, Finn met Teddy's hard gaze. "Ready."

They nodded to each other and rose up to assess their attackers. A row of three approached them as they reloaded their rifles—two human women and a goblin.

"Right," Teddy muttered, indicating one of the humans.

"Left," Finn added—the other human.

"C-center," Mara said shakily, rising between them and aiming her own crossbow.

They fired. Hit. Hit. Hit. The soldiers dropped. Teddy whistled sharply again and they ran, glancing back toward their enemies as they did.

"Cover!" Finn shouted as they reached a small creek.

They slid down behind the bank just as rifle fire rained in their direction. They pressed their backs up against the safety of the bank and assessed their weapons in dismay. In their haste, they hadn't properly secured their quivers, so their bolts had nearly all been scattered on the ground as they ran. Only two bolts remained, both in Mara's quiver. She handed one to each of the men.

"Best for you to do this now, I think," she said quietly.

Finn glanced at Teddy. "There's a lot more than two of them."

"We're outnumbered here. That's a fact. We're going to have to fight them hand-to-hand or just run and keep running," Teddy muttered.

Finn looked in the direction they'd been running. There was a long trek left to go before they would be out of the park, and even then, they had no way of knowing what awaited on the other side. But they knew what danger was on this side, and it was not one they would be able to defeat. He returned his gaze to Teddy, but nothing need be said. There was no choice.

The old man groaned and hung his head. "Oh, I hate running."

"We'd better get to it," Finn grumbled. He loaded his crossbow and Teddy did the same.

"Fire quickly and try to take out one of them," Teddy instructed. "Then we'll drop the crossbows and run and not stop running until we're out of this park."

"I'm sure Hodd loves giving us new crossbows after every trip here," Mara said shakily.

"Ah, well. He did say he'd give us whatever we needed, so he opened the door," Teddy answered absently. "You ready?"

He glanced at Mara, who nodded, then at Finn, who nodded. The men sheathed their blades. Mara broke into a run as the men rose, fired, and dropped the crossbows to join her. Bullets whizzed past them as they ran. Teddy groaned and stalled for a moment but continued to run. Finn shouted and swore but continued to run. Then Mara screamed and fell.

They stopped. Teddy's pant leg was dark with blood and Finn had blood trickling down his arm, but Mara lay on the ground and clutched her side. They looked back toward the line of reloading or approaching enemies. Teddy swore and whistled sharply once more, and their horses burst through nearby bushes.

"Finally!" Teddy shouted. "Come on, boy," he ordered Finn.

Finn mounted the first, and Teddy helped him to haul Mara up behind him. Teddy heaved himself up onto the other horse, and they galloped out of the park and away from Pitfall.

⚜

None of the soldiers had stopped to get horses before heading to the park, so they had a sizeable lead once they rode away. With Mara barely hanging onto consciousness and Finn tending to her, Teddy led the way out of the park and toward where they had stashed their belongings.

His head spun. *This is twisted, even for Gaele. I know of sibling love from her younger years. I know of the pain of betrayal from her teens . . . and from the look in Kara's eyes when she looked at Mara.*

He glanced over at his niece, unable to hold herself up on her horse, Finn's arm keeping her steady. He shook his head, and the sea elf met his gaze briefly before nodding behind him. Teddy turned. In no time at all they had already made it almost to the river, but they were nowhere near the bridge they'd crossed to enter Pitfall. At this part of the river, a shipyard was tucked up against the water.

"Right," Teddy said. He glanced up the edge of the river and pointed at a cluster of bushes. "Finn, take Mara there and wait for me. Give me your horse."

"You can't go on your own," Finn hissed.

"I can and I will," Teddy snapped. "Look at her. We can't drag her all over the place. We can't make her ride on horseback out of this cursed land." Teddy pursed his lips as he looked at Mara. "I'll be there and back as fast as I can."

Finn handed Teddy the reins before dismounting and pulling Mara down into his arms. Teddy wrapped the reins around his saddle horn and urged his horse forward and across the water. He breathed deeply, trying to keep himself calm and convey that calm to the horses as they crossed. When the leading horse's hooves pressed them out to dry land, he praised the horse and gave him a moment to catch his breath before urging him forward once more.

When he reached their hiding place, he quickly dismounted and slung the bundles of supplies onto Finn and Mara's horse, secured them, and, groaning at the strain from the shot to his leg, got right back on his horse and headed back across the river.

In the dead of night, the shipyard would be abandoned but for a few guards, if that, so after Teddy returned with their belongings, Finn stayed with Mara while Teddy approached the shipyard. It was a shed-sized building with a six-boat dock attached. Quickly and quietly, Teddy snuck up to the building and looked in the window. There was just one guard inside, and as he peeked around he saw one more on the dock. Easy.

Teddy crept into the building and behind the inside guard and put his arm around the guard's neck, covering the human's mouth to keep him quiet until he passed out. When the guard went limp, Teddy laid him down gently and crossed the dock to execute the same move on the other guard. With one sharp whistle, he alerted Finn, and the sea elf carried Mara to the smallest of the ships in the yard. He laid her down gently on the deck, the men gathered the remaining supplies from the bushes, and they let the current take them away from Pitfall.

Finn took the helm as Teddy went to Mara. They would need to patch up their wounds, but there was little they could do on a moving ship, in the dark, while fleeing certain death. She groaned and stirred as he peeled the uniform shirt back to examine her belly, and her eyes snapped open.

Mara felt her wrist for the friendship bracelet her sister had made her. Since coming to Ambergrove, fiddling with it had given her such comfort, but there was just a light ring on her skin where the bracelet had been. It was really gone. Her eyes filled with tears as she turned to look at Teddy.

"I know," he said softly.

He reached down to hold her as she cried, and she stared miserably back at Pitfall as it grew further and further away ... and her dear sister with it.

# Chapter Five

# The Bonds of Family

Once the ship had floated far enough downriver, past the only real kink in the stream, they tended their wounds. They'd been wrapped, at least, to stem the blood flow and keep them clean. Upon further inspection, Teddy's shot to the leg was little more than a graze. He quickly slapped some poultice on it and covered it back up.

Finn had been shot in the meat of his left shoulder. The bullet had gone clean through, so Teddy quickly cleaned the wound and stitched it closed, commenting that a few more to the same spot and the scarring would be its own armor. They tiptoed around Mara as they worked. The sky was just beginning to brighten with the promise of sunlight, and Mara had cried herself to sleep not long before. Finn and Teddy wouldn't risk waking her by talking, but now they needed to take the opportunity to care for her wound. She stirred as Teddy pulled the uniform shirt back and began to remove the hastily-applied bandage.

"M-my sister, Teddy. How could this have happened? What did Gaele do to her?" Mara whispered.

Teddy pressed his hands into Mara's side and felt the hard mass of a bullet. He clenched his jaw. She still had a bullet in her side, and there was no way they could extract a bullet on a boat. They would have to wait until they got back to Questhaven. Thankfully, it wouldn't take them more than another day to get to the cove, and they could get to Questhaven soon after on *Harrgalti*.

"Gaele got to her, Mara," he said softly.

Teddy sighed and began preparing the wound.

"But how?" Mara pressed, "Why didn't she go to Aeunna? She should be safe at home with Freya, waiting for us to get back. She should be eating Freya's muffins Dad used to make for us and training with Cora and being judged by Aengar—all of it. Just *safe* there."

"That's not how it works, Mara," Teddy said.

"What do you mean?"

He sighed and rubbed his neck, taking what time he could to clean the wound before answering, "When someone comes to Ambergrove from Earth or to Earth from Ambergrove, they don't go to a particular place, they go to a particular person—their family."

"But—ah—but why would Kara go to Gaele? I'm the closest family she has! She should have come to me! Or to you, like I did. Dad didn't even know his mother," Mara said bitterly.

"I have a theory about that," Finn interjected. He turned to look at them from the helm. "That night when— when we met Gaele, you two and her were in the same place in the middle of the night."

"Meaning?" Teddy asked, pausing with the jar of Freya's poultice in his hand.

"We all left at the same time, and none of the three of us turned back. What if Gaele did? What if that night, your sister appeared at that camp, coming to you, but you just didn't see her?" Finn asked.

"Ohhh ..." Mara made a heartbroken sound and looked miserably up at Teddy. "We just left her there, Teddy. Gaele had just killed Kip. Who knows what she might have done to her? And we just left her there!"

"Hey, now." Teddy cupped Mara's cheek and wiped a tear, casting a sideways glance at Finn before turning back to her and beginning to apply the poultice. "We had no way of knowing what would happen, and it is not your fault whatever did happen. Gaele poisoned her on her own, just like she tried to poison you. She saw Gaele and not us. No matter the story, aren't you more likely to believe the first person you heard it from?"

"Based on what she said to you, Gaele painted Teddy as a murderous, poisoning monster and you as a lost soul he brainwashed—someone who cannot care for her anymore," Finn said. "Ironic that she described exactly what she's doing to Kara." He shook his head and looked back across the water.

"If Gaele got to her first, how am I going to get through to her?" Mara asked quietly. "To be perfectly honest, right now I don't care about stopping Gaele. I just want to save my sister."

She tried to sit up, and Teddy pushed her down and began wrapping her wound, corking the opening so it wouldn't seal before they got the bullet out. "That's what Gaele wants, Mara," he said gently. "She wants you to lose focus and let her go on with her schemes."

"I don't *care* what she wants!" Mara repeated, dropping her head back to the deck in exasperation. "The way she looked at me, Teddy. My Kare Bear. I just want to fix this."

"We will," Finn reassured her. Teddy turned to glare at him. "I'm not saying it will be easy," Finn added hastily, "but we will."

Mara nodded miserably and felt again for the bracelet on her wrist. "I can't believe she took it."

"Maybe it's good that she took it," Teddy said.

"How?" Mara asked, leaning forward again. This time, Finn removed his uniform shirt and chucked it at Teddy, who stuffed it behind her for support.

Teddy sat back and took Mara's hand, twisting the wooden ring on her finger to reveal the tiny bindrune. "Do you remember what I said about the necklace Kip had made for you? What it meant?"

"Yeah, you said that there was a little bit of both of us in it and that it was meant to bond us forever. What does that have to do with this?"

"How did you get that bracelet, lass?" Teddy asked.

"Kara gave it to me on my sixteenth birthday. It's a friendship bracelet. It's a thing kids make that means you're supposed to be friends forever," she explained.

"So, it's a symbol of your bond," Teddy said.

"Yeah, I guess it is," Mara replied.

"Now, Mara, Kara made that as a present for you, as a way for you to remember every time you looked at it just how much she loves you and what bond of family you share. Nothing we said to her got through to her. Nothing. But when she saw that bracelet, she stopped. That stopped her.

It made her think for just a moment. ... So, what could she be thinking now?" Teddy finished.

"Even though she took it, that bracelet is a bond that will keep the two of you together," Finn added.

"Kara will know that. She will," Teddy said softly.

"And if she doesn't?" Mara asked.

"She will." Teddy patted Mara on the arm before standing. "Now, you get some more rest. We'll meet up with Ash and Keena soon and be back to Questhaven to get you patched up. We'll figure something out then."

Teddy turned and met Finn's worried gaze—one that mirrored his own.

⊕

A flying mass of fur met their little ship before they spotted *Harrgalti*. Keena was so excited to see them, she nearly tipped the little Pitfall boat over in her excitement. It was too light to hold her, so Teddy tied a rope to the front of the ship, let her take the other end in her mouth, and she pulled the ship the rest of the way to *Harrgalti*.

Ashroot dropped the anchor so she could try to help them switch over, but they couldn't climb onto *Harrgalti* with their injuries. Especially not Mara.

"You have to be very nice and still, Keena," Teddy said firmly.

She stood very still on the deck of their little ship as Teddy hefted Mara onto her back. When her mama was safely on, Keena gently flew up to land on *Harrgalti*. She laid down on the deck so Ashroot could help Mara off—if just to slide her onto the floor until the men boarded—and Keena went back for Teddy and Finn.

"What *happened*, Mara?" Ashroot asked.

Mara opened her mouth and closed it a few times, unsure of what to say. "My sister," she said finally. "My little sister, Kara, came to Ambergrove and is in the clutches of my grandmother. She pointed a gun at me, and she tried to kill Teddy. She hates us, and she's in so much danger."

"Ashroot! Need your help with this!" Teddy called.

Ashroot left Mara on the deck and ran to help Finn as Teddy raised the anchor. Before casting off, Keena let out a great roar and set the smaller ship ablaze. They would not bring something like that back to Questhaven for fear it would put them in greater danger. Mara watched the smoke rising as she fell back asleep.

⊕

When Mara woke, the sun was peeking out over the horizon, and Fang was hauling *Harrgalti* onto the beach at Questhaven. She rode on Keena's back all the way to the main tent, and Finn and Teddy laid her on the table while Ashroot scurried around to prepare a sedative tea and tools for surgery.

The process would be much like what Mara had done when Finn had been shot in the belly. Teddy would have to remove the dead tissue, open the wound enough to see and remove the bullet, repair any damage, and stitch her back up. Teddy had to hunt for the bullet, but that was because it had missed Mara's organs and had been moving around in her belly.

He made sure she was free of infection, added a disinfecting poultice for good measure, and stitched her back up before carrying her to her tent and laying her gently in her bed.

⊕

The next time Mara woke, Teddy was sitting in a chair by her bed. He'd brought the writing table into her tent and had various materials strewn across it. She stirred, and he stood and helped her to sit up before returning to his chair.

"What's all this, Teddy?" Mara asked weakly.

Teddy patted the writing table. "Ah, well, this is a few things. I've written to Freya about what it is we've discovered. I'll be heading out to Gylden Grotto shortly to pass that along to her. But before I do, I … uh … have something for you. Something from your da."

"From my dad?" Mara's eyes widened. "How do you have something from my dad? Did Kara—"

"No, no, these aren't from Kara," Teddy replied quickly, grimacing as Mara's face fell. "Your da—your dad—sent quite a few letters and things with you that were to be given to you at specific times. You know about some of them. This is a small thing that Toren told me to give you if you ever lost all hope. I considered giving it to you after Kip's death, but I didn't see how it would help then. This is better anyway."

He handed Mara an envelope. On the seal, it said: *For when things seem most dark.* She gently ripped it open and tipped it toward the bed. Out tumbled little, plastic, glow-in-the-dark stars, like the kind she used to have on her ceiling when she was little. She picked one up and cracked a small smile before enclosing it in both hands and peeking in to see if it still glowed. It did.

She peeked inside the envelope to find two more items. First was a picture of Mara, Kara, and Toren using a candle to roast marshmallows in a makeshift fort underneath those plastic stars. Kara couldn't be much older than five. The other was a short note:

> Mara,
>
> The time will come when things will seem hopeless. This always happens on a Ranger trial. When you're faced with the darkness, remember this. This was the night of that awful storm that took out the neighbor's house. Sara and your mother had gone out and were sheltered there, but you, me, and Kare Bear hunkered down at home. You both were so scared of the storm, but we stuck together. We got through it together, and these stars lit our way when nothing else could. Don't be afraid to go back to your roots, Mara. Sometimes the childish thing is the right thing. Sometimes the light comes when you make it. Don't ever lose hope.
>
> —Dad

Mara smiled and wiped away the tears running down her cheeks. "He always did know the right thing to say," she said shakily, handing Teddy the note and picture.

Teddy looked down at it and gently traced the features of Toren's face. Two little girls with missing teeth and chocolate on their faces squeezed their dad from either side. "You all look happy," Teddy choked.

"We were. I wish I could get that day back. I wish I could remind her what we are to each other before it's too late," Mara murmured.

"Maybe you can," Teddy said, glancing over the note. "Maybe it's all in here, if you just look for it." He handed note and picture back to her.

"But I'll tell you one thing—Gaele and I never had any moments like that. Never. Even before we lost our parents. She's never been warm. We never acted like this—like we loved each other. She doesn't have that warmth in her, and although she's good at pretending, Kara will have to see that the love she pretends to have for your sister doesn't reach her heart."

Mara looked at the picture, flipping it to the back in search of some hidden answer. "I guess so," she said quietly.

"Well, let's just get you mended first and then we'll find out what to do to make things right. I understand why your top priority now is saving your sister—as it should be—but we do have to make sure we don't sacrifice our cause in the process, you hear?"

"I hear you, Teddy," she whispered.

"Right then." Teddy stood and patted his legs. "You get some rest and think on what your da has told you. I'm going to take this to the grotto for Freya." He held up his letter and gave her a reassuring peck on the forehead before leaving the tent.

*What a mess*, Teddy thought as he steered *Harrgalti* toward Gylden Grotto. He patted the letter at his chest. *It will break her heart to learn she has another niece here, and that Gaele has her hooks in the girl. Maybe she can think clearly where I can't. Maybe she'll know what to do.* He grimaced. *Toren. Our Toren would be devastated to see his daughters at odds, but what can we do to stop it? How do we save her without discarding the goddess's mission?*

"A sign would be appreciated!" Teddy shouted into the empty sky. Nothing but silence answered him. "Of course, it doesn't matter," he muttered.

Suddenly he heard flapping and turned just in time to duck as a giant owl landed on the ship's wheel. Teddy straightened and looked the owl over and noticed something human about her—and something very feral. Then she said, *I am not at your beck and call, my son.*

Teddy's eyes widened, "G-goddess, I never—"

*Of course, you never,* the owl snapped. *I borrowed this owl friend so I can get you a message and prevent you from running this quest off the rails in your own shortsightedness.*

"But, Goddess, she's my niece," Teddy said quietly.

*You realize you are talking to the mother of the forest dwarves—both those girls included? Don't tell me what is at stake.*

Teddy avoided the owl's gaze. "But what about Kara? And the mission?"

The owl shifted her feet and dug her claws into the wheel. *I cannot say. Mara is forbidden advisement on a Ranger trial. Just . . . don't think you have to throw away one mission for the other. Perhaps the final goal is one and the same, and to complete one is to complete the other.* She paused. *Perhaps.* She spread her wings. *Don't call on me again until the forbidden lands are free.*

The owl flapped her wings just once before disappearing, leaving Teddy more bewildered and grumpy than if she hadn't appeared at all. He was still scowling when he steered *Harrgalti* up to the familiar docks.

If Hodd was surprised to be seeing Teddy again so soon, he didn't mention it when he strode up to meet the green man when he arrived at Gylden Grotto. A messenger was already ready to take the letter from Teddy, and the bald man gladly passed it off.

"No dragonwolves this time?" Hodd asked as he clasped arms with Teddy.

"Not this time," Teddy replied.

"Should I be worried about them—or you?"

Teddy shook his head. "Worrying helps no one. We are in a predicament, but the dragonwolves are safe and sound. Well, they were when I left them."

"Come, brother, and tell me what ails you." Hodd stretched a hand up to Teddy's shoulder and guided the big man back to his hall.

Although Teddy knew he could trust the mining dwarves as their brethren, especially Hodd, he also knew that too much information told to anyone can only do harm. As he sat opposite Hodd at a small table and drank a warm drink, he told Hodd what he would.

"We went looking for whereabouts of my treacherous sister," Teddy explained. "We got the information we needed and traveled inland only to find it was someone else we knew. A friend—a good person my sister is taking advantage of."

Hodd took a sip of his own drink and swallowed. "Aye? How so?"

"She's young. Only a teen. She was confused, lost, and alone. Gaele took advantage of that and poisoned her mind into thinking that we're the bad ones, and she's her, well, family, so to speak."

"I see. Is there no getting to her? Even with a message from a bear or a hedgehog or something?"

"No, no. She's not a true forest dwarf." Teddy shook his head. *At least, not yet.* "We'd need to communicate with her some other way—but we can't send a messenger like I do here because it's not safe. Who knows what Gaele would do to your messenger, if you even found someone willing to go?"

Hodd took another sip of his drink then leaned back and stroked his beard. "I'm sure there would be someone up for the task here, but risking another's life on a mission he won't come back from—one with low odds of success—is not a decision a leader makes."

"Too right," Teddy said quietly. "I'm sure we'll find another way ... somehow." Teddy stared into his drink, thinking of what the goddess had told him. He dimly heard Hodd speak, and he shook his head and looked up. "What was that?"

Hodd chuckled. "I was saying that I'm sure those people in the forbidden lands use some other form of communication that we aren't aware of. Some fancy Earth thing. Perhaps if you could get into a city and see how they run, maybe you can figure out a way to send her a message their way, and their people will be none the wiser."

Teddy blinked and grinned at Hodd, then he raised his mug, and they clanked their mugs together. "Hodd, brother, I think that may just work."

✦

*Mama, I don't think this is a good idea,* Keena whimpered.

Mara lay across Keena's back as the dragonwolf slowly walked through the forest. "It's okay, Keena—ah." She winced at a twinge of pain in her stomach. "This is what I need to do to figure things out. You trust me, don't you?"

Keena whimpered and tucked her tail between her legs as she walked. They didn't speak again until Mara could hear flowing water. She instructed Keena to let her get down at the edge of the spring, and then Mara sat on the ground with her back to the boulder.

*Help me now,* Mara thought. *Whatever god or spirit watches over this spring, help me now. Help me find a way to save my little sister.*

Keena paced in a circle a few times before laying down, and soon she was asleep. Mara's thoughts ran away with her as she pondered what Kara had said, what Teddy had given her from her father, and what Fang had told her about the power of the spring. She begged for some sort of help or sign to show her what to do, but the night was silent.

She leaned over to look in the pool, hoping to find some small comfort in the sight of Kip's hammer—but she couldn't see it. The water wasn't murky. Where could it have gone? She began to panic. If this last piece of Kip was gone, maybe Kara would be gone too. That wasn't the sign she wanted. Surely the hammer was around there somewhere. She pulled herself to the edge of the pool and slid into the water.

She groped around for it, whimpering softly the longer she searched, sticking her head underneath and trying to see, but she saw nothing. No sign at all. Finally, she stopped searching. She guided herself to the edge of the water and sat, leaning her head back against the rocks, and she stared up at the stars as her vision blurred.

Eventually, she began to see the glow-in-the-dark stars in the sky instead of real ones. So many shapes danced before her eyes. When she looked down, she sat at the edge of a campfire. It was familiar. She felt a warm hand in hers and turned to see the impossible. Kip looked back at her and smiled.

"What's wrong, Mara?" a man's voice said.

Mara turned to see her dad sitting across from her on the other side of the fire. "Dad! Dad, it's me!" she cried.

He didn't seem to hear her. He gestured to the empty spot on the log next to him, and Kara appeared there. "I didn't want Kara to be here on her own," he said. "I came with her to make sure she got here safe."

As he squeezed Kara, Mara shook her head. None of this was right. She turned to Kip, but he was gone. It was dark, and her hand was empty. "Daddy!" she cried out. It was a child's voice.

She saw him appear in front of her, not in a forest, but in her bedroom. He held a little Kara in his arms. "There's a storm coming," he said. "Come with me and Kara. We'll be safe together, I promise."

Mara took his hand, and her surroundings changed again. A scented candle sat in front of her. Her hand was sticky with melted marshmallow as she held a fresh one in her hand and a stick in the other.

"I can't get it, Daddy!" Kara cried.

Mara watched as her dad put Kara's marshmallow on a stick for her and held her hand out over the candle. Mara stuck her tongue out in concentration as she stuck her own marshmallow on the stick and held it out next to Kara's. She watched in awe as the marshmallow browned and then blackened and caught fire. She pulled the stick away and held the marshmallow toward her face, trying to blow the fire out.

"It's too hot, Daddy!" she cried. She could feel the heat all over her body, and she looked around for help to make it stop, but she couldn't see her daddy anymore. "Daddy! Daddy, it's too hot! It's too hot!"

❖

"Calm down, Keena! I don't know what the problem is, and you dragging me all over the island is not going to help!" Finn cried.

Keena had his shirt sleeve in her mouth as she whimpered and pulled him to a part of the island he'd never been to before. They came to a clearing, and he could hear groaning, but he couldn't see anyone. He lurched forward toward the sound, but Keena yanked him back just before he tumbled over a cliff. He looked down.

"Mara!" he called. He rushed around to the edge of the water and jumped in. "Keena, what's she doing in the water?" he shouted.

"It's too hot. It's too hot," Mara murmured.

Finn felt her forehead and swore. The water was cold, and she had an open wound. A fever was burning inside of her, and the person who could best help her was out at sea. He hauled her up out of the water and hefted her onto Keena's back. They walked back to camp, and he held onto Mara as she tossed on Keena's back, stuck in some kind of nightmare.

"It's alright, Mara," Finn told her. "We're heading back home."

"Home," Mara muttered. "Home. I'm home. Daddy, where are you? Where's sissy? Sissy? Kara!" she cried.

Finn just looked at her in alarm as she shivered and he hoped upon hope that the fever would bring her sister back to her when no one else could—and that when he got back to camp, he and Ashroot could bring Mara back to *them*. As he listened to her cries, he quickened his pace.

# Chapter Six

# Kara

Rain began to pour as Kara rode her horse through the walls of her grandmother's stronghold and up toward the manor house. She made herself smile as citizens of the capitol approached to greet her, hurrying as best she could up the cobbled streets and to the boundaries of her grandmother's home. She had never been good at pressing forward when people wanted to talk to her. She nodded to the guards as she rode past them and continued up to the stables. A goblin man in worn work clothes appeared as she led her horse into his stall.

"How are you today, princess?" the goblin asked.

Kara dismounted and patted her horse. "Fine, Steve," she said with a sigh. "And don't call me princess."

Steve cackled. "Oh, no!" He held his hands up in mock defense. "When a woman says she's fine, a war is about to start. Do me a favor, will you? Just don't hurt my horses, prin—captain." He grinned toothily at her and scurried away to greet a guard returning a horse to another stall.

Kara sighed and turned to begin untying her saddle. "What am I going to do, Flintlock?" she asked the horse. Flintlock whinnied and lipped at her arm. She sighed. "Yeah, I don't know either."

She heaved the saddle and blanket from his back and hooked it over the stall door. His whole back was slick with sweat. She grimaced. After she'd seen her sister, Kara got on the horse and rode, and she kept riding until she got to her grandmother's home. She grabbed a pail and rag and began wiping the horse down, feeling a pang of guilt to have pushed him so hard.

*What now?* she wondered. *What am I going to say to her when I see her? I wasn't supposed to be back for another week. Will she be happy to see me or will she scold me for leaving my post? Will she tell me the truth when I ask?*

Flintlock nudged her and whinnied. "Okay, okay," she said, setting down the pail and picking up a towel. She rubbed him down and brushed him, and by the time she was done, Steve strode by and pressed something into her hand before continuing on his way with her saddle in tow. How he could lug saddles around all the time when they were half his size, she would never understand. She shook her head and gingerly fed the horse his apple slices before giving him one last pat and leaving the stall, nodding to Steve as she went.

As Kara began the final trek up to the manor house, she looked back down at the city sprawling below. The city was like its own little mountain, and the way the streets wound around with the leader's home at the peak in the center reminded Kara of the greatest city in classic fantasy books. It wasn't made of white stone like that one, but the Earth-like city rose high into the sky and seemed mighty. She wanted this city to be like that one. It was the roost of a ranger who became a king, a classic hero who would lead the people well. *Isn't it though? Isn't Gramma good?* Kara asked herself.

Soon, she would find out. She'd summon the courage to ask her grandmother the truth about Mara and about Teddy. Kara stretched her gaze past the buildings and to the fields beyond. Far in the distance she could see the blackened land that was so common here—the bare trees and decaying life. Around the capitol, however, there was so much green and so many colors. Farmland stretched out in a ring around the city, and she could barely see the dots of the draft horses working in the fields. One of her favorite places, a flower meadow to the east, was beautiful even miles away.

Kara sighed and turned her gaze to the manor house. One of many surprises upon her arrival to Ambergrove and her grandmother's kingdom was that the Great Harbinger didn't live in a castle. She was sure the land would be full of castles. Even after she learned that this land followed a skewed view of Earth, she was still surprised to see the manor house. It looked to her like something an English lord would live in, and when she first approached the house, she did imagine for a moment what it would be like if her own Mr. Darcy emerged from it. Or Bingley. He was nice too.

She shook her head at the memory. So much had changed in her these past few months in Ambergrove. The romantic nonsense of a silly teen had abandoned her after just a few days living here. She wasn't that girl anymore. She sank a hand into her pocket and thumbed the worn bracelet she'd taken back from her sister, and she blinked back tears. Apparently, this land had changed everyone.

She willed her feet forward. Following a loose stone road, it was about a quarter mile up to the manor house from the stables. She could see a line of soldiers by the entrance and servants busying themselves cleaning the windows, brushing the stairs, and tidying the flowerbeds. Kara focused her gaze on the manor house and tried to ignore the eyes on her as she made her way up the path.

The house was four stories high, not counting the attic space. It was built with a greyish-tan stone that was scrubbed monthly. The roof was grey metal and had a row of six chimneys—why it still needed so many hearths when every building here had electricity, she didn't know. Long windows lined the front of the manor house down to the giant front door with a grand staircase leading up to it. At the center, in front of the staircase, was a life-sized marble statue of Haeyla, the Great Harbinger.

Kara walked up to the statue and paused, looking into the soulless eyes of stone and trying to imagine what she would say to the real person. Nothing came to her. She took a deep breath and walked slowly and deliberately toward the manor house, ignoring the surprised looks and murmuring from the soldiers and servants. The butler, an old, brown-skinned man with a long, white beard, bowed deeply when she walked up the grand stairs and to the door. He opened it for her when she reached it and said, "It is nice to see you returned home, miss Kara. The Great Harbinger is in her hall."

"Thank you, Reginald." She procured a coin from her pocket and handed it to the old man as she passed.

Reginald smiled at her and dipped his head. She wasn't sure she would ever feel comfortable with the idea of having servants, but she hoped she at least treated them well. She sighed and stepped over the threshold. The foyer was massive, with a crystal chandelier hanging over another grand staircase. More than anything, she wanted to just go straight up those stairs and hide in her room and let someone else tell Gramma she left her post, but she knew she couldn't.

Kara steeled herself and made herself walk to the left instead, down the long hallway that led to her grandmother's hall. Fancy tapestries and paintings lined the walls, separated by light fixtures. While walking down the hallway, those images told the visitor the story of Gaele. How she was betrayed by her family at a young age, losing her son to the corruption of his uncle. How she became Haeyla and made her way out to this land on her own, claiming what was feared and forbidden as her own and pledging to unite Ambergrove under her banner. How she spent decades gaining followers, taking in shunned and forgotten peoples to repopulate the forbidden cities and build her own nation. How she then became the revered Great Harbinger.

It was meant to leave visitors more at ease when they came to the hall, so Gramma said, but all it did was intimidate Kara. She stopped in front of the large double doors, took a deep breath, and opened one. A tall, red-haired woman sat at the end of the hall, in a grand chair on a raised platform. A hint of greenish hue to her skin was all that would betray her dwarven ancestry. She'd insisted to Kara many times before that it wasn't a throne room, but it did sure look like one. A hearth fire blazed behind Gaele despite the warmth of the day, and an old woman in rags knelt on the floor in front of Gaele, crying.

"… and if you ask me again, I will have no choice but to make an example of you and your family in the Famine city square!" Gaele was shouting at the woman. The hall door closed behind Kara with a loud thud. Gaele glanced up at the sound and hastily added pleasantly, "Now run along, my dear, and dry those tears."

The woman bowed deeply and retreated, glancing up at Kara with watery eyes and a puffy, tearstained face as she brushed past and out the door. As Kara slowly walked toward her grandmother, the woman was all smiles.

"Kara, my lovely girl! How nice to see you. I wasn't expecting you yet," Gaele said pleasantly.

"What was all that about?" Kara asked.

Gaele stood and came down to hug Kara and said with a dismissive gesture, "Oh, that was nothing. Happy tears, Kara. She was so grateful for my help, but she didn't want anyone to know. I was joking with her about telling everyone you see. All is well." She gave Kara a kiss on the forehead.

"No, it isn't," Kara whispered.

Gaele pulled back to look at Kara. "What is it, dear?"

"I-I saw Mara," she said quietly.

"You *what?* Didn't I tell you what she would do to you if she found you?" Gaele asked furiously.

"You did," Kara began timidly. "You did, and some of it did go that way, but …"

Gaele sighed and cupped Kara's face in her hands. "But what, dear?"

"She … she didn't want to fight me," Kara said quietly.

"Of course, she *acted* like she didn't want to fight you. It was a trick, Kara. Poor thing." Gaele pulled Kara back into a hug and squeezed.

"But she didn't try to fight me at all," Kara said into her grandmother's chest. "Neither did Uncle Teddy."

Gaele's grip tightened painfully around Kara's shoulders. "Tederen, Kara!" she snapped. "Not uncle, just Tederen. Tederen was there?" Kara flinched, and Gaele's grip loosened and she stepped back.

"They came to Pitfall and found me in the park there. The garrison told them where I would be."

"They did?" Gaele's eyes blazed briefly. "Well, then they must be punished for the treason and the danger they caused you, my dear."

"No. They didn't mean to, Gramma. Honest. Mara and the sea elf were dressed like guards and said that they were there to deliver a prisoner directly to me. They were just following orders."

But Gaele wasn't listening. She waved dismissively at Kara and raised a hand to beckon a guard over from the door. A blue-skinned woman strode over obediently.

"Yes, Great Harbinger?" the sea elf asked.

"Go to Pitfall and question every soldier in the garrison. Those who directed the raiders to Captain Kara must be punished for treason." Gaele turned back to Kara. "Was there a fight? Did you call for assistance?" Kara reluctantly nodded. Gaele turned to the guard and commanded, "Any soldiers who did not come to the captain's aid should be punished as well."

"Yes, Great Harbinger."

"Very well. Gather supplies and your chosen soldiers and see it is done."

The guard saluted her commander and left. Kara could feel the color drain from her face. Gramma only had a few sea elves among her guard. They were ruthless. If she was sending a sea elf, the guards in Pitfall would be lucky to come out alive. *I shouldn't have come here,* Kara thought miserably.

"Oh, you're shaking like a leaf!" Gaele said gently. "Come over here by the fire."

Gaele led Kara to sit beside the hearth and rubbed her shoulders. Kara began to cry. "I'm so sorry, Gramma."

"Hey, hey now. No need for tears, my dear. You are safe now."

"But ... but what about Mara?" Kara asked.

"What about her, dear?"

"Well, she ... she's my sister. She didn't try to fight me at all. Maybe if I could just talk to her—"

"It's not safe, granddaughter. She's not the person you remember," Gaele said gently. "I know you want to love your sister, but she doesn't love you anymore. Not like I do."

"But I think she does, Gramma. Really."

"No, Kara. It's a trick, like I said. I'm your family now, remember?"

Kara hesitated a moment, then reached into her pocket and pulled out the worn bracelet.

"What's that thing? It looks like trash," Gaele snapped.

"Uh, well. I mean it does now, I guess," Kara stammered. "It's a bracelet. I made it for Mara for her birthday the last day I saw her on Earth. It's a friendship bracelet. It's a token of love, and the whole thing about them is that if you really care about the person, you don't take the bracelet off. It has to wear away to nothing and just fall off. She was still wearing it, Gramma. What would she gain from wearing this all this time later if she didn't mean it? If she didn't really care and miss me?"

Kara smiled softly, but her face fell when she saw her grandmother's expression. There was a fury in her gaze Kara had never seen before. Gaele reached out and snatched the bracelet from Kara's hands and held it up. "This means nothing, Kara! It's the silly creation of a silly little girl. She doesn't have it anymore. Your link is gone, and you will never get it back.

It is time for you to give up this foolish dream of having your sister back. She's nothing. *This* is nothing!" Gaele brandished the bracelet for a moment and then threw it in the fire.

Before Kara could even cry out, it was gone. She began to sob. She had no words. That bracelet had made it all this way, all this time, and her grandmother had just destroyed it without a thought.

"It's all a lie, Kara, and it's time you learned that. Just go to your room if you're just going to sit there and cry. Go!"

With one anguished glance at her grandmother, Kara fled to her room.

"Leave me!" Gaele commanded.

With a quick salute, the remaining guards in the hall filed out. Gaele turned and grabbed her throne, roaring and throwing it against the wall so it busted into splinters. She grunted and picked it up piece by piece, casting it into the fire. Hot embers came back at her and singed her arm, but she ignored them. When the throne was completely engulfed, she took a deep breath and stormed out of the room.

She strode down the hallway to the front door, calling, "Reginald!"

The butler appeared.

"I need a new throne—chair—for the hall."

"It will be done."

"Good. Tell everyone I am not to be disturbed," Gaele commanded.

She turned toward the grand staircase. Steps rose to the left and right, but in the center was the door to the lower level. She opened the door, flipped the light switch to illuminate the descending stairway, and headed down to her command center.

At the bottom of the stairs, she flipped the command switch, and the large room came into light. Maps and figures lined the walls, and at the center was a large table with a tactical map of all Ambergrove rising out of it—the whole world in miniature there for her to see, down to the trees, hills, and ponds, with figures to represent assets positioned throughout her realm.

"Mara is more resilient than I'd hoped," Gaele grumbled. "I'll have to accelerate my plans if I am to keep Kara in my grip."

She perused the upper corner of the map. Six small ship figures were clustered in the westernmost lake. The workers in Famine would have to redouble their efforts. They would need twice that many ships, and they would need explosive weapons to eliminate their greatest obstacle and allow their fleet to access the other lands. With the new weapons on their ships, not even the sea elves would stand in her way.

Gaele sighed and looked up at the ceiling. "Kara is weak, but her love for her sister is stronger than I thought. It could be the undoing of everything I've built here. I don't understand, great goddess. She's supposed to be the future. My legacy. There has to be a way to break the bond she has with the other one. I'll have to have someone watch her to make sure she minds me from now on."

Gaele scanned the map and picked up a small horse figure. She grinned.

Kara lay curled up on the bed in her room. It had been some time since she'd cried herself sick. Never had she been so confused. It had not been easy to let go of Mara when she woke up the morning after Mara's sixteenth birthday and found her gone. Her dad had no choice but to tell her what had happened, even though she didn't believe him for months. He wasn't supposed to tell. That was the rule. Children of Ambergrovians on Earth went to Ambergrove at the end of their sixteenth birthday if that's what was in their heart. That's why Mara had gone. Telling Mara anything about it may have changed her future.

*Did it change mine?* she wondered. *Would I have come here if Mara hadn't disappeared and forced him to tell me about this place?*

There was no way to know. She liked what she knew of the fantastical, but she liked the life she had too. If she'd have known she'd come to a world where all her family seemed to hate her, she would never have come.

But why hadn't Dad told her anything about his mother? She knew that answer, really. He'd never known his mother. Teddy had never talked about her, and he was raised by Teddy and his wife. She hadn't come into the picture at all. When Kara had come to Ambergrove and her grandmother had taken care of her in the forest, the old woman had explained the terrible things her family had done to her, and how they had corrupted Mara into helping them.

But had they? She had never seen such anger in her grandmother's eyes as when she cast the bracelet into the fire and sent her away. She'd expected to see that sort of look from Teddy when she saw him in Pitfall, but she didn't. She had tried to kill him, and the worst look on his face was disappointment. Why was Gramma so mad? What if everything she'd said was a lie and Mara was the good one? How would she know?

She had never felt lonelier in her entire life.

A few hours later, Kara left her room and snuck down to the kitchens. The old cook, Adam, a round-bellied giant man, had a soft spot for her ever since her arrival. When she walked in, he offered her some chocolate-sprinkled doughnuts—her favorite.

"I made them for you as soon as Reginald informed us you'd returned early. I was sure whatever caused it would bring you here for some sweeties," the old man explained.

"Right you are, and, boy, is it a doozy. I don't know how to clear my head, but I figured I could start with chocolate."

"You can't ever go wrong with chocolate, little one. Never." Adam grinned toothily at her, and she realized just how many empty spaces there were in the cavernous mouth of an elderly giant man.

"What should I do, Adam?" she asked, taking a large bite of her doughnut.

The old man turned away from her and walked to the fridge. When he returned, he held a cluster of carrots in one hand. "I've found with you the best thing is usually for you to talk it out with that horse of yours. Sometimes I swear you can actually understand each other. Maybe he can help you find the answer."

He handed her the carrots. "Thanks, Adam," she said. "And thanks for the sweets. What would I do without you?"

"Probably starve!" he joked. "Now get on with you. I need to get started on supper. Go on, go on."

She nodded to the old cook once more before fleeing out the door and to the stables. Flintlock whinnied when she approached. "Yes, yes, I have something tasty for you, bubba," she told the horse.

She snapped one of the carrots in half and held it out in her palm, and he gently lipped it away. She stood there and broke apart the carrots, feeding them to the horse in silence and laughing as he nuzzled her and lipped at her clothes searching for more.

"There's no more, bubba. Look." She held her hands up in front of her so he could see they were empty. "You eated it, bubba."

The horse blustered.

"Yes, much like princesses, they always want more than what we have to give," came a raspy voice.

"What is that supposed to mean, Steve?" Kara snapped.

"Nothing, princess," the stable hand said quietly. "What brings you here to see him?"

"I have a ... personal dilemma, Steve, and thought maybe Flintlock could help," Kara told him. She grinned as the horse nudged her again.

"He made you smile, at least, princess." Steve paused. "Maybe you can take him on a ride? Perhaps to the meadow? A nice ride this time. Slow."

She gave Steve a look. "Yes, I'll go nice and slow." She patted Flintlock's neck. "Do you want to go for a ride to the meadow, boy?" she asked him.

He blustered and nudged her in response.

"I guess that's a yes!" Steve cackled. "I'll go get your tack for him, princess."

⊕

"You're sure?"

"Yes, Great Harbinger."

Gaele sat in her new throne—somehow, she was always surprised by Reginald's efficiency—and grinned. "Excellent. You have done well."

"Thank you, Great Harbinger," said Adam.

"Thank you, Great Harbinger," said Steve.

Kara took her time riding through the city and down to the meadow. She always did, and Gaele figured she always would. She couldn't resist stopping to talk to people or play with children. Her need for connection was her easiest quality to exploit.

Gaele had more than enough time to get herself ready in the meadow before Kara arrived, and the old woman sat with her back to the city while she waited for the sound of hoofbeats. When Flintlock finally plodded into the meadow, Gaele began her charade.

"Oh. Great goddess, please help me," Gaele cried, reaching her hands up to the sky and sobbing loudly. "I was just so afraid of my precious Kara getting hurt that I hurt her myself. I'm just doing my best, but ... now she'll never forgive me!" Gaele began to wail.

For one awful moment, she thought Kara would turn away from her or that, worse, it *wasn't* Kara, and she was making a fool out of herself in front of one of her followers. *If that's the case, I'll make sure they're not around to tell anyone,* Gaele thought bitterly. Just as she was about to break the charade and turn, she heard the thud of a dismount and felt hands on her shoulders.

"Oh, Gramma, I know," Kara said quietly.

"I'm so sorry I lost my temper, dearest. You know that isn't like me." Gaele didn't turn, but she knew Kara's face was filled with anguish. *Good.*

Kara squeezed her from behind, and the girl hardly breathed as she said, "I know you just want what's best for me. I do, but I'm just so ... confused."

Gaele bit back a grin. "I know you're confused, my dear. But I'm here to look out for you, just like all the people under my charge and in my household."

"I know, Gramma."

Gaele turned so she could look into Kara's eyes, showing the girl her puffy, tearstained face. "Why don't you just stay here at the manor for a while, dear?"

"W-what?" Kara asked.

"Just for a little while. Just to keep you safe while you work out these feelings you're having. You can rest here and be around people who care deeply for you until you feel better."

"But I—"

"Just until you feel better, dear," Gaele insisted sweetly. "It's for your own good."

Kara tipped backward and sat on the ground, crestfallen. "I can still do my job, Gramma. I can. You don't need to—"

"Hush, dear." Gaele pressed a finger to Kara's lips. "Hush, now. It's settled. Let's go for a ride together, hmm? Just you and me."

"Uh ... yeah. Sure, Gramma." Kara stood and walked toward Flintlock, looking around her as she walked.

Her eyes widened in shock when Gaele approached Flintlock herself and swung up to mount the horse behind her. Gaele snaked her arms forward underneath Kara's and took the horse's reigns. As she urged the mount forward, she tipped her head forward and her silent personal guard fell in behind her.

⊕

Kara had known as soon as her grandmother took Flintlock's reigns—something was wrong. *She* was wrong. She had crossed some invisible line simply by seeing her sister, and as punishment, she would be stuck at the capitol until she learned her lesson.

Kara's room was guarded by two soldiers at all times. Another sat outside the window in case she took that route. When she left her room, she was accompanied by an escort. All meals were had in the banquet hall with her grandmother. She had quality time with Gaele every day to help remind her that her grandmother only wanted what was best for her.

Kara sat on her bed with her knees tucked to her chest and rocked back and forth. She had to learn her lesson to earn her freedom. She repeated one thing in her mind as she rocked: *Mara's bad, Mara's bad, Mara's bad ...*

## CHAPTER SEVEN

# LIGHT IN THE DARK

Mara sat at a little plastic table with a pink tea set in front of her. She didn't know why, but she was upset. Her lip quivered.

"No, Mara!" a woman snapped. "Proper girls do not cry at the table. If you want me to take you somewhere nice, you cannot act like a child."

Mara looked up. She *was* a child. She was in her childhood living room. Sitting across from her, looking quite proper, was her older sister, Sara. Sara had a pink princess dress on and looked like a lady—despite showing her missing front teeth when she smiled.

*Hang on*, Mara thought. *Sara lost her two front teeth when I was eight. I remember, because we couldn't go on vacation until she let Dad pull them. But where's . . .*

Mara looked to her right. A young Kara sat in the chair next to her, wearing a purple princess dress, finger firmly up her nose in search of treasure. Looking down at her own clothes, Mara saw that she was wearing a light blue princess dress.

"Mara, don't slouch!" the woman commanded. "Kara, stop that!"

Mara watched as her mother stomped around the table and grabbed Kara's hand, smacking the hand a few times before letting her go. Kara began to cry. "W-w-want D-dad-d-dy!" she wailed.

Mara began to cry harder. She remembered this day. This was when—

"Honestly, Mara! What is the matter with you? You can't sit right, you make a mess, and you cry and cry about everything! Why can't you be more like Sara?" her mother shouted. "Kara, you disgusting little girl, you will never amount to anything in this world without—"

76

"WHAT IS GOING ON HERE?" Toren roared. The girls' father stood in the doorway, and his face was crimson with rage.

The color drained from Kenda's face. She began softly, "Well, you see, Toren, I was just telling—"

"I heard what you were telling them, Kenda! You have three daughters. Three! All of them are different and wonderful, and they all deserve unconditional love from their mother without being dressed up like dolls and made to be your little playthings!" Toren shouted. He looked down at the frightened faces of the girls and said gently, "Girls, why don't you go to your rooms and get changed. I'll take you to the park, okay?"

"Yaaay!" Kara cheered, hopping up immediately and running out of the room to go get changed.

"But I want to keep my dress on!" Sara whined.

"You can stay here with me, my angel, and we'll be good girls together," Kenda told her sweetly.

Toren growled and gritted his teeth before saying calmly, "Sara, dear, please take Mara and go to your room so Mommy and I can talk. You can come back here after. You don't have to take off your dress."

"Okay, Daddy!" Sara said brightly. She daintily stood and grabbed Mara's hand to lead her away to the bedrooms.

Mara pulled at her sister's hand and wrenched herself free, but her dad appeared in front of her. "You didn't hear this part, Mara," he said, his voice echoing in her ears. "Sara pulled you away, remember? You weren't here. Mommy and Daddy fought, and then I came to get you and your little sister. Let's do that."

He patted Mara on the head, and the scene changed. When he pulled his hand back, Mara was sitting in the backseat of the family car, and he shut the car door and drove away from the house.

In a blink, he was opening the door again, all smiles. Mara unbuckled, and she and Kara hopped out of the car and each grabbed one of their dad's hands.

"What sort of adventure do you want to have today, princesses?" Toren asked them. He swung their hands playfully.

"I like being a pretty princess, but I don't like the *rules*, daddy," Kara said.

"Well, Kare Bear, you can be any kind of princess you want out here," Toren told her.

"She can?" Mara asked.

"She can! And you can!" Toren said brightly. "Do you want to make crowns and be princesses?"

"Yes! Yes!" they cried.

"Well, come on, princesses!" he replied.

Toren led the girls into one of the trails, and when they needed to go single file, he held Mara's hand and Mara held Kara's hand. They marveled and pointed at the woodland creatures they passed—before Kara scared them away with her excited screeching and jumping—and they stopped and hopped off the trail when they reached a creek where beautiful, delicate, white flowers grew in abundance.

Toren knelt by a cluster of the flowers and beckoned his daughters to crouch beside him. "Now, these are called arrowheads," he told them.

Kara crossed her arms. "They don't look like arrowheads."

Toren chuckled and tousled her hair. "Sometimes you have to use your imagination, Kare Bear. Look here at the leaves."

Toren pressed his fingers on one of the lower stems and plucked a leaf. He pressed at the base of the leaf, cracking its hold on the stem and slightly straightening it, and then he held it up for the girls to see. The pointed leaf and thick stem did somewhat resemble an unfletched arrow. Kara gasped in awe.

"These are way more than just pretty flowers," Toren explained. "You can look at the leaf and stem and remind yourself to be strong. To fight for things that are important. If you dig up the tubers, they're like baby potatoes you can eat."

"Poh-tay-toes?" Mara asked with a grin.

"Yes, Mara, poh-tay-toes," Toren replied.

Mara hadn't noticed then, but now she saw the weary look he gave her.

She was sure he had come to regret introducing her to the masterpiece films during her quoting-movies-all-the-time phase.

"Don't kid yourself, Mara. Some things never change," an echoing voice told her.

*This is true.*

"The thing we care most about here is the pretty flowers," Toren went on. "These are flowers that grow in sacred threes. You know—"

"These things always happen in threes," the girls chorused.

"Ah. Well, they do. Three is a really important number. Why do you think I had three girls?" Toren said brightly. "Now, the threes can be loads of different things. It's up to you to pick what your threes are—the three most important things to you as princesses. Can you think of three things?"

Kara scrunched up her nose as she pondered, and Mara frowned.

"What about goodness? Being good?" Mara asked.

Toren held up a finger and turned to Kara.

"Aminals?" Kara asked.

Mara smiled. It would take another year yet before Kara could say "animals" properly. Toren held up a second finger, and both he and Kara looked at Mara.

"Family," Mara squeaked.

A slow grin spread across Toren's face as he raised a final finger. "Alright, forest princesses. Goodness, animals, and family. Let's pick some flowers to make your crowns, eh?" Toren looked directly at Mara, and in that echoing voice, she heard, "Remember, forest princess. Remember what you chose."

Toren helped his daughters to pluck a few stems each and showed them how to weave little flower circlets with them. Kara cried out after a few attempts, unable to get hers to stay together, so Mara set her own flowers down and held her sister's hands to help her make hers first. When they were done, Toren placed the circlets on their heads—wearing his sample one at their insistence—then they grabbed sticks and pretended to be mighty warrior princesses.

"We are the rulers and protectors of the woods!" Mara shouted importantly.

"You will not harm our trees or squirrels!" Kara shouted, waving her stick at a bug.

Mara looked out into the forest and pointed her stick sword. "Oh, no! It's a dragonwolf! I'll protect you, Kara!" she said, moving to stand in front of Kara and raising her stick.

"Ahh! Don't get me, dragonwolf!" Kara cried.

"Oh, wait, I don't need to protect you from dragonwolves, because dragonwolves are good," Mara said. She lowered her stick.

"Oh. Yeah, I 'member," Kara said.

"But trolls aren't!" Toren shouted. He made big, stomping steps as he came toward them, with his arms in a monster position—his fierce trollness somewhat muted by the flowers resting on his head.

"No! Not a troll!" Kara cried, giggling.

"Never fear, Kara! We are the people of the woods, and we will not be gotten by trolls!" Mara said.

Toren straightened and looked at Mara, and when he spoke, his voice was different again, echoing in her ears. "You see? Even when you were little, you both wanted to be forest dwarves. Both of you. Together. You were my little woodland princesses. When you are together, you can fight off any monster. You're family."

❖

"Who's our family?" Kara asked.

Mara heard it, but it sounded so far away. She blinked, and when she looked again, she and Kara were sitting at the dining table in their home, and Toren sat across from them. Kara held up an assignment from school. It was a picture of a tree with little boxes on it. A family tree.

Their school had a policy about siblings. Whenever possible, the siblings would have different teachers to make sure that the schooling was fair for the student—and the teacher if the family was full of difficult students. This had worked out well for Mara, because she didn't have a teacher who assumed she would be a girly girl and think learning was silly. It had mostly worked out for Kara, so she, too, could have her own identity and not be reduced to "Sara's Sister" or "Mara's Sister" by the teacher.

However, it did mean that she was the first of the girls to be given this assignment. She was supposed to write her sisters' names and her parents', but she was also supposed to write grandparents.

"Our family is us. You and your sisters, your mother, and me," Toren said brightly.

"No, but who's this?" Kara asked, showing him the paper and pointing at *Paternal Grandfather* on the tree.

Toren paused awkwardly and said, "Well ... that would be Teddy."

"No, Teddy is your uncle, Dad. You've told us that before," Mara said.

"He was basically my dad," Toren answered quickly. "Anyway, it doesn't matter."

"It matters to me," Kara said.

"And me," Mara added, crossing her arms.

Toren sighed deeply, and when he spoke, his voice was an echo once more. "I wanted to tell you then about my mother, but I couldn't. I couldn't tell you anything that might accidentally change your future in Ambergrove. But in not telling you or Kara what she was, I left the door open for her schemes. Gaele put her name on this blank family tree when she found Kara in the forest, and your little sister had a hole filled in at last. It should have been different ..."

Mara blinked. When she opened her eyes, Toren wasn't looking at her. He was looking at Kara. He was giving her names for her chart, like he had when this happened. She wouldn't know until coming to Ambergrove that none of the names her father said were real. But she should have.

"...you can really just make it up for this," Toren finished awkwardly. "Besides, it's not your family here that matters." He pointed at the paper. "It's your family here." He rested his hand on his chest. "Am I here, Kara?" he asked.

"Yes, Dad," Kara said, smiling. "And you are, too, Mara."

"You know what?" Toren said. "Give me this." He took the paper from Kara and ripped it up. "I'm going to talk to that teacher and I'm going to tell her that you're not going to do this assignment. We're going to do something else instead."

Kara sputtered and laughed, looking at the shredded bits of her assignment. "What are we going to do, then, Dad?" she asked.

"You and me and Mara are going to make something. Something fun and full of love that shows what family really is. How about that?" he asked, grinning. Only now could Mara see that the light didn't reach his eyes.

*He knew he shouldn't have torn up the assignment or told Kara to defy the teacher. He so badly didn't want us to know our history, but who could blame him? Mara thought. His father was a mystery, his mother a monster, and the death of his wife's father was on his shoulders. And if he'd told us about Ambergrove, would that have changed the Oracle's visions for Aeunna? Still, something good did come out of this day.*

"Let's see, uh ..." Toren began, looking around. "Aha! Why don't you girls start off by finding one thing around the house. Find a little thing that can easily fit in your hand—something that represents who you are," he instructed. "Go on, go on."

Mara hunted around the house for quite a while. She and Kara each brought him something and held it up a few times, and he just kept shaking his head and telling them to look some more while he worked on something else on the dining table. Mara learned later that he had been stalling to actually come up with a plan, but back then she just thought it was meant to be a very, very important choice.

A few hours later, Mara and Kara returned to the table with their little items, and Toren explained to them what they would be doing. "First, show me what your pieces are," he said.

Kara hesitated, so Mara held hers up first. It was a maple tree seed. Her dad called them whirlybirds, but the kids at school called them helicopters.

"Why did you pick that?" Kara asked.

"I just really like these," Mara said sheepishly. "I really like going out to the woods and just walking through the trees when it's windy and these are all falling and flying around."

"That's nice, Mara," Toren said, smiling at her and giving her a pat on the shoulder. "And yours, Kara?"

Kara, who had newfound confidence in her own piece after seeing Mara's, held up a little gum wrapper folded into an origami bear. Mara giggled. She'd forgotten about that phase. After getting a piece of gum as a reward in school, Kara's seat mate had folded his gum wrapper into an origami crane. Until the teacher rearranged the seating chart after winter break, Kara became a gum chewer, and she checked out an origami book from the school library so she and her friend could make new things with their wrappers.

"It's a bear because I'm Kare Bear!" Kara cried, grinning. "What's yours, Dad?"

"Yeah, what's yours?" Mara repeated.

Toren held up a little bowler hat. "Oh!" Kara exclaimed. "That's your badger hat!"

Sara had been given a Monopoly game one year for her birthday, and when they saw that the hat piece was defective—instead of a top hat, it was a bowler hat—they demanded that their dad always play the hat piece in honor of his favorite television character, Badger. This made perfect sense to Kara, and to Mara at the time, but she knew now that he had picked it because it was his Ranger name.

"What are we doing with these, then?" Mara asked.

"Girls, you need to know what family means. That what's important is that people who love each other come together and are on the same side no matter what. So, I made a game so you can work to be on the same side," Toren explained. "But I need you to help me finish putting it together."

"How are we going to do that?" Kara asked.

"Well … there's a little bit of drawing and a little cutting and taping, and then … hmm, I can't remember, have you girls ever asked me if you could play DUNGEONS & DRAGONS?" he asked.

"YES!" they shouted in unison.

"Great, because we're not doing that, but we're going to use some of the stuff. Now, I need— What?" Mara and Kara both glared at him. "Sorry, sorry. It was a joke," he said. "I'm funny."

"You know, if you have to say that you're funny, it means you're not," Kara said.

Toren made a mock wincing sound. "Oh, no, I'm pretty sure I am."

"Okay, funny guy, what do we need to do?" Mara asked.

They spent the next two hours putting the game together. What was like DUNGEONS & DRAGONS was the character sheets and the dice. They would be using some of their dad's spare dice sets to play, and he had created special character sheets for them.

She would learn later just how loosely based on DUNGEONS & DRAGONS it was. For now, at least, she learned the stats. Characters had six attributes: strength, dexterity, wisdom, constitution, intelligence, and charisma. For the purpose of this game, all the dice were linked to a particular stat—four-, six-, eight-, ten-in-the-hundreds-, ten-, and twelve-sided dice respectively. The twenty-sided die would be used for something special at the end.

"What special thing?" Kara asked.

"You'll figure it out when we get there," Toren told her mischievously.

They continued with their character sheets. They rolled each die once and wrote the stat number on their sheet, they drew in their game pieces, and then they listened while Toren read off a list of questions for them to answer. The trick was that the questions were going to be specifically about the person they were playing the game with, so Kara answered about Mara and Mara answered about Kara.

"Why is the d00 so different?" Mara asked when they got to the percentage die. "All the other things were nice, but this one isn't."

"Yeah, how does it help with family bonding to say what bad thing the other person has done?" Kara pressed.

Toren smiled warmly. "Tell me, Kara, what happened to my crystal dragon statue?"

Kara mumbled.

"What was that?" Toren asked.

"I broke it because I played with it when you said not to," Kara said sheepishly.

"You did. And I was upset because it was a rare, sentimental thing I've had for a really long time. But you broke it, and that hurt me when you did that. I knew you didn't mean to break it, and you knew you did something wrong. There's no reason for me to be mad about it. You're my daughter, and I love you. Sometimes the people who love you can do little things that hurt—little things, mind you—but that doesn't mean you aren't family anymore. You take a little bit of bad with a lot of good." Toren tousled Kara's hair and added, "A little bit of *mischief* with a lot of family."

"No, no, too late! You already said bad!" Mara said.

"Okay, you're both little beagles who eat newspapers." Toren rolled up his paper and bopped Mara on the head with it, then Kara. "Bad puppies. Now, can we finish these?"

"Yes, Dad."

"Yes, Dad."

They finished up their last few responses, furrowing their brows and leering at each other while they tried to answer the last one, and then their character sheets were ready.

Next, they would need to build the game board. Kara brought her special store of markers, Mara collected old papers—sign-up sheets for the first of their mother's pyramid schemes—and Toren dumped a bunch of things out of a box, broke it down, and made the board for them to tape the papers onto.

"Here, Kare Bear. You're the artistic one," Toren said, handing Kara a pencil.

"Hey!" Mara protested.

"What? You know it's true!" her father said.

Kara swiped the pencil from his hand. "That doesn't make it nice."

He showed her his doodle of the game board, sat patiently while she laughed at it, and then explained the board to Mara as Kara worked.

"This is a simple game, like Sorry or Parcheesi. You each start on a side. One of you will move on yellow spaces and one on blue."

"I wonder why the rest is green," Mara said sarcastically.

"Remember, though, he's *funny*," Kara joked.

"Alright, alright." Toren made a face of mock offense and continued, "The circle in the center is the finish, but you aren't just going to go around the board once."

"I thought you said this was simple," Mara said.

"Well . . . maybe there are some complex parts. Like this one. So, you're going to play around the board, starting here, and using your d4 to roll for movement." He held up the four-sided die. "Once you have your piece all the way to the center, your character sheets come into play," he explained. "You're going to go to the middle, then the other player is going to read to you what they put for their d4—strength—stat. Once they read their answer, you will move your d4 die into their d4 space to complete your first round."

"How many rounds are there?" Mara asked.

Kara held up the game board. There were seven dice squares on the left and seven on the right—one for each stat and a final for the twenty-sided.

"You're going to go through each stat, go around the board, read answers to the questions, go around again. Each of the questions have to do with the two of you as family together, so you can talk about it and do family stuff between rounds. You know, if you want," Toren said.

"If we want. Yeah, write that down as a game rule, Mara," Kara grumbled.

"It'll be fun, I promise. It'll be nice." Toren grinned at his girls and experienced the first angsty eye roll—from those two anyway. "Let's just play," he said as Kara finished coloring in the game board.

Kara placed the board on the coffee table, Toren sat on the couch beside the table, the girls each took a side on the floor, and they began to play.

Mara watched as the game pieces slowly moved across the board, and the voices around her became hazy. Suddenly, she was on her feet, standing in a blue square. A loud thud startled her, and she looked up to see a twelve-sided die spin and land right next to her. Kara hooted from up above and a giant, foil bear head moved past Mara's face to land on a yellow space nearby.

She stood on the game board in alarm, shouting to try to be heard, jumping out of the way as the twelve-sided die bounced around her and Kara's piece moved. She lunged forward, crossing off of the blue track and onto the yellow, chasing the foil bear around the board. She skidded to a stop in the green center circle, and Kara cheered.

"What do you think the future holds for you and the other player?" Kara asked.

Somehow, she stared directly at Mara, the ant on the game board. Mara heard herself say her answer. "We will get to play D&D with Dad together all the time."

She felt a pang of sadness. That's what both of them had wanted back then. They'd had a chance to play with their dad. He taught them about a year later, and from that day on they would go to Jim's house to play every other Saturday.

They'd been so excited that first day, and every day, when they had played the game with their dad. If she'd known when they played on her birthday that the game would be her last with him—and perhaps Kara—she would have done things differently. She would have paid more attention. She would have held onto those moments.

"You didn't know," her father's voice echoed. "How could you have known?"

"You could have told me," Mara whispered.

"Yes, but family is not measured by togetherness, Mara. I didn't need to have you right here with me to love you. I needed you to be you. To set you free to live the life you were meant to live. That's what families do."

"But I miss you."

"That's the love, Mara. It's always going to be there. Now—Kara is about to roll her final roll. You want to pay attention to this part."

Mara looked up as a twenty-sided die came down toward her head. She dove out of the way, and it bounced and rolled to a stop. "That's it!" Kara cried. "Now what?"

Kara turned to Toren, who said, "Now you read the last responses to each other. Why don't you go first, Kara?" To Mara, the echoing voice added, "Yes, I know that's not the order we did before. Humor me."

Kara cleared her throat and sat up straight. "Okay. One motivational thing for Mara to hear." Kara glanced at Toren and back to her sister. "Mara, you should know that Daddy loves you even if you don't act like Mommy wants."

"Too right!" Toren said happily. "I love my little girls! Mara, tell Kara what you wrote."

*What I wrote.* Mara felt weak. She struggled to stand on the game board. Her character sheet fell to the table for her to see, but she didn't need to read it to remember. Her voice broke as she said, "Kara, no matter what that paper says, we love each other, and we'll always be together." *Always.*

"You did it, girls!" Toren shouted. "Brava! You came together as a family, and you won our game. Don't ever forget about the bond you have. When you forget, just remember these." Toren held up the game pieces. Then he disappeared from his seat, reappeared on the game board next to Mara, and added in an echoing voice, "You can always come back to each

other if you work to get back together. Don't let Kara be left out in the cold."
He held her hand and placed the game pieces in it, now the appropriate size.
He smiled at her, and she could see both warmth and pain in his eyes before
her surroundings began to blur.

"Cold," she heard again, echoing. "It's cold. So cold."

Mara shivered and heard muffled voices around her.

"She's awake!"

"Her fever's broken!"

"C-cold. So cold." Mara opened her eyes and peered around her,
blinking rapidly as things came into focus. She saw Finn and Ashroot, a
worried Keena, she saw that she was in Questhaven, and her eyes grew heavy.
She shook her head and forced her eyes to open.

"Easy there, Mara." Finn helped her sit up and pressed something into
her hand. A cup.

Awake, at least for now, and sweating, she realized that all she wanted
in the world was to drink the whole cup. As she gulped it down and where
she was became clearer to her, she felt a pang of sadness to realize it had all
been a dream. She wasn't going to see her dad again, but Kara ...

"You yammered on while you fought the fever. Something about
princesses and dice and—what?" Finn stopped and raised a brow.

Mara blinked and splashed the rest of the water on her face, wiping her
hair back out of her eyes and waking herself up. "I know." She panted. "I
know what we have to do."

## CHAPTER EIGHT

# MIGHTY FINE SHINDIG

When Teddy returned from Gylden Grotto, he praised Keena, Finn, and Ashroot for their quick thinking. The ice bath, Ashroot's teas, and the care they had taken in keeping Mara protected after her trip to the spring had surely saved her life. They yammered over each other to tell Teddy about all the strange things Mara had said when she was delirious with fever, but he waved them away.

"She'll tell us what she needs to tell us when she's ready," he said.

Mara slept for a few more days to recover from her sickness. Then, as they all sat in the main tent eating a bracing stew, Mara did her best to explain the journey she'd had through her distorted memories and how, in her dreams, her dad had told her what to do.

"Well, what do we need to do?" Finn asked.

"We need to get some things. Things we will only be able to get in Chaosland in a thriving city. And we need to make some things. Perhaps a blacksmith in Gylden Grotto can help us with that," she explained.

"Hang on!" Finn cried. "Hold up. You said we need to go into a thriving city in Chaosland? Again? When you're barely clinging to life after our last visit? You're just going to casually mention that like it's no big deal?"

"It *is* a big deal," Mara replied, "but it's necessary."

"Explain, lass," Teddy said, setting down his spoon to give her his full attention.

She told them about the games she had played with her sister—both the game they had invented with their dad and when they had pretended to be woodland princesses.

"Not far off, were you?" Finn joked.

"No, I guess not," Mara replied. "I'm sure our dad laughed it up watching us all those years."

"I know I would have," Teddy said.

"How is that going to help, though? You remembering the things you did as children?" Finn asked.

"Who we are now is because of all the things in our lives up to this moment. If I can remind her of who she was, who we were, maybe I can get through to her and help her see that I am on her side."

"What in her past will help you? Those things you saw in your dreams?" Finn asked.

"What better to remind her of the bond you have shared since childhood than to remind her of that childhood?" Teddy asked.

Mara nodded. "I think the best way to get through to Kara is to make her remember these moments we had as kids. Only, to do that, there are going to be some things we need from an actually stocked store. Then we have to figure out how to get them to her."

"I know how to get them to her," Teddy said. "Well, I don't, but I have a plan."

He explained to Mara what Hodd had said about using their sort of messenger, and they began to formulate a real plan. Mara made a list for them of all the things they would need. Some they could find on their island, but they needed to make sure the mining dwarves could help them and make sure they could get the rest before they got started. Mara gave Finn and Ashroot the task of searching for special, white flowers. She would have to go to Gylden Grotto herself to explain what needed to be made, so Teddy went back so she could rest and recover while he sailed, and Keena went along, not wanting to miss a good opportunity to see Hodd—and his giant treats.

"You want me to do what?" the blacksmith asked. Mara held up her crude drawing, and the dwarf just shook his head. "You'd be better off with someone who does finery doing something like that," he said. "Try the jeweler across the way. Forde. He may be able to help you."

"Thanks for your help!" Mara told the blacksmith.

She was feeling stronger after her additional rest time on *Harrgalti*, but it was still slow going for Mara. She set the pace as they descended into the mountain toward the jeweler, and Teddy and Keena trailed behind—at least until the tunnel became too small for Keena and she decided to start searching the upper tunnels for the giver of steaks instead. When Mara and Teddy arrived at the jeweler's shop, Mara repeated her request to Forde and showed him the drawing.

The jeweler peered at Mara's crude depiction of game dice. "I recognize that one," he said, pointing at the traditional six-sided die. "Never seen any of them before, but I think I can manage," he added, gesturing to the other dice in the set. "What do you want me to use?"

Forde pulled a padded tray of gems out from under a back table and lifted the cover to reveal an assortment of colors and types. Mara pointed immediately. "That one," she said. The jeweler picked up the large piece of rose quartz and handed it to her.

"Are you sure?" he asked.

Mara turned the jewel over in her hand and nodded. Pink had always been Kara's favorite color, and the dice she had at home were pink—though they were cheap resin, whereas these would be real gemstone.

"You aren't taking these to the forbidden lands, by chance, are you?" the jeweler asked.

"Uh ... why would you say that?" Mara asked slowly.

"It's just that I know you've been going there to try to defeat the evil that's there. I even heard a complaint about you from a resident," Forde said slyly. "My son—little scamp—likes to mess with those fancy ladies when they come by for fine jewels. However rarely they do come by. He swiped this from the last lady."

The jeweler handed Mara a folded-up piece of paper with a wax seal. It had already been opened. Mara unfolded it and gasped. Then she read aloud, "Lady Catherine, you are cordially invited to Midnight Manor at the top of the hill in Darkness the eve of this coming new moon. There will be a feast, and Lord Peter will be showcasing his collection of replica

Earth arts for auction. Masquerade attire is required. Please dress yourself in finery and join us for this event. Invitation must be presented for entry."

Mara looked up at Teddy. "However did you get something like this?" he asked Forde.

The jeweler smirked. "It is as I said. My son does love to mess with them. As do I. Please take this and make good use of it, yes?"

Mara pored over the document as the gears turned in her brain. When Teddy nudged her, she looked up at Forde and cried, "Oh, I will!" She then pulled the jeweler in for a hug, much to his surprise and discomfort.

"Yes, yes. That's quite enough," Forde said awkwardly. Mara released the man, and he continued, "If you do something about that thing and come back here after, I will make sure these are ready for you when you return."

Mara thanked the jeweler one last time. Then, with a quick glance at Teddy, she set off down the winding pathways in search of another shop.

⊕

She hadn't really expected the seamstress to have something for her to use. Stereotypes about dwarves growing up had told her that female dwarves were manish. It was even common in mainstream fantasy for the female dwarves to have beards. She hadn't seen any bearded ladies on any of her trips to Gylden Grotto, though she had seen some in dresses, but none in what she would consider ball finery.

The seamstress's shop had tall windows, and one displayed just that. The left window displayed men's clothes, mainly pants and shirts with some leatherworked items, though Mara grinned ear to ear when she saw the kilt in the window. The right window displayed everyday women's clothes—most the same as the men's—and also dresses and skirt ensembles Mara would consider normal for a fantasy world, and one big layer-cake dress.

When she stepped into the shop, she was immediately greeted by the seamstress, a stocky, coal-skinned woman with her grey hair tied back in intricate braids. She wore a simple red skirt and plain, white shirt. She grinned when she saw Mara.

"I wondered when the famous Dragonwolf would come walking into

92

my shop!" The woman hugged Mara like they'd been friends all their lives and added warmly, "I am Nyla. Tell me, what brings you to my shop today?"

"I was hoping you would be able to help me with this," Mara explained, handing the woman the invitation.

Nyla read it over. "Well, *Lady Catherine*, what sort of finery were you wanting?" She handed the invitation back.

"I have no idea. I'm completely at your mercy. I just need things that will allow me to blend in with the people going to this event."

"To truly fit in, you need to have a custom dress, not one that looks like you bought it pre-made and not made special. Lucky for you, I have one I've been working on that should suffice. We'll get you sorted, don't worry." Nyla patted her back and led her through the shop to a dressing room.

Nyla brought out a pair of red heels and a red mask that sort of reminded Mara of a phoenix, and then she retreated into a storeroom for a while. When she returned, Mara was fitted for a giant, frilly, red dress. She sure looked the part.

When they set sail again for Questhaven, Mara was giddy. She'd been formulating a plan, but now she had a way into Darkness.

✦

"You can*not* do this!" Ashroot cried.

Mara sat at the table in the main tent of the Questhaven camp with her companions. Finn and Ashroot had discovered the northern river on the island was lined with arrowhead flowers, and they had been excited to divulge this to Mara—until she revealed how she wanted to get the remaining elements from her dream.

"Mara, the last time you went into a city dressed in a disguise, you nearly died! This time, Teddy and I won't be with you to help you. Are you insane?" Finn asked.

"No, Finn. I'm realistic. This here is our best shot! This invitation fell into our laps. We'd have to be crazy *not* to use it!" Mara replied. "It's not like I'm going into this stupid party. I'm just using it to get around Darkness without being hassled by guards."

Teddy groaned. "I'll admit, this does present an exciting opportunity, but you can't expect to just go into it all on your own!"

"What else would you suggest, then?" Mara asked. "This is our ticket. There isn't another."

*Mama?* Keena interjected.

They all turned to look at her, even Finn, though he wouldn't understand what she said.

*What if Teddy and Finn come on the big boat and wait for you outside the city or in a sneaky place, and if you need help then they can fight the bad men and I will take you to them so you aren't alone?* she suggested.

There was a brief silence. "That's not a bad idea," Mara replied.

"What's not a bad idea?" Finn asked.

"Yeah, well it isn't a good one either!" Teddy told Mara before hastily turning to Keena and adding, "Sorry, Keena."

"What's not a good idea?" Finn asked.

"It will work, though, won't it? And then I won't be completely alone, and we can do what we need to do," Mara snapped.

*"What will work though?"* Finn shouted.

"Sorry, Finn," Mara muttered.

She explained what Keena had said and Finn added, "Hey, that'll work."

"See?" Mara said to Teddy.

"Fine," Teddy replied. "Fine, we will do your crazy plan and hope it works and you don't die."

⬥

It took exactly three steps in that red dress with her fancy shoes on before Mara regretted her decision. She would need to make sure nothing gave her away, so she left all her weapons with the men on the outskirts of the city. However, her dress was bulky enough that she could hide her signal horn under her skirts without any sign. No matter how hard she tried, she still couldn't part with her father's dagger, so she tied a piece of cloth around her thigh under her dress and slipped it in as well.

A concoction of Ashroot's worked as concealer and natural makeup, covering her scars. She had to blink back tears when she did her hair, because in order to not look at all like herself, she left her hair down, and Teddy had washed it with a mixture of Ambergrovian temporary hair dye that made it dark brown instead of russet red, but the last time she had curled her hair in that way and left it down was when Kip had told her he loved her.

She shook off the memory and accepted the invitation from Teddy, donning her mask and taking a deep breath, doing her best to appear regal and commanding as she walked toward the street and into Darkness.

No guards stopped her, though a couple raised their brows when they saw an elegant lady letting her hem drag through the dirt. She made a point of hiking up her skirts and walking delicately after that—as delicately as she could, at least. Her ankles wobbled slightly with every step, like a newborn deer, and she made a conscious effort to keep her skirts hiked just enough to be out of the mud and not enough to show her ankles—though every few steps she jacked her ankle and bit back a curse.

*If I die after all this time in this dark land because I fell down in these accursed shoes . . .*

A smiling man stepped into her path and held out a hand. "Would you like some help, miss?" he asked.

"Do I look like I need your help?" she snapped, straightening herself in the shoes, wobbling a little, and trying to look like someone of importance, as she imagined Lady Catherine would.

The smile vanished. "Never mind, then," the man replied quietly as he turned and walked away.

She really did need help, though. Sure, she was in Darkness, but she had no idea where the general store might be and needed someone to guide her there. How would Lady Catherine ask? Lady Catherine would probably just send a servant. Who would be safe for her to ask?

As she walked up the road and looked around at the people, trying to maintain an air of superiority as she frequently tripped over air itself, she saw a child peeking out from an alleyway with a dog poised defensively beside her. *That should work.*

Whereas fake guard Mara or average citizen Mara couldn't pity the homeless, fake lady Mara would be all for it. If there's one thing rich people do, it's charitable acts just for the sake of being seen as charitable. As Mara walked toward the alley, her shoes got the best of her, and she wobbled, staggered, and began to fall, thinking only that she'd jinxed herself and was now going to die by shoe.

She saw a flurry of fur and fell not on hard stone, but on the dog's back. He pushed against her to steady her, and when she straightened, she saw the girl still cowered in the alley, while her dog had prevented Mara from falling entirely.

*You look about like I would walking around with those things on your feet. It's a good thing these people notice only themselves,* the dog grumbled.

He was a large, fluffy, wolf-like beast, and Mara resisted the urge to pet him—barely. "Oh, goodness!" she exclaimed delicately. "Why, I almost fell. Thank you for your help."

*What's a forest dwarf doing in a place like this?*

"Oh, now look at me. Talking to an animal," she said, shaking her head. She peered into the alley like she was seeing the girl for the first time. "My, little one! Thank you for sending your pet out to assist me."

*Yeah, the human did it,* the dog grumbled. *Nice save, forest dwarf.*

"Y-you're welcome, miss Lady," the girl whispered.

Mara tried to crouch next to the girl and wobbled slightly. *Daeda save us,* the dog huffed. He padded forward and braced his body against hers to keep her upright, giving her a light nip on the leg to show he was grumpy about it.

Mara ignored him, smiling at the girl instead. "Say, would you like some coins for a nice supper?"

The girl's eyes brightened, and she nodded.

"Well, how about I give you two coins for keeping me from falling in the dirt and ruining my dress and two more coins if you can tell me where I might find a general store," Mara said brightly.

The girl stuck out her lip. *She doesn't know that,* the dog told Mara needlessly. *I know where it is. I steal food from there sometimes.*

Mara tried to look like she didn't understand the dog, but she noticed that as dirty as the girl was, she did look well fed. Of course, this dog was a good boy. "Oh, what is it, dear?" Mara asked the girl sweetly. "No, no, it's okay. How about you just give me a little hug for them, eh?"

She smiled at the girl, and the girl grabbed onto Mara, and Mara held her tight until the girl let go. "Thanks, Lady," the girl whispered.

Mara took out a handful of coins and handed them to the girl. "I thought I smelled some bread nearby. Why don't you look for a nearby bakery while I say goodbye to your friend here?"

The girl nodded and skipped away with her spoils. The dog looked at Mara. *You do not blend in here at all, forest dwarf,* he said. *You walk like you just learned how to do it.*

"Hey, I did just learn how to walk in these silly things," Mara retorted quietly. "Listen, I just need to get some things from the general store, and then I won't need any more of their money. If you can tell me where the general store is, I will leave the rest of this there for you to take, for yourself and for the girl."

*And if I don't?* the dog asked suspiciously.

"Then I'll leave it at whichever store I find, and hopefully you'll be the one to find it," she said quietly.

The dog wagged his tail ever so slightly and proceeded to give her directions to the general store. When she was just about to leave, he added, *Make sure you don't fall and die on the way there, walking as you do.*

"You know, if I see you again, I'll leave these shoes for you too," she said.

Now forced to stand on her own again, she was back to wobbling. She sighed, and she heard the throaty laugh of the dog, but she began her trek up to the general store and didn't stop until she'd walked right in. As she entered, she nodded curtly to the shopkeep before perusing the stock. She found a few sheets of copy paper and a cardboard box—why someone had a cardboard box with them when they came to Ambergrove, she didn't know. There were also pen and marker sets. She set the supplies in the box and turned around to look for more.

A tall, dirty man stood inches away from her, and his eyes were hungry. "What's a pretty lady like you doing here in this part of town?" he asked, reaching out a hand and touching the folds in her dress.

Mara saw red, but she couldn't react. She had to remain Lady Catherine. She screwed up her face in a look of disgust. "Sir, unhand me or I will have the guards come for you at once, and you will never see the light of day again. How dare you presume to touch *me*?" she snapped.

He didn't let go. "Now, sweetheart. There's no reason to get feisty. We can be friends here," he said.

She did the only thing she knew a fancy woman would do to hurt a man.

She pulled her arm back and slapped him in the face with all her might. Although it wasn't a part of regular fighting skills, Cora had taught Mara the value of a good slap, and the key to proper execution. Hand rigid, arm perfectly vertical, and no break in momentum. The hardest slap doesn't stop *at* the face, but *through* the face.

The man staggered and fell, crying out as he tipped over a display of pickles and they shattered on the floor around him. "What's going on over there?" someone yelled.

When the guard came around the corner, the man was stumbling to stand, and Mara was feigning a look of fear. When the guard chased the man away and she was alone, she picked up one of the few surviving jars of pickles and delicately slipped it into her box before continuing through the store. To her surprise, there was actually a s'mores section in the store. Marshmallows, graham crackers, and chocolate bars were all lined up on the same shelf. She slid these into her box.

Using more of the money they had stolen from Robert's guards, she paid for her spoils and left the store. As promised, she dipped behind the store and placed the small purse on the ground behind a trash can. When she turned down a side street to see if she could find the post office to speak to someone there before heading out of Darkness, she ran into another woman in a fancy dress. As the woman gasped and stumbled, Mara reached out to help her steady herself.

"Oh, dear!" the woman said. "I am so sorry for my clumsiness!"

"No, no, pardon me!" Mara replied, groaning inwardly. "I must learn to watch where I am going."

The woman looked her up and down and exclaimed, "Oh! Are you going to Lord Peter's gala as well? I must say, I got all turned around on these streets, and I would appreciate your help in getting there. We could walk together!"

Mara smiled at the woman and hoped she didn't look like an axe murderer while doing it—because she sure felt like being one just then. She glanced around quickly for an escape, but there were guards coming up the road, and there was no easy place to hide. She would have to actually go to the thing she was pretending to go to.

"That would be great!" Mara exclaimed a little too enthusiastically.

"Wonderful! My name is Christianna." The woman hooked an arm in Mara's, and they walked up the hill together, Mara still awkwardly carrying her box of goods.

✤

*Kara would think this looks like Darcy's house,* Mara thought as they approached the manor.

Lampposts lined the stone path up through the gardens to the manor house. Mara scanned the area for some sort of escape as Christianna excitedly dragged her closer and closer to the door. When they reached the staircase leading up to the house, a servant opened the front door for them and beckoned them through the halls toward the ballroom. A guard sat at a table by the door, and Mara's heart began to race as they approached.

"Invitations?" he asked, holding out a hand.

Christianna finally unhooked her arm so she could open her purse and present her invitation. Mara had chucked hers into her box of supplies, along with her signal horn, when it seemed she wouldn't need it anymore. She awkwardly sat the box on the table and rummaged through it, trying to hide the horn as she did. She handed the guard her invitation, and he glanced at it and passed it to someone standing behind him before reaching out to take the box.

"What are you doing?" Mara snapped as she shot a hand out to grab the box.

"Miss, I am taking your personal effects. You surely do not wish to carry this cumbersome and unsightly thing into the master's hall." He gave her a scornful look one would not typically give someone in the station she was pretending to be.

She blinked and released the box. "Very well. But if any of my belongings are lost or damaged, I will see to it that you never work again," she told him in her best holier-than-thou voice.

"Yes, miss."

She tried to watch where he went as he stood to catalogue her box, but Christianna had snaked her arm into hers again and was excitedly pulling her toward the ballroom door and the man with the invitations. He pounded a staff on the floor twice, and the door opened.

The ballroom was filled with light from extravagant chandeliers. String lights also snaked around giant pillars. A band was somewhere in the back, playing beautiful, stringed melodies. Men dressed in fancy, tailed suits stood in clusters or danced with the women—who were still all dressed in more intricate dresses than Mara's. A cluster of women looked Mara and Christianna up and down as they stepped into the ballroom. The man pounded his staff twice again.

"Lady Catherine and Lady Christianna!" he announced.

The music hadn't stopped, but somehow everyone heard, and suddenly dozens of eyes were on Mara. She could feel herself beginning to sweat. *This was a mistake.*

---

Mara had one goal as Christianna unhooked her arm and left her alone in that ballroom of prying eyes—blend in long enough to get out. She'd run through what she knew of events like these in her mind. She hadn't been introduced to anyone and thus was not socially permitted to talk to them. *Good.*

She busied herself at the buffet table before moving to stand in the shadow of a secluded pillar to eat and wait. It was torture to stand for what felt like hours in those shoes, but at least she hadn't been spotted—and no one there would watch her try to walk in them. As clusters of people moved to stand on the other side of the pillar and filtered away, she caught many snippets of conversation.

Lord Christopher and Lady Martha were trying to get a divorce—an Earth custom only practiced in Chaosland. Lord Peter was holding this auction so he could gain more prestige with the Great Harbinger. She'd been cross with him because more of his patrols had been taken by the raiders than any others. Lady Donna had released one of her servants because he had taken an important package to the post office, and it had been lost because he hadn't filled out the correct paperwork. Man, was mailing care packages to her sister in Famine such a hassle.

*Finally, some useful information*, Mara thought. Then another voice broke through.

"I wonder when Lady Catherine will arrive. It's not like her to miss an event like this. She especially loves masquerades," said one woman.

"I heard her announcement, but it is so hard to find people at masquerades. We'll have to just look for her after the lord and lady are presented," said another.

*Okay, time to go.*

As Mara started toward the door, a trumpet sounded. The music stopped. All the dancers who'd been floating around like leaves in the wind stopped as abruptly as their music. A giant in a blue suit stood at the doorway with a giant woman in a large, blue dress on his arm. Both wore red sashes.

"Presenting the lord and lady of the house, Lord Peter and Lady Rebecca!"

As the lord and lady stepped into the center of the room and drew all eyes to them, Mara threw away her remaining food and slowly made her way around to the door, holding one hand on her stomach. There's a fine line between running a convincing bluff and making a spectacle of yourself, and Mara was toeing that line as she feigned sickness.

As she slipped through the crowd, she could hear Lord Peter's address. "Thank you, honored guests, for attending this event. We will have many fine items up for bid tonight, and I trust that by the end of the night, you will all have fine words to convey to our Great Harbinger about your hosts."

*Yeah, like that will do any good*, Mara thought.

She shook her head and ignored the rest as she arrived at the door. The guards by the door shared disapproving glances, but one opened the door to let her pass anyway. When she stepped out into the hall, there was a woman making a scene at the nearby table.

"What do you mean I need to have my invitation for entry? Don't I look like I belong, you halfwit serving boy?" she raged, slamming a fist on the table.

Mara gingerly stepped behind her so the man could see she was waiting to talk to him. He snapped his fingers and a guard appeared to restrain the woman, and as they tried to drag her out, he went back to get Mara's box.

"Here you are, Lady Catherine," he said as he handed her the box.

*"What?"* screeched the woman. *"I* am Lady Catherine!"

For a brief moment, Mara stared at her. She glanced at the guards and made a decision. Kicking off her high heeled shoes, she turned on the spot and ran for the exit.

"Get her!" Catherine screamed.

"Bring her back alive for questioning!" someone shouted.

As Mara burst out the door, knocking down some guards as she did, she shoved a hand in the box, pulled out her signal horn, and blew.

⊕

Mara beelined for a large bush in the garden and crouched behind it as she assessed the enemy advance. Guards began to pour out of the manor house, and everywhere people were shouting. Mara set the box on the ground, hiked up her dress, and drew her father's dagger from its hiding place.

"Sorry about this, Nyla," she muttered.

She stabbed into the dress and pulled, cutting the material off around her knees. *Better.* She tucked the box back under one arm and snuck through the garden. She could hear shouting coming from the entryway to the manor.

"Get me a rifle!" a man shouted.

"Lord Peter, please come inside where it is safe," a timid voice replied.

"No! I want to take her down, but I want her taken alive, do you hear me?"

There were sounds of a struggle and loud cursing. Mara poked her head through a bush to look back as Lord Peter was forcefully dragged back into the manor house by guards, while Lady Rebecca fretted about his appearance in front of the guests. Guards began to press guests back toward the house and fan out into the garden.

Mara took a deep breath and kept moving, holding her father's dagger at her side as she went. Bush after bush, she snuck through the garden, and just as she was nearing the outside edge, a gunshot rang in her ears. She heard the bullet as it whizzed past her. She turned.

The guard pointed the rifle directly at Mara's chest. "I didn't have to miss!" she called. "Lord Peter wants you in alive."

Mara tested the weight of the dagger in her hand, weighing her options. They weren't good. She quickly looked around in the skies. No sign of Keena. *Well,* she thought, looking the human up and down, *at least we should be evenly matched as I play for time.*

She set her box down on the ground and dropped her father's dagger into it before settling herself into a fighting stance and raising her fists. The guardswoman lowered her rifle and set it to the ground beside her before raising her own fists.

"This is how you want to do it?" the guard asked as they began to circle each other.

Mara shrugged. "This way, one or both of us might live. I'm all for living. I don't want to go all my life just to die in a dress."

The guard smirked and lunged, jabbing with her forward hand and swinging hard with her other hand. Mara ducked and came into harsh contact with the guard's thrown knee, knocking her backward. She rolled and jumped to her feet. Then she shook her head in an attempt to clear it and patted a hand to her busted lip.

"Rookie mistake there," the guard said triumphantly. "Too many of those and I won't be able to bring you back to my lord alive. At least not in one piece."

The guard threw her head back and laughed, and Mara took the opening to use her favorite hand-fighting move Cora had taught her. She took two steps forward, planted herself, and raised a foot to drive it forward. The guard looked down just in time to lean back, so instead of a mighty, flinging kick, Mara pressed her leg forward to push the other woman to the ground. The guard grabbed Mara's foot as she fell, and Mara twisted herself free, kicking the guard in the face in the process, and barely stumbling to a standing position as the guard hit the ground.

Mara took her own opportunity to sneer at the guard, for the sake of prolonging the fight, but it was short-lived. The guard looked up from her resting place on the ground and began to cackle. Mara turned to look behind her. Human, goblin, giant—half a dozen guards flanked her. As she turned to look back at the woman she'd been fighting, more filtered in on the other side. She was surrounded. She could see the guests were up at the house, standing at the edge of the garden despite their prior warnings.

All eyes were on her. There was no escape. She couldn't wait any longer for Keena. Just as she considered a mad dash to the box for her dagger, a loud, roaring howl filled the air. *Finally.* There was a thundering crash behind Mara as Keena landed hard behind her. Keena whipped her spaded tail, knocking some of the soldiers back. Then she took a deep breath and roared toward the manor house and up into the sky, sending a great column of fire in each direction.

It was a spectacle if there ever was one. Soldiers tripped over themselves as they fell back toward the house. Mara turned to Keena and grinned. She darted over to pick up the box, and then the dragonwolf dipped herself down to allow Mara to swing herself up onto her back. With one last roar, they rose up into the sky. Mara removed her mask and cackled as she tossed it away into the air and they flew to safety.

# CHAPTER NINE

# A LEAP OF FAITH

After a thorough scolding from Teddy the whole way back, they spent the next few days at Questhaven making final preparations. The s'mores ingredients stayed in the box, not requiring further preparation, but Mara sat at the table in the main tent for hours at a time trying to recreate the game board and character sheets. She meticulously colored in the spaces, as if one stroke outside the lines would mean failure.

The others were also busy at work. In addition to filling out her own character sheet, and Kara's, as they were before, Mara had insisted sheets be made for Teddy and Freya as well—Kara's true Ambergrovian family. Teddy also decided to make one for Kara's kind grandmother in Nimeda so she would know more about the grandmother who would truly love her as a grandmother should.

Finn had a little doodle of an origami bear head from Mara and was attempting to replicate it on test paper before using the gum wrapper. As he pondered how best to make it look like the picture, he munched on the pickles Mara had brought as well.

"This is too complicated," Finn said after scrapping his fifth origami bear. "Why couldn't she just pick something off the ground like you did, eh?"

"Because my sister was a lot more creative than I was. Also, she was in fourth grade when she made it, so a big, tough man should be able to do it," Mara replied.

"Hey, what about this?" Teddy grumbled. "'What makes us stronger when we're together?' Why do you have soft questions like this?"

"Because it was made for soft little girls and not grumpy old men," Finn said.

"Hey, just fold your shiny paper why don't you?" Teddy retorted.

Mara shook her head. On and on they went.

Keena and Ashroot were searching through the island with the wolves, trying to find a maple tree and looking for something that would best represent the Ambergrovian members of Kara's family. Keena flew overhead while Ashroot and the wolves combed through the forest.

When Teddy finished with the character sheets, he sailed alone to Gylden Grotto to retrieve the game dice for Kara and take the ruined dress back to Nyla. Mara was too nervous to tell her about how she had thrown away or ruined all the things the woman had given her. By the time Mara had finished the game board and scrutinized Teddy's character sheets, Finn had folded a serviceably bear-like creature, the others had returned with their suggested game pieces, and Teddy was on his way back to the island with the dice.

❖

"About time you showed up!" Finn joked as Teddy walked up to the camp from the beach. "What took you so long?"

Finn, Mara, and Ashroot all sat at the table with the items for Kara laid out in front of them. Keena was playing with a stick nearby. Teddy looked at Mara and beamed. "The people of the grotto wanted to have a celebration after your success at the party thing." He put a hand to his head. "We were up a little late."

Finn cackled. "Maybe you ought to go sleep it off in your bunk, old man."

"Not the worst idea," he replied. "But we need to finish this up first."

He strode into the tent and took a seat at the table.

"So, what did they say?" Mara asked.

Teddy grinned. "They're glad someone stuck it to the rich folks and can't wait for one of them to come back to the grotto and tell their version of the tale." He reached in his pocket and pulled out a pouch. "These are from Forde. They seem to be what you wanted."

He handed the dice bag to Mara, who immediately dumped the contents into her hand. Seven perfect, pink dice. "This is better than I could have hoped for," she said.

"I figured." Teddy chuckled and stuck his hand back in his pocket. "Bonus. Forde's boy, Hamr, was impressed and glad for his mischief to come to something. He wanted me to give you this as a thank you." He handed Mara a small crystal dragon. "He was disappointed to not have tried dragon*wolves* yet, but I figured you'd appreciate it all the same."

Mara nodded vigorously. "I know just what to do with this."

"Perfect!" Finn said. "Why don't we go through the rest of this then, so the old man can take a breather?

Teddy glared at him, but Mara said, "No, you're right." She turned her head and called, "Keena Keena! Come here and show me what you and Ash found!"

As Ashroot unfolded a small piece of cloth on the table, Keena charged the tent and came to a halt, plopping down to sit beside her. Ashroot flipped the cloth open to reveal a perfect maple seed and three other pieces. Mara picked up the maple seed as Ashroot picked up a piece of sea-washed glass and began to explain. "Your grandmother Inola is the matriarch of a village by the sea. She's been smoothened over time and worn down by the things that have happened in her life, so we chose this."

"She's a bit rougher around the edges, but okay," Teddy said.

"Teddy," Mara scolded.

"What? I said okay!" Teddy said innocently. "Next, Ashroot?"

Ashroot held up a small, reddish-orange root piece that was cut in the shape of a hammer. "Okay, miss Freya is an amber root because that is a core plant used to make healing tinctures. Also, this one is shaped like a hammer because you don't want to cross her."

"Too right!" Teddy said with a chuckle.

"Too bad there's not a towel-shaped one. Or a shoe," Mara joked. "What about Teddy's?"

"Um ... yeah, so ..." Ashroot avoided their gaze. Mara was sure if she could see through the fur, Ashroot would have been blushing.

She handed Teddy an acorn with no cap. Keena wagged her tail and said, *It's shiny and missing the part on top, just like you!*

Mara snorted and Ashroot smiled sheepishly.

"It's because you're bald!" Mara cackled.

"Really, Ashroot?" Teddy asked, leering at her.

"Well, that was part of it, yes. Just a part, though," she said hastily. "Oak trees are ones that last. They're strong and they protect. And your relationship with Kara is just starting to bud, like an acorn."

Teddy's eyes narrowed. "Fine, then. That makes sense."

Mara, Finn, and Teddy drew the game pieces on the character sheets.

"What do we need to do next?" Finn asked.

Mara gathered the pieces and placed them all in the box before answering, "I think all that's left is to make a circlet from the flowers you and Ash found by the creek. And I need to write my sister a letter to go along with all of this."

"Why don't you do that first?" Teddy suggested, laying a hand on Mara's shoulder. "It should take time, and it will. We can make the flower circlet when you're ready."

Mara nodded and looked around at her companions. "Thank you for all your help," she said in earnest. "With your help, I may be able to get through to her."

*Family works together and protects,* Keena said, tipping her head to gesture toward the pack of wolves heading slowly together back into the forest.

"Well said!" Teddy called.

"What is?" Finn asked.

"She said you should make the supper while I take a nap in my tent," Ashroot told him.

Finn made a face and laughed. "No, she didn't."

"No, that's what I heard," said Teddy.

Mara nodded and Keena copied the gesture. "That's exactly right," Mara added.

Finn looked around the table and sighed before standing and walking over to begin building a fire. "Just remember you all asked for this," Finn called back.

Teddy winced theatrically. "Ooh, we did, didn't we?"

Mara laughed and collected some writing supplies before heading out into the forest and toward the spring.

✦

"I thought this would help," Mara said. "I thought by just being here, I would know what to say. How to get through to her."

She looked around her. No one was there, but she wasn't trying to talk to a person who was there. She looked into the spring. Her head was clear this time, and still Kip's hammer was gone. She should have taken better care of it. Just like she should have taken better care of him. And Kara. She took the worn photo out of its special pocket in her shirt and sighed. *Kip would know what to do.* She frowned and kissed the picture before returning it to its safe pocket.

Mara took a deep breath and began to write. She wrote about her guilt, about Gaele and Teddy, about trusting in their bond and remembering all the things they'd done together. She wrote about the past and the future. She wrote until her eyes filled with tears, and then she folded up the letter and took a deep breath.

✦

The next morning, they loaded up *Cronecrusher* and headed out into open waters. Due to her size, Keena could no longer ride in the dinghy with them, so she flew ahead with Mara's strict instructions not to fly over Chaosland or land there until they had also reached it.

As they entered the larger of the two coves between Fear and Darkness, they saw Keena jumping up and down and playing on a small sandbar just at the outside ring of the cove.

"Perfect!" Mara said. She pulled out a piece of paper, drew a small, crude map, and marked the sandbar with a note for Kara. They sailed past and into the cove with *Cronecrusher*, and then they loaded their extra supplies on Keena's back, and Mara began to lead them toward the center of the island in the direction of Pitfall.

"Why exactly are we going to Pitfall?" Finn asked. "Why can't we just leave it at a posty-whatsit in Darkness for her?"

"Post office," Mara corrected. "If we leave it somewhere Kara often goes, and we leave her name on it as the *sender*, whoever finds it will just take it back to her, assuming she lost it or something."

"Ah." Teddy nodded. "And where are we going to leave this package?"

"Well ..." Mara shifted awkwardly. "I have two proposed places. Either we can find some sort of way to get close to the barracks again and slip it somewhere near there," Teddy's face told her that was a firm no, "or we could leave it on the bench where we found her last time. That park ranger said that she normally goes there, so she may go there and find it herself or the ranger will go there just making his rounds and assume she left it there by accident."

Teddy shook his head.

"I think it's a good plan," Finn replied, looking at Teddy. "What's the problem?"

"I just hate how the people from Earth use the title of Ranger so loosely," he said.

Mara opened her mouth to explain and thought better of it. Park rangers were actually probably the closest to what he knew as a Ranger anyway. At least their job was to protect and manage the park. "Any other comments about this plan?" she asked.

The men both shook their heads, so they carried on toward Pitfall.

⟡

Since they had been into the park and back out, they knew a good way to get back to that grove without running into any guards. At least in theory. Just in case, to lessen their chances of being spotted, Mara and Finn snuck into the park while Keena and Teddy waited just outside of the city and watched for signs of trouble.

More guards seemed to patrol the park since their last visit, and they had to be absolutely sure not to be spotted in there, or it could ruin everything. They snuck around the back of the willow wall and listened. Silence. Finn pulled some branches back as Mara slipped into the grove.

There was no one there, but Mara stared at the bench where she had first seen her sister in Ambergrove. As she set the box down, her hand lingered on Kara's name written on the top. *Please listen, little sister,* she thought.

She heard a rustle and approaching footsteps, so she quickly slipped back through the wall to where Finn stood waiting. They couldn't wait to see if their plan was successful. It was too dangerous. Finn tugged on Mara's shirt sleeve, and they snuck back out of the park to where Teddy and Keena waited for them and made themselves begin the long trek back to Questhaven.

⊕

Kara sat on her favorite bench in Pitfall's park and stared at the box in her hands. She'd received a message from the park ranger that indicated that she left a package on her previous visit, and he had it waiting safely for her in his station whenever she wanted to come retrieve it. She was going to tell him that she had left no package, but she was intrigued. She thought that maybe some of the soldiers in the barracks were finally warming up to her, despite the punishment they'd received on her behalf. It had only been a few days since Gramma had told her she finally learned her lesson and could leave the capitol.

But she knew that handwriting as soon as she saw it. *Mara's bad, Mara's bad,* she thought. She took the package anyway, and now she sat wondering how it could be a trap—because surely it was. But Mara had seemed so earnest before, and Kara and her grandmother hadn't been getting along very well in recent weeks while Kara had been under house arrest. She sighed and pulled the box open.

A folded-up piece of paper rested on an assortment of items. She pulled the paper out of the box and set it to the side. The first item she pulled out was a little circlet of white flowers. *Like Mara and I used to wear when we pretended to be woodland princesses,* she thought, cracking a slight smile. She lifted the circlet and set it to rest atop her head—a perfect fit.

Next were the other loose items. The glowing first caught her attention, and she picked up one of the small stars and peered at it. It was just light enough that she could see the other, bulkier items in the box. "What?" She whispered harshly, nearly tipping the box to the ground in her excitement to pull out the chocolate bars, marshmallows, and graham crackers.

It took all her effort not to stop and build a campfire right there in the grove. *S'mores.* She hadn't had s'mores since she was little. Now that she knew the ingredients were here—even if it may just be in limited quantities—she was going to have to hunt around for other things she might be missing. She reluctantly set the food down and picked up the next thing in the box.

A crystal dragon, like the one her dad had when she was little. It fit in her hand, so it was smaller than the one she'd broken. She gently set the dragon down beside her and picked up the next thing in the box. She took the small, velvet bag and tipped the contents into her hand. Pink dice. Then she opened a small, plain, wooden box and marveled at the items inside: glass, a root, and an acorn, but also …

She stared at the whirlybird and origami bear in her hand, and then she slowly put them back in the box, set the box down, and picked up the final items. She blinked and realized she'd been crying as she tried to focus her eyes to read the character sheets. She had an aunt back in her dad's hometown. She had another grandmother—one who was sweet, kind, and a good leader. She looked at the game pieces as she examined each sheet, matching the people to the pieces and trying to know them.

Finally, wiping her tears, she delicately placed all the items back in the box besides the letter. She took a deep breath and unfolded it. Out fell a printed picture, and she understood why Mara had given her s'mores and plastic stars. She'd almost forgotten that night in the dark. She smiled at the happy girls in the picture, and then she looked back at the letter and read:

> *Kare Bear,*
>
> *I hope this letter finds you safe. Please read it. I know Gaele has told you bad things about me and about Teddy, but you will always be my little sister. Dad probably didn't tell you about Gaele because he didn't really know her, and maybe Teddy should have explained her history better to Dad, but he didn't. What we knew our entire lives, what we knew when dad made the Family Green game, was that Teddy was like his dad. He's the one who is good. He's the one who will love us unconditionally.*

*If you can't trust him, trust me. Remember when we were woodland princesses together? We were just playing, but when I told you I would protect you, I meant it. There are three petals to those flowers, remember? One of those is family—you and me. When the power went out and we made s'mores together, we were together through the darkness. We made a game together that was all about family and how close we were together. Do you remember my last response? Take a look. No matter what that family tree said, no matter what Gaele says, we love each other, and we'll always be <u>together.</u>*

*You broke dad's crystal dragon and he still loved you. I left you to come here. I didn't do it on purpose, and I missed you every day. Love <u>me</u> still. I'm here now. All I have thought about since I saw you in that park was hugging my little sister and getting her home safely to Aeunna, where her real family is. Where Dad meant for you to be.*

*You went to family that night when you came to Ambergrove. You went to Teddy, like I did. You went to me. But we didn't see you; she did. Had it been any other time, we would have brought you home, not Gaele. We didn't see you then, Kara. We didn't know you were right there with us. But now you have a choice, Kare Bear. I won't fight you. You will always be my baby sister. But I am going to defeat our grandmother to fulfill a prophecy. The one that took our dad away from his home. And when I'm done, I will go home to Aeunna.*

*I hope you will come with me. You are embroiled in something so dangerous, and Teddy and I just want you to be safe and home. Remember, Kara. Remember. Help us defeat her and save yourself. Please.*

*I'm enclosing a map with a marker on a neutral and safe place. If you're with me, leave a note for me there, and we can decide what to do. Remember, we were supposed to be friends forever. I didn't take my bracelet off. I didn't cast you out. I wasn't there for you when you needed me, and I will spend my whole life regretting that, but I would never leave you by choice. I will never leave you again. I love you, Kare Bear.*

*Mara*

Kara stared at the paper until it became too dark for her to see, and she held onto the last page. The map marked an X, a place that was supposed to be neutral and safe. *But why tell me it's safe unless there was a chance it wouldn't be?* Kara thought. *What would Gramma say? She'd say it was a trap. She'd say that they were trying to hurt me. Just what they would say about her.*

She thought back to the last time she'd seen her sister and her uncle. She couldn't bring herself to hurt Mara then, but she was prepared to kill Teddy. She wanted to keep herself safe from the monster Gramma had described. But neither of them had tried to hurt her then. Gramma wouldn't lie to her, would she? After the darkening sky had gone completely dark and it was impossible to see without the guiding streetlights, she folded up the letter, set it in the top of the box, removed the circlet, and carried the box back to the barracks.

⬦

"How long do we wait before checking for a sign from your sister?" Finn asked a few days after they got back to Questhaven, after Mara had spent the whole journey pacing and grumbling.

"We need to give her time. It won't be overnight," Teddy reasoned. "We should give her at least a full turning of the moon."

"A whole *month*, Teddy? Are you nuts?" Mara cried.

"Specifically, acorns," Finn quipped.

Mara glared at him.

"At least a month, Mara. Chaosland is not small, and we don't know what will be in her way if she tries to help us. Would you rather wait or would you rather miss her by a day and lose her?" Teddy asked.

Mara kicked at the ground and sat. "Fine. One month then."

"At *least*—"

"Quiet you!" Mara told Finn.

A silence stretched on. Then Teddy cleared his throat and rubbed his hands together. He grinned. "Well, I know what we can do to pass the time!"

Mara groaned. "Don't say tr—"

"Training!" Teddy declared. "You could use some. Come on, it won't be so bad."

Training after not really doing it in a while, and after having a stomach wound, *was* actually so bad. Teddy kept them at it, and it proved to be a pretty effective distraction for Mara. As if they didn't burn off enough steam with day training and occasional night training, Finn had insisted on another distraction—setting the ping pong net back up.

Mara felt a twinge of pain when she held the paddle Kip had made, but it was brief. A walnut was coming at her before she knew it. They even got Teddy to play with them this time, though he was a better match for Ashroot than he was for Mara or Finn. He blamed his old bones.

"It's more than your bones that's old!" Ashroot told him as she hit the walnut back over to him and won her game.

✧

Mara didn't figure Keena would say no if she asked the dragonwolf to come with her to the grotto, but when Mara explained that she wanted to fly there, Keena became so excited she wouldn't stop jumping until Mara was ready to go. There were just a couple days left before they could go check the sandbar for a reply from Kara, and Mara couldn't take another training day.

They soared high over the clouds. Mara breathed deeply and listened to Keena's wings flapping as the clouds turned to mist on her face. It was a quick jaunt to Gylden Grotto by dragonwolf. As always, when they arrived at the docks—Keena landed gracefully in an open bay—Hodd came out to greet them. He congratulated Mara on her victory at Darkness and told her Forde and Nyla both had news for her if she wanted to keep Keena with him.

Hamr met her on her way to see his father and ran out to give her a high five. Then he hugged her like she was long lost kin. "Oh, you should have seen her!" he cried.

"Her who?" Mara asked with a grin.

Hamr straightened his back to stand regally. "The great and wonderful Lady Catherine, madam, of course."

"She came back?" Mara asked incredulously.

"Yes! Stormed all the way up to the counter and was screaming at my da about someone stealing her invitation and that it had to be him." Hamr stroked an imaginary beard and said in a deep voice, "Miss, it is not my problem if you are unable to keep track of your belongings. If you've just come to insult me, please leave my shop."

"Ha! And what did she do?" Mara asked.

"Got all crazy eyed and rambled on about how somehow one of the raiders had her invitation and ruined Lord Peter's masquerade, and the only way she'd be able to go to another fancy party is if she won their favor. Left the shop with all the diamonds da had ready." He grinned. "Oh! Also, some lady named Christianna told a thrilling tale about being alone with the barbarous raider on an abandoned street and barely making it to the party with her life."

"What?" Mara cried. "The only reason I actually went to that stupid party is because that girl grabbed my arm and wouldn't let go of me."

"That's not how she tells it. She was in constant danger. She's the honored guest at the next gala in every one of those cities. Had to get a bunch of custom dresses ordered. Speaking of—you need to go see Nyla. Go on, go on." Hamr shooed her away with a wink and a grin.

The seamstress greeted Mara with a smile when she entered the shop. Mara waited and felt the finery while Nyla finished a kilt fitting for an exceptionally wide dwarf. As soon as the door shut behind him, the woman turned to Mara and frowned. "You disrespected my gifts, Dragonwolf," she said.

"I know, and I'm very sorry," Mara replied.

"Sorry?" Nyla asked, taking a step toward Mara. "So sorry you sent your poor uncle here to face my wrath?" Mara just stared at her. "So sorry you laughed while you threw my mask away?"

Nyla stormed behind the counter. Flabbergasted, Mara asked, "How did you know that?"

"You told me just now," Nyla snapped. Mara raised her brows in surprise, and Nyla shook her head and reached underneath the counter. The mask. "No, Christianna traded it to me in exchange for two of my best dresses. Thinks it's valuable because it belonged to you. Doesn't realize I'm the one who spent three days making it," Nyla grumbled.

"I am sorry, Nyla," Mara said quietly.

"Yes? Well ... young Christianna has garnered a lot of business for me thanks to your little escapade, so all is forgiven. I just hope you don't need any of my finery again." Nyla grumbled.

"Yeah, me too," Mara said. Nyla glared at her. "No, I didn't—"

But Nyla was bodily pushing her out the door, and the woman was strong. The door slammed. Mara sighed. "Never can say the right thing, can I?" she muttered. "I just hope Kara listened more than she did."

She made herself walk away, and her feet carried her to the tavern and to dozens of mining dwarves who wanted nothing more than to brawl and to listen to her tell them all about the gala. She was grateful for the distraction as she waited out her final hours before judgement day.

# CHAPTER TEN

# HAEYLA'S ROOST

Teddy guided *Cronecrusher* up to the small sandbar Mara had marked and watched as his niece paced and hopped impatiently, rocking the little dinghy.

"Do you want to topple us over before we get there, lass?"

Mara sighed and jumped over into the water, splashing knee-deep as she strode up onto the sandbar. Teddy glanced at Finn as blue hands replaced his green ones on the rigging. "Go on," Finn murmured.

Teddy jumped off the dinghy after Mara, no longer trying to hide his own impatience to find any information he could about his youngest niece. A large driftwood log rested near the center of the sandbar, and the forest dwarves strode together straight to it. They skidded to a halt beside the log and glanced at each other.

"Well, see what's inside, Mara," Teddy said quietly.

Mara sighed, feeling the weight of recent months settling firmly on her shoulders. She closed her eyes and stuck one hand inside the log. Nothing. She grappled around a bit before curling her fingers around what felt like a branch. She held it tightly and pulled.

Not a branch—a tube. Like a scroll case she'd seen in a television show once. Mara plopped down on the ground and clutched it in her hands. Kara had left a message after all.

Teddy sank down to his knees next to her and rested a hand on her arm. She unlaced the leather straps and pulled out a roll of paper. Sighing, she unrolled it and read.

"What did she say?" Teddy asked after a moment.

Tears filled Mara's eyes. "She said that she's not sure what she should believe. So much has changed and so much confuses her, but she knows ... she can always count on me." She sniffled. "She says that she's afraid of Gaele, because Gaele has done some things that scare her."

"Of course, she has," Teddy muttered.

Finn, having pulled the dinghy safely ashore singlehandedly, called to them as he approached, "Is she going to help us?"

Mara looked back down at the paper, flipped it over and looked at the second page—a map. "Yes!" she shouted. She handed the map to the men as Finn reached them. They examined it as she read, "I cannot get between you two, but I can get you together. I'm including a true map showing the location of the capitol, Haeyla's Roost."

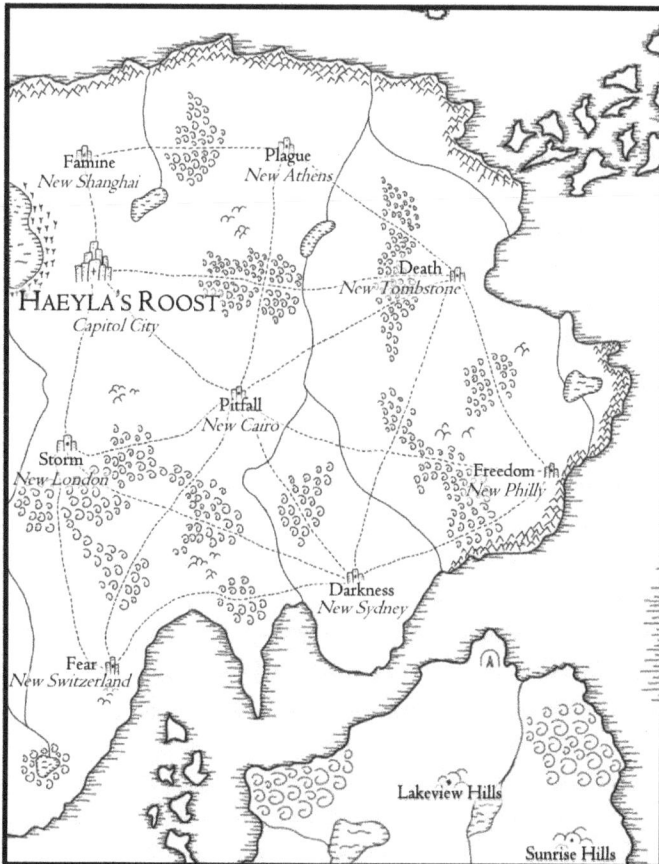

Teddy pointed to the spot on Kara's map as Finn pulled out his Chaosland map. "Here." Finn pointed. "The map we have shows that land as desert. She just wiped it off with sand."

"Doesn't even trust her own people," Teddy muttered.

"Would you if you were an evil mastermind?" Finn asked.

Teddy grunted. "Suppose not."

"But how could there be a whole city there not on any map? What goes on there?" Mara asked.

Finn shrugged. "Only one way to find out."

"Did she say anything else, Mara?" Teddy asked.

"I have marked a spot on the map outside the Roost. Go to that meadow on the day after the next full moon. I will make sure she is there." The last part, Mara did not say aloud: *I love you, Big Sister. I hope we can both be free soon.* "We will be, Kara," she whispered.

❖

Having limited transportation without stopping in another city, it would take them weeks to get to Haeyla's Roost. They returned to Questhaven with the news for Ashroot and scrounged up supplies for their journey. They wouldn't have time to return to Gylden Grotto beforehand, so they would have to make do with what they had. Teddy allotted two days to see Ashroot, resupply, and sleep in real beds before they began the long walk.

Mara woke early the first morning to find the men had both decided to savor their time in beds before they would be forced to sleep in the dirt for weeks. Keena stirred when Mara left her tent.

*Mmm . . . where are you going, Mama?* she asked.

Mara scanned the island around her. "I'm just going to go make a loop around the island before the others wake up. Do you want to come?"

Keena lurched to her feet, making Mara chuckle before beckoning her pup to follow her into the forest. It had been a while since Mara had traversed the whole island. She'd been to the spring, sure, but she hadn't explored. If they were going to finally be completing their quest and heading home, she wanted to explore.

She hopped up onto Keena's back, and the dragonwolf lumbered out of the camp and to the left, looping up to the overlooking cliff and along the river. They saw a few morning doves as they padded by, but nothing eventful really happened—until they made it to the northern dock.

None of them had been to the northern dock in nearly a year—not since Teddy, Finn, and Kip had defeated the shipload of goblins who had attacked Moon and tried to steal her pups. Now, a large ship was docked and large people with skin in hues of greens and reds poured out of the ship and bustled around it. *Forest dwarves*. Mara swore. Never did she imagine forest dwarves would come to Questhaven, and whatever brought them couldn't be good. She gently shushed Keena and they came in closer to listen to the voices.

"... well, what do you think we're going to find here, Willem?" a haughty woman asked.

"I don't know, Eile. They just said that here is where to go to prove we belong with the members of the new world order."

*The new world order*, Mara thought furiously. *Gaele. They are here to join Gaele.*

"Just think, Agrona, before you know it, we'll be living like kings in a city and never have to work again."

"We'll be living like Earth humans!"

"Right! It's a cushy life for us, lads. Who cares if it costs a little chaos to get it, eh?"

Mara couldn't think. Her brain refused to work in her favor. She was furious, more furious than she had ever been in her life. She nudged Keena forward, and the dragonwolf leapt a little into the air, spreading her wings and dropping back to the ground in front of the newcomers with a snarl and a puff of smoke.

"I care," Mara snarled.

In that moment, the shipload of forest dwarves saw a harrowing sight. Mara, fiery-eyed and scarred, sitting astride an angry, draft horse-sized dragonwolf. The captain blanched. Another sailor wet his pants with fright. Some drew their weapons before the captain shouted, "No! Stand down!"

Mara hopped from Keena's back, trying to look fearsome as she did. "Do you have any idea who I am?" she hissed, slowly approaching the crowd on the dock. Having left without gathering anything, including her bracer, she raised her left hand to show them her father's bracelet.

"You're a rich wildlady?" someone asked.

She stopped and surveyed the group. In the early morning light, standing so close to them, she could see that they were all just kids. Well, teens. They didn't look much older than Kara. Kara, who had been taken in by lies and corrupted by a force she just didn't understand. Mara sighed and when she spoke, her voice was measured.

"I am Mara, daughter of Toren the Badger, the last Ranger of Aeunna."

The captain gasped, and her eyes darted from Mara to Keena. "Y-you're the Dragonwolf," she stammered.

Mara nodded.

"But weren't you supposed to go up to the Dragon's Teeth?" someone asked.

"I did that. I earned three companions—a forest dwarf, a gnome, and then a sea elf—and I sailed through the Dragon's Teeth. There, Aeun gifted me my darling Keena, a true dragonwolf, and she set me on my path here." Mara leered at each of them before adding, "Here ... to rid the land of the poisonous rule you have come here to be a part of."

Not one of the forest dwarves before her had the sense to look sheepish. If anything, they grew taller. One greenish man, Willem, puffed out his chest as he said, "Yeah? And why shouldn't we be a part of it, eh? The Great Harbinger has promised a peaceful life with all the ease of the Earth folk."

"It's easy for you to throw stones," Eile sneered. "You've lived a life with air conditioning and lightning power. You've lived a life without care. What do you know about it?"

Mara pressed her thumb into the wooden ring on her finger and looked at the thin, white ring around her tanned wrist where her sister's bracelet used to lay. When she looked back up at Eile, Mara's eyes were filled with tears—tears of loss, or anger, or a hopelessness in the task before her. "I know more than you can imagine," she whispered.

"Eh?" Willem asked, chuckling.

Mara glared at him and strode forward. "I've seen a good man who was pulled from his home by a human who thought more about the conveniences of Earth than her own humanity. I've seen that same man have to teach his daughters not to be consumed by the conveniences available to us. I watched a man, a man whom I loved, *die* for the sake of this corrupted vision. I watched my little sister try to kill her own family because she was misled by a bitter beast. I've lived with Earth's conveniences. Are they really worth the loss they cause here?"

She pointed in the direction of Chaosland. "All you will find there are broken dreams and death. Will you enslave others to force them to your way? Will you murder others, watch them starve, for the sake of your own greed? Only darkness waits for you there. The only hope of a better life for our people and all of Ambergrove is to bring Gaele down."

"Wait." The captain raised a brow. "Gaele? The leader in the forbidden lands is Gaele, mother of Toren?"

*Of course, they would know that and not anything else I'm telling them.* Mara snapped, "Yes."

"Why should we believe you, a part human, over another forest dwarf, the mother of the Badger?" Eile asked.

Mara chuckled drily. Freya had called her foolish for having the Great Silver Bear leave his token across her chest, but now it was easy to reveal the deep, clawed scar to these wayward dwarves. Mara snatched the collar of her shirt and yanked, showing Eile and all the others the swipe from the Great Silver Bear. She clicked at Keena, who took a few steps forward and roared, sending fire up in the air in front of her. "I *am* a forest dwarf!" she shouted. "Gaele was born in Aeunna and spent her whole life trying to get away from it. She tried to poison my father to her ways, but when she found him to be good, and brave, and true, she left instead. She came here to raise an army of people she could control. *I* came *to* Aeunna. I faced trials for our people. So did my father. I am telling you that Aeun is with *us*, not Gaele. Gaele's fortress is called Haeyla's Roost. Is that really the person you want to follow?"

*All the animals fear the Great Harbinger,* Keena growled. *She is no friend to us. You are supposed to be friends to us.*

Eile took a step back and looked at the ground.

"Well?" Mara snapped. "Are you friends of the animals and the values of our people ... or are you a disgrace?"

Willem shifted awkwardly. "Well ... what would you have us do then? Keep struggling to survive?"

Mara stepped forward. "Willem, is it?" He nodded. "Willem, what village do you hail from?"

"Brynmor."

"Well, Willem, when I came to Ambergrove, I was thrust into this world and given responsibilities. One of those responsibilities was to guide the forest dwarves when they need guidance—to lead them and to help them. All of them. When I am finished here, I will go home, and when I do, I will visit Brynmor. When I visit Brynmor, I will come to help ease the lives of the people who live there. I expect to see you there when I do."

"So, you just want—" Eile began.

"Pack up the ship, lads!" the captain ordered. "We're shoving off." She walked up to Mara and held out a hand. The two women looked fiercely into each other's eyes, and both liked what they found. Mara reached out a hand, and the captain clasped it in a strong shake. "Agrona," she offered. "I will tell the people of Brynmor that you are here and fighting for us. We will return home and wait for your success."

"Good." Mara smiled. "I look forward to seeing you there soon."

The captain chuckled and turned, and the young forest dwarves loaded up into the ship and cast off, following the shoreline back in the direction of home.

❖

"What?" Teddy shook with rage. "I thought we were past this, Mara!"

"Past what?" Mara cried as Keena cowered behind her.

"Past you needlessly risking your life and the success of this entire quest because you can't handle—"

"I can handle it, Teddy," Mara replied severely. "I can. I didn't go out there in a blind rage. Those were *forest dwarves*, Teddy. They're supposed to be my people. One forest dwarf turning on everything they were brought up to believe and value is bad enough. My *sister* being taken in is worse. I won't have more of my people lost to Gaele. Not one more."

Teddy opened his mouth and closed it again. Opened and closed. Opened.

"You know she did the right thing here, Teddy," Finn scolded, arms crossed. Teddy turned to look at Finn, who returned his gaze with brows raised.

Teddy scoffed. "Alright, fair enough," he said. "But you didn't know they wouldn't be hostile. That was stupid of you, Mara."

"Maybe it was, Teddy. But they were kids. Kara's age. They were easily taken in by Gaele's charms and didn't know any better. I came out to them as a friend and as their future leader. That was much more effective than bows and swords would have been."

"You're not the Ranger yet, lass," Teddy said softly, cracking a smile despite himself.

"Maybe not, but I will be."

Mara wanted no more goodbyes. They had farewelled their fill last time. She simply waved to the wolves and gave Ashroot a wordless hug before boarding the dinghy with Finn and Teddy. Keena lingered as *Cronecrusher* made its way out to open sea, licking the wolf friends she was leaving behind. Only when she had become a spot in the distance did Keena take to the sky and fly to the dinghy.

There was no need to discuss their dark destination. Although carelessness in itself can always mean death, Mara felt that she had lost the one person she had to lose during her trial. She would make sure she didn't lose another. Kara would make sure Gaele was alone and out in the open. Soon it would be over. She gazed at the map her sister had given her and found it difficult to see.

*What if Gaele found out that Kara decided to help us?* she worried. *What if Kara is locked up somewhere and we're headed into another trap? What if it is just a trap?*

"You've got that look." Finn moved to sit beside her and nudged her with his shoulder.

"What look?" she asked.

"The look that always tells the old man it's time for some old man advice," he replied.

"That's a look?"

"It sure is!" Teddy called over his shoulder as he tied a rope to the small mast of *Cronecrusher*. He turned to sit opposite her and crossed his arms. "What are you thinking?"

Teddy leaned forward, rested his chin in his hand, and peered at her. Finn poked his head forward beside him, and they both stared into her eyes. Then Finn snapped his fingers and said, "Got it!"

Before Mara knew what was happening, Finn had stood, rocking the boat, snatched her by the shirt, and pitched her over the side. Thankfully, she wasn't wearing her armor. Unthankfully, the water was surprisingly quite cold. She gasped and sputtered as she splashed to the surface—just in time to see Teddy clap Finn on the back and hear, "That's exactly what she needs, boy!"

"Why do I need this?" Mara squeaked.

"Because, lass, you were 'what if'-ing yourself into a panic," Teddy said kindly. He and Finn reached out to pull Mara back up into the dinghy.

"Pulled you out of it, now, didn't I?" Finn asked, grinning.

"Yes, I suppose you did," she grumbled. "But that doesn't make it nice!"

"When did we ever say we were nice?" Teddy asked.

Mara pointed. "You did! When I came to Ambergrove and you promised I was safe with you."

Teddy looked up in mock bewilderment. "Really? That doesn't sound like me."

"My people tried to kill you, so I, for sure, made no such promises," Finn added.

"True, but I recall your own narrow escape from a swim when you first saw us, buddy," Mara snapped.

"Actually, I do think it *is* your turn," Teddy remarked.

"No-no-no-no!"

Too late. Teddy grabbed Finn and bodily threw him overboard. At that moment, Keena flew down low to investigate and fled in a flurry of flapping when Finn burst forth and released a string of curses. Mara grinned.

✣

Miserable weeks passed as they crossed Chaosland. Teddy grumbled about the charade, Finn grumbled about the walk, and Mara grumbled about the time it took to make the long trek. They watched the moon cross the sky and fill, and they quickened their pace.

Bleary-eyed and breathless, they could see the skyline of Haeyla's Roost appear just as the red sun rose behind it. It was certainly an imposing sight. Were it not for the doom that hung over it, it would look to Mara like the famous white city of fantasy. She was sure it looked like that to Kara. What Mara saw was a dark fortress with smog pouring out of every chimney. It was the evil queen's lair at the top of the mountain with all her people between them to take the fall.

They gave the city wide berth as they passed it on their way to Kara's meadow. The meadow was truly a beautiful sight, even cast in the shadow of Haeyla's Roost. So much in Chaosland appeared dead or dying, poisoned by Gaele's people. The meadow was bright and green, filled with little violet flowers. They settled themselves under a large tree in the center of the meadow and waited for Gaele to appear.

✣

"It is a monstrous thing, isn't it?" Finn asked. He pointed needlessly up at the capitol city. "I mean, the sea elf capitol is the head of the serpent, and the castle is up on a hill, but that's just a hill. This is …"

"This is Gaele," Teddy grumbled.

"What I don't get is how this meadow is here," Mara said.

Finn turned and looked around them. "How do you mean?"

"Well, look at it. Down in the lower part of the continent there was grass and some trees. A little bit of life. But Death was just that—death. All the plants were grey and dead or dying, and there were no animals. How can we be here, right next to her capitol city and be in a beautiful meadow surrounded by farmland?" Mara asked.

127

"Maybe she does have Haeyla or Toren on her side—the god Toren," Teddy said quietly. "If she does, there will be quite the fight ahead of us."

"Aeun said she wouldn't help me, so if Gaele does have divine help, there's a great chance we'll lose," Mara replied.

"You'll lose," Finn corrected.

"What?"

"You will lose, not us," he repeated. "This is the climax of your trial. We're not supposed to help you fight her. You have to fight her on your own."

Mara groaned. "You know, that's just like you and the Dragon's Teeth, Finn! Waited until the last moment to drop the bomb on me. Thanks a lot."

"Hey, it's not his fault, Mara," Teddy said. "You weren't paying attention. You got distracted thinking about your sister and helping her, you forgot what we were supposed to do here. What *you alone* were supposed to do here."

"Man, if only someone had told you that as soon as you saw her in Pitfall," Finn quipped.

Mara glared at him.

"Again, not my fault," he said. "But now we're down to it. She could enter this meadow at any moment, and you have one big decision you have to make."

"What's that?" she snapped.

"If you are going to kill her," Teddy said firmly.

Mara gasped. "What?"

"She is a plague on this world. When she couldn't take over the forest dwarves, she disappeared," Teddy explained.

"But—"

"And she came here to this land. She now plans to conquer everyone," Finn added. "Where will she go if you don't kill her? What new terror will she wreak?"

"Don't you people have jails or something? Somewhere we could put her to just wait out her life in punishment?" Mara asked.

"How many people are in this land? Tens of thousands?" Finn asked. "They adore her like she is a goddess among them. Do you think they will just let her sit in prison without waging a war to set her free?"

Mara looked up at the capitol city. "No, I guess not," she said quietly.

"Sometimes the only way to prevent more blood is to spill some,"

Teddy said. "If you don't stop her, and for good, Ambergrove may all fall to darkness."

"You have killed so many soldiers in the year we have been here," Finn said.

"Don't remind me."

"You have," he repeated. "What's one more? The last?"

"What's one more? Really?" she snapped. "I'm not going to kill of the sake of killing. Wasn't that the very quality in me that got you to come on this trip? Eh? I don't enjoy it, and I will gladly live out the rest of my days and never do it again if I can get away with it. Besides, she's my grandmother."

"In name only," Teddy said. "Had you been here instead of Earth, she wouldn't have kissed a skinned knee like Inola would have. She wouldn't have protected you from a child's nightmares. She wouldn't have held your hand while you were bleeding or kept you safe from harm. She wouldn't have carried you to safety while you were overtaken by fever or injury or enemies or gone out into the night on a perilous journey alone for nothing more than to help you. She wouldn't have stood in line to be tortured just to spare you the pain. Inola, Freya, me, Keena, Finn, Kip ..." Teddy's voice cracked. "We're your family. Us and Kara, when we bring her out safe. But Gaele? You don't owe her a single blessed thing."

"You don't have time to decide," Finn whispered, tapping Mara's boot and pointing behind her.

Two figures appeared on the path from the fortress to the meadow. They were deep in conversation, laughing and patting each other as they approached. When the two figures neared and Mara could clearly see the face of her dear sister and the woman who'd tried to take her away, she rose and rested a hand on the head of her small axe. *Decide.*

"Gaele!"

# CHAPTER ELEVEN

# THE EARTH QUAKES

K ara stood apprehensively outside the Great Harbinger's hall. She could hear muffled shouting inside as her grandmother spoke with her senior captains. Whatever her plan was to spread her rule beyond this land, it had taken a serious turn in recent weeks, and she was preparing for the endgame. Unfortunately, her plans didn't seem to align with what was happening, and the captains were bearing her wrath.

*No use waiting. You told Mara you'd have her at the meadow. It's time to get her there.* Kara took a deep breath as she entered the hall.

"Great Harbinger, forgive me, but the southern raiders have made it difficult for supplies to come north to Famine for the ships. With them on the loose, we—"

"Forgive you?" Gaele snapped. "Don't talk to me about the southern raiders, James, after you allowed them to escape with a few cuts and bruises *and my location* when they were captured."

Kara stopped at the door. She'd heard about that. She was surprised the giant was still allowed under her grandmother's service after he walked into the camp where Mara and her companions were imprisoned and they escaped while he was there—after he revealed to one of them where the Great Harbinger herself would be found when she camped near Death. Kara had first met her grandmother in that camp after the ensuing fight with Mara and her people. Revealing such information would be a banishable offense under the best circumstances, and after the sea elf captain had returned from Pitfall and detailed the pain she'd put the garrison through, simply for being tricked by Mara or for not getting to the battle in time, Kara realized the Great Harbinger's punishments were not going to be the best of circumstances.

So why had this man gotten off so easily? She'd asked about it early on, when her grandmother was nursing her wounds from that day. He was the one who'd brought the giants to her realm and convinced them to follow her. Without him, she'd still have cities of people and legions of soldiers at her command, but with him she was mighty. That was how her grandmother told it.

When she saw Kara standing in the doorway, the fiery anger in Gaele's eyes fizzled out. "Leave me!" she commanded, waving dismissively to her captains.

The soldiers tipped their heads and raised their right fists to their chests in respect and then obeyed. When Gaele looked at Kara, she was all smiles.

"Good morning, Gramma," Kara said as pleasantly as she could.

"Why good morning, my dear!" Gaele replied sweetly. "What brings you in to see me? Is it already time for our lunch?" Gaele reached into her pocket and checked her watch.

"No, it isn't yet, Gramma. I was just wondering if you and I could go out for a picnic together for lunch. Just the two of us out to the meadow. It would be nice."

Kara crossed her fingers behind her back and hoped upon hope that her grandmother would not sense her nervousness. Gaele only smiled.

"Well, of course we can, Kara! Have Reginald inform Adam to prepare a picnic for us," Gaele said pleasantly. "Go on now, go on."

Kara smiled and retreated to get Reginald, glad of the chance to stay away from her grandmother until it was time to head to the meadow. Once Adam was put to the task of putting the picnic meal together, all that was left to do was wait.

Kara hid in her room until it was time. She had hidden most of Mara's gifts on the road, too cautious to bring them into the capitol city, but she kept the crystal dragon with her. On Earth, according to the Celts, dragons symbolized protection. She felt safer with it there and had even named it Icewind like it was a real creature. As she waited, she clutched the dragon to her chest and tried to breathe evenly.

When it was time to get ready to go, she was thankful that she had always wanted to play adventurer. In the months she had been on Earth after Mara's disappearance, Kara's father had taught her how to use a sword, and when she'd come to Ambergrove, she'd insisted on always carrying one until Gaele forced her to carry a rifle and pistol instead. From the moment she'd seen Mara, she'd wanted to carry a sword again. She'd justified it to her grandmother by telling her that she'd had to use the rifle to block Mara's swings when they'd fought. Gaele had the best blacksmith in the dwarven lands forge it for her—or so the old woman had said.

She donned her sword belt and slid the sword into its place. The crystal dragon she wrapped carefully in cloth and stuck in her money pouch. It was certainly strange to spend time on her appearance when there was so much at stake, but at least it was distracting. She stood in front of her mirror and stared at her reflection, smoothening out wrinkles in her pink button-down shirt and trying to wipe the mud off her jeans. She'd never understood the reason for the vests, but she slipped into the grey thing anyway. She swept her red hair back and tied it into a high ponytail. She grimaced when she noticed how chipped her nails were. She couldn't help peeling and picking at them when she was nervous, and she'd certainly been nervous lately. She sighed and looked down at the collection of earrings on the dresser. Over the months in the capitol, she'd met many goblins and accumulated more piercings as a result—and a variety of rings to go in them. She decided to fill her piercings with rings instead of studs, inserting three on the left and five on the right. Finally, she sighed and left her room behind, heading down to the foyer to meet her grandmother.

Gaele was all smiles when Kara arrived and had a serving girl, Anna, holding the picnic basket.

"Oh. I thought it would just be us," Kara said sheepishly.

Gaele smiled and made a look of mock disapproval. "And have us lug our own supplies? Really, Kara."

"I don't mind. I used to love being the one to carry the picnic basket. It makes it the best family outing for me. Please, Gramma?"

Gaele stared at Kara for a moment, and then smiled and nodded to Anna, who handed the basket over to Kara. She buckled a little at the weight, surprised something so small weighed so much, but it was necessary to go alone. She hefted the basket with a grin, and she and Gaele walked toward the meadow, toward Mara, and toward Kara's own freedom.

✦

"How—?" Gaele glanced from Mara to Kara. Shock shone full across her face as she met Mara's red-faced glare across the meadow. Clearly, she hadn't expected Kara to stand up to her, and that miscalculation would be costly. She looked at Kara, who had already begun to sweat with fear. She shook her head and frowned before saying mournfully, "Kara, you promised me you wouldn't turn on your family."

Kara's fear turned to anguish as she opened her mouth to speak, but Teddy rose and shouted, "She hasn't, Gaele!"

Gaele raised a hand as if to strike Kara, and the girl flinched. Kara let out a small cry as the hand came closer and jerked when Gaele simply patted her gently on the cheek. The old woman turned to face Mara and glared through her, crossing her arms. Kara shivered.

"I see you *do* have a real dragonwolf," Gaele commented.

Keena made herself large behind Mara. *Yes, she does*, the dragonwolf said fiercely.

Gaele made a sound of disinterest and looked back to Mara. "So, what's your plan, granddaughter?" she asked.

"I told you not to—"

"Right, right. Don't call you that." Gaele waved dismissively. "Okay, *Mara*, what is your plan? Are you going to have your beast burn me to a crisp? Are you going to fell me with one of your crossbows or have someone else do it like I—"

"I will not do anything like you do," Mara spat.

Gaele shrugged, unfazed. "Very well, but then what? Do you expect to take me peacefully? Do you think I'll just ride back to Aeunna with you and forget my own ambitions? Do you think I'll give you Kara just because she led me here to you? You know I'm more stubborn than that. I take what I want, and I won't be finished just because you tell me to be."

"Will anything ever make you stop?" Teddy asked, disgusted.

"Hmm … you know what? I can think of something," his sister replied.

133

She spun to face Kara and slowly walked toward her, stopping inches away from Kara. The girl trembled as Gaele reached out a hand, gripped the sword at Kara's hip, and drew it, swinging in one motion to face Teddy again. Teddy drew his own sword and strode past Mara.

"No, Tederen!" Gaele commanded. "Not you." She turned her terrible gaze back to Mara and grinned.

"Give me the sword, Teddy." Mara tried to keep her tone firm. She hadn't used a sword outside of practice since ... well, since her last duel. He just looked at her. "Give it to me," she said more forcefully. "You know I have to be the one to do this."

Teddy sighed and tipped the handle in her direction, the proper way to pass a blade. "I just hope you know what you're doing."

"She does." Finn had sat quietly through the entire exchange, but he now stood in solidarity and nodded.

Mara tipped her head in his direction, took the sword from Teddy, and faced her grandmother.

❖

It wasn't supposed to go this way. He was supposed to come with Mara to keep her safe. Yet he'd handed her his sword with hardly a beat to think about it first and allowed her to stand in front of *Gaele*. Gaele, who had already shown her apathy for her blood a hundred times over. He'd wanted with all his heart to be able to return to Freya when this was all over, but he hadn't expected to. If it came down to him or Mara, he wanted it to be Mara who made it home.

Fear crawled up his neck. *Toren would be so disappointed in you if he were here*, Teddy told himself. He looked at Mara, head held high, brandishing his sword. Mara, determined, stepping fearlessly forward. *No, he wouldn't. He's right here. That fire in her eyes. The sense of duty. There is my Toren. Right there.*

❖

Mara raised Teddy's sword toward Gaele as they strode forward to meet each other. "Are you sure you want to go down this road, Mara? Once you hurt your family, there's no turning back," Gaele sneered.

"I know that," Mara said quietly. "I've known that since you killed the man I loved just so you could break me."

Gaele's smile vanished as she raised her sword to meet Mara's. They clicked the blades together once as a formal start to their duel, and then they began to circle each other.

"You know, Mara, swords have not been my weapon of choice for decades, but that does not mean that I don't know how to use one," Gaele warned.

She whipped her sword around in a butterfly shape. Mara blocked it and flicked the sword away with hers. Man, it made the muscle burn in her arm just to do that. *Thank you, Teddy, for your relentless training the past month.* Without it, she might be fatigued from just that first sweep.

"Go ahead and get the fancy stuff out first," Mara quipped. "It will make it much easier for me in the long run."

Teddy cheered on the sidelines, and Keena whimpered. Mara didn't swing, but Gaele did. There were two benefits for Mara in this match. First, Gaele hadn't used a sword since she left Aeunna. Even though Mara hadn't used a sword in battle since her last duel, she had trained more recently than Gaele. In skill, they would be evenly matched. Second, Gaele hadn't used a sword since she left Aeunna. That meant that she only knew Aeunnan techniques. Mara had only been trained to fight with Aeunnan techniques. However, she'd spent her entire life on Earth watching period and fantasy movies and shows—countless musketeer, King Arthur, and Robin Hood renditions and fantasies of all types. She'd also seen swordplay firsthand at her favorite festival growing up.

Most of those sorts of things include a "do not try this at home" warning or are made under the assumption that no one would be stupid enough to try it at home. But Mara wasn't at home—she was in Chaosland, and this was a boss battle. The only way to win was to use the special tricks she'd learned along the way. She'd played enough games to know that. She'd just need to wait for the right moment to strike.

She blocked Gaele's swing with a move she'd seen in one of the King Arthurs. Gaele glared at her. "You know, Mara, this is your problem. You're not a real forest dwarf like I am. The people are going to see that."

"No, Gaele," Mara snapped. "I am more of a forest dwarf than you will ever be, because I fought for it." She tapped her chest with her free hand. "I fought for them, and I will continue to do so. For them, not for myself."

Gaele swung, and Mara parried and quickly thrusted the sword forward—a fencing move called riposting. Gaele flicked her sword away just in time. The fight wore on for a few moments. Mara nicked Gaele's arm; Gaele nicked Mara's leg. They exchanged small cuts on their arms and legs—and Gaele's cheek and Mara's neck—before Gaele growled and swatted Mara's sword away with force.

"You won't take from me again!" Gaele shouted.

"Me take from *you?*" Mara growled.

"Yes!" Gaele snapped. "My son, Toren, was taken from me. He was meant to be the chosen one. Now you have corrupted my Kara, but I'm telling you that I will not let her go."

She swung viciously, but Mara growled and blocked. "You lost them both for your own greed, Gaele, but they were never yours."

Gaele turned to Kara, who was sobbing on the sidelines. "Dearest Kara, I implore you to see reason. Your sister is evil and unstable. Look at her. I'll forgive you for what you did. You don't have to disgrace our family too."

Mara swore and brought her sword down hard. Teddy growled and shouted at Gaele. Kara whimpered. Gaele focused all her attention on Mara as she let loose a series of furious blows. In a split second, Gaele had knocked Mara to the ground. Stunned, as Gaele thrust her sword, Mara rolled out of the way and stood.

Suddenly, Mara heard Finn's voice, and it was forceful. "Mara! You cannot give way to your anger. Remember what anger did to Candiru! Let it go, and fight with a clear head."

*Candiru, warrior champion of the sea elves.* Mara had dueled this formidable foe in the final round of the Serpent's Gauntlet. She'd been severely outmatched, but she'd won the duel anyway because she'd taunted the sea elf until anger had gotten the better of her. Gaele grinned. Mara took a deep, calming breath. And another. *Find her weakness. Don't let her use yours. Find her weakness.*

Gaele thrust her sword, and Mara focused on her movements as she parried. She breathed heavily as she watched for an opening and—there; found it. As Gaele thrust her sword forward, she put all her weight on her front leg. Mara stepped to the side and stabbed the leg, making Gaele stagger and swing wildly. Mara twisted her sword around the hilt of Gaele's and gave it a flip, sending the sword high in the air and Gaele to the ground. Mara sidestepped as the sword came down, knowing she wasn't dexterous enough to catch it. When it hit the ground, she kicked it as far as she could and turned to put her own blade at Gaele's throat.

Except for the women's panting, there was silence for a moment. They glared at each other, and Gaele spat. Mara shook her head. "I'll admit you did have me for a few months, Gaele. I let the chaos take the reins for a while, but it did not and will never consume me. Never."

"That's what you think. I—"

"No, you won't," Mara snapped. "You're done. You're finished here."

Mara looked around the meadow and saw Kara's tearstained face, Teddy's furrowed brow, Finn's eye of expectation, and Keena's tail between her legs. She looked at the hate in Gaele's eyes as the old woman lay on the ground at the end of Mara's sword. *Decide.*

Mara stabbed her sword into the grass. "I'm not going to kill you, Gaele. You have caused so much pain, but you're finished here. I'm sparing your life, but we'll find some other way to punish you for all the bad you have done."

Mara turned away from Gaele and began to walk away, toward her sister. Finally, finally to Kara.

"No, no, *no!*" Gaele shouted. "How dare you? I am not finished. I decide when I am finished, not you. I am the Great Harbinger. *I decide!*"

Mara smiled softly but didn't turn. She'd done it. It was over.

⊕

Gaele lay on the ground where she fell, stunned and furious. *How dare she? How dare Mara turn her back on me? On all I've done and all we could be? On all Kara could be? How dare she think that she could just leave me here to start again, as if that were the end of it? No. I make my own end.*

Time stood still as Gaele drew a tiny pistol from her vest pocket. *I decide.* She pointed the weapon at Mara.

⊕

"Mara, look out!" Kara screamed.

Mara turned to search for the danger, but what she saw was Kara bolting across the meadow. Kara pushed Mara to the ground as she ran past. "Kara, NO!" Mara cried as she fell.

Gaele grinned and fired.

"NO!" Mara screeched. "NO MORE!"

The sound Mara made was almost inhuman. Gaele watched in horror as the bullet slowed, stopped in the air, and fell to the ground. Still Mara screamed, clutching the dirt and the grass in her hands, unaware of what had happened.

"How could you?" she cried. "How could you try to kill your granddaughters, especially after you were shown mercy?"

Gaele opened her mouth to speak.

"No! No more!" Mara pounded her fist on the ground. "You are done here, Gaele! You do not belong in this world! Your poisoned cities do not belong in this world! Your followers do not belong in this world! *I swear, Gaele, I will make sure Ambergrove is free of you forever. I will wipe this whole continent clean if I have to. YOU ARE FINISHED HERE!*"

As she spoke, the ground began to shake. Where her hands pressed into the dirt a great rift opened up. The cracking moved steadily toward Gaele, who scrambled to stand, but she was too late. The ground broke beneath her, and a green light burst from the chasm as it opened. Gaele scrambled to grab onto something, but the ground just split further. She fell.

The cracking didn't stop there. Mara watched as the split widened and Haeyla's Roost began to shake and crumble. They could hear the distant screams as the entire city toppled to the ground and was swallowed by the green chasm. The shaking grew stronger around them, and Finn and Teddy fell to the ground. Kara screamed.

Teddy leapt from the ground, bellowing, "Hold on, lass!"

He staggered and lunged, gripping her arm just as the quaking caused her to topple into the chasm, but the quaking didn't stop. Finn lunged forward and helped Teddy drag Kara out and to safe ground. The quaking grew stronger and stronger as they watched everything they could see but the plant life disappear into the chasm. When it had all fallen, the rumbling changed. The beam of light from deep within burst into the sky and rippled above them, all around them, like the northern lights.

The rumbling shifted, and Mara watched as the chasm thinned and closed. Then the lights shot away in all directions until the rumbling spread away like a wave. All went still. Mara found that she could finally move again. She lifted her hands from the ground, and they were sore and hot to the touch. She looked at where Finn and Teddy sat on the ground, bewildered, with Kara in their arms between them, sobbing. Mara looked to where Haeyla's Roost had stood. Where moments before had been a fortress—a city—now there was flat plainland. Gaele, and everything she stood for, was gone.

## Chapter Twelve

# One Door Closes

Mara sat on the ground, frozen and disbelieving. She looked at her sister, now sobbing in Finn's arms, and she looked at the emptiness around her. She swore. *What happened here?* It was impossible. She looked toward the empty plainland where Haeyla's Roost had been just moments earlier. There was no rubble. There was just nothing but empty land, like it had never existed. *What could have caused this devastation? Where did that green light go? What . . .*

Her sister's crying broke through her thoughts. Where Finn sat holding Kara, there wasn't even a dirt patch to indicate that she'd almost fallen to her doom. Teddy looked wildly at Mara, and she shook her head slowly. *Who could have done something like this?* She felt pain all over her body. Some of it was familiar, like the cuts from Gaele's sword. Some of it was strange. Her whole body ached like she'd been awake for days doing hard labor. Her hands were raw and hot, and when she tried to bend her fingers, they were stiff. As they all sat bewildered, a white flash burst forth right next to them and a familiar figure—at least to Mara—appeared.

"What are you doing here?" Mara snapped.

The figure stopped. "Now, is that any way to talk to a goddess?" she asked.

Teddy scrambled forward and knelt low. Keena burst from her hiding place at the edge of the meadow and greeted the goddess Aeun. The goddess stretched out a hand to pet Keena, then she cupped the dragonwolf's face in her hands and pressed her forehead against Keena's.

"What happened here?" Mara asked. "What did you do?"

Aeun sighed and turned to Mara. Butterflies flew out of her dress as she moved. "I did not do this," she said simply.

"Then who did?" Finn asked. Kara had stopped crying in the shock of Aeun's appearance, but she still held onto him and so he still sat.

Aeun glanced at Mara, who waited expectantly. "That is something for you all to learn in time."

Exactly the answer she expected to hear from a goddess. "That's just some bu—" Mara began.

"For now," Aeun said loudly, "I have some business to discuss with you."

Mara waved a hand as if to say, "Fine, then get on with it." She knew she should be more respectful toward a goddess, especially the matron of her people, but the events of the past few moments had sucked all patience from her.

"You will learn in time," Aeun told her. "For now, look around you." Aeun waved a hand.

"What happened to the cities? To the people?" Teddy asked.

Aeun turned and smiled at him. "All are gone."

"What?"

Aeun turned back to Mara. "You were tasked with defeating the Great Harbinger and ensuring that her poison did not spread to other lands in Ambergrove. You have achieved more than we could have hoped. This land has been wiped clean of everything from Earth that had corrupted it. The cities are gone. With them, their electricity, their weapons, their customs of poverty and unbridled greed. All is gone. It has been erased."

Kara squeaked, "But erased how? Gone where? They're not ... dead?"

"No, child, they're not dead. Even your treacherous grandmother still lives." Aeun replied. "They have been banished from this land, and they will now see just what they thought was so admirable about Earth."

"You mean you sent them to Earth?" Finn asked incredulously.

"I did not—"

"Right, right, you did not," Mara snapped.

"Won't she just do the same thing on Earth?" Kara asked quietly. "What about the other races? Giants and goblins? They don't look human at all and—"

Aeun held up a hand. "That is none of your concern. Without her power, she's just a person—one no one will follow. Just leave it at that. She will not harm anyone again."

Mara's mouth hung open in bewilderment. Aeun approached Mara and grasped Mara's left hand with both of hers. The goddess ran a thumb over Mara's ring and pursed her lips. Then she pressed a hand into Mara's forearm. Mara felt a twinge of pain. As quickly as it came, it was gone. Aeun moved her hand to reveal a leafy triskele pattern tattooed into the skin on Mara's forearm in amber lines.

"Congratulations, Ranger," Aeun said softly. "Ambergrove is indebted to you."

Even in the largest city in her realm, Gaele had never been accosted by such constant noise. The last thing she remembered was the earth splitting beneath her feet. She woke up under a metal bridge. There were trees nearby, like there were in the parks in some of her cities, but she knew right away that this was not one of them.

Bright, colored lights shone everywhere. Loud, metal beasts patrolled all the roads and obeyed the colored lights. Bumping sounds like drums came from tall buildings spotted with lights. It was all too much. People walked by in the oddest clothes, and they all had lit rectangles in their hands.

Gaele began to talk to herself, first mumbling then shouting. "I don't understand. What is this? I am the Great Harbinger. I came to rule this land and to conquer the rest of the world. I am the Great Harbinger. I have thousands of followers. I am the Great Harbinger. What are they looking at? I am the Great Harbinger!" She clutched her small pistol in her palm.

One of the metal beasts approached her, and she stared at it with wild eyes. Red and blue lights flashed, making her squint and cover her eyes as two people emerged from the beast.

A woman in blue clothes walked toward her. "Ma'am? Ma'am, are you alright?"

"Ma'am, do you know where you are?" another woman in blue asked.

"I am ... I am in my realm and ready to take my ships to the mainland!" she said haltingly.

The women in blue shared a glance. "Ma'am, have you been drinking this evening?"

A crowd had begun to form around them. Gaele turned away from the lights and tried to look around, tried to understand. As she looked out among the crowd, she saw a small human who reminded her of Steve.

"Ma'am, can you tell us your name?"

A switch flipped. The sounds faded away as Gaele turned to the women in blue. "My name? I am Haeyla, the Great Harbinger of Chaos. All will be under my rule! All will embrace chaos!"

There was a pause. Scattered laughter filtered to her ears from the crowd. One of the women in blue said, "Uh-huh," as if to a child. Gaele felt her face redden with rage.

She raised a hand, and her sleeve fell down to reveal the pistol she held. "Silence!" she shouted. "I am the Great Harbinger! How dare you? I am the Great Harbinger! I am—"

Gaele was on the ground and her pistol was ripped from her hands. One of the women in blue was on top of her, pulling her arms back. Before she could catch her breath, she had been manacled.

"Target secured. Code 4," the other one said.

They heaved her to her feet. "Alright, *Great Harbinger*, do you have a license for that firearm?"

"License? The only license I need is my—"

"Okay, that's a no."

"Haeyla, you are under arrest. You have the right to remain silent. Anything you say can and will be held against you in a court of law ..."

The woman kept talking, but Gaele didn't hear her through her own shouting. She was dragged over to the metal beast and hauled inside it. When they closed her in, she continued to shout, "No, I am the Great Harbinger. You cannot treat me like this! I am the Great Harbinger!"

As the beast left and the crowd of people dispersed, one remained. A small man stumbled forward underneath the bridge and looked down at his reflection in the water. His skin was no longer yellowed, but a whitish brown. His ears were small and round. His hair was black. He splashed at the water, but the reflection remained the same. *What happened here?* he thought. *The Great Harbinger, taken away in manacles, completely powerless. Metal beasts everywhere. No. It can't be ...*

A beautiful woman stood nearby and grinned. As she walked away, butterflies came out of her dress. *Good,* she thought. *All around the world, the corruptors of Ambergrove are realizing that the world they idolized is nothing like the one they left. Some will learn how to live here. The sensible ones will. But Gaele?*

The woman chuckled and then faded away into white light.

✤

"Does this mean what I think it means?" Teddy asked, shocked out of his respectful posture. He strode over to stand beside Mara, grasping her arm and inspecting the new Mark.

"It does," Aeun said. "Mara has successfully completed her trial and has earned the title of Ranger. She is the Dragonwolf of Aeunna. You can go home."

*Home. Freya.* Teddy took a deep breath and blinked back tears. *I'm coming home, honeydew.*

Aeun smiled and looked around her dramatically. "Mara, you and your companions have done a great thing. With your dedication and sacrifice, you were able to defeat this scourge and drive it out. With the modernities gone, particularly the power of Earthfolk, you have opened the door for other heroes to begin to piece our world back together. There are strange times ahead."

"Strange how?" Teddy asked.

"Without Earth to corrupt and consume the power of magic, our great magics will return to the land. Already, all over Ambergrove, there are magical creatures in the sky and sea. There are elementals in the very wind. Magic is returning. A new world begins now, and it will be beautiful."

✤

Aeun's words shook them all. Ambergrove reborn. A new world begun. It shook them so severely, they didn't realize when the goddess gestured that it was time for her to leave.

"Where are you going?" Kara stood, wobbling a little. "You can't just say something like that and leave. What will you do now?"

Aeun's eyes blazed at Kara's "you can't just", but she cooled and gave the girl a smile. "If you must know, now I will return to my brothers and sisters, and we will do something we should have done a long time ago. We will close the bridge."

"Close it?" Teddy asked.

"Yes." Aeun sighed and clasped her hands together. "Yes, it is about time we sever the link between our worlds. We should have done it before we became too weak. Now that the slate is fully cleared, it is time to close this door forever."

"But ... you can't just close it!" Kara cried.

Aeun's gaze hardened as she looked back to Kara.

Kara sheepishly dropped her gaze and turned to her sister. "What about our dad?" Kara pleaded.

*Oh, Kara,* Mara thought miserably. *She didn't know that, for her, that link had already been severed. Or maybe ...*

"Aeun, I have a favor to ask of you," Mara said.

Aeun glared at Mara. "I have my limits, Ranger, but please divulge."

Mara glanced at her sister and then her uncle. "We will never see our dad again. We know that. In that way, the door closed as soon as we came here—or, as soon as he left here, for Teddy."

"That is correct," Aeun said.

Kara gasped and whimpered.

Mara frowned. What a terrible way for Kara to learn about that. She went on, "But can he see us? Or hear from us? Will you allow us to somehow just let him know that we're okay and everything worked out, so he doesn't have to worry about us forever?"

Aeun stared at Mara, unblinking, before turning and pacing. Butterflies and honeybees flew out from her dress into the paradise of the meadow as she paced. Mara's breath caught, and she waited. Finally, after a few loops around their area of the meadow, Aeun turned away from them and waved her hands. There was a white flash. When she turned back around, Mara's camera was in one hand and writing utensils were in the other.

"I will permit this one link, out of respect for the service you have done for our world here today. Do not ask anything else of me." She handed the camera to Mara.

❀

"I don't understand this," Finn said.

"Don't press the button yet!" Mara cautioned. "There's only one photo left. It needs to count."

She showed Finn again how to operate the camera, and then Mara backed up to stand with her uncle and sister. Teddy stood in the center of the meadow with one arm around Kara and the other around Mara. Keena stood behind with her wings outstretched. Mara took a deep breath as Finn counted down. *Five.* She thought about the first day she arrived, about how lost she felt without her dad, and about Teddy stepping in and taking care of her. *Four.* She thought about meeting Kip and the sacrifice her dear gnome had made to protect her and to help her to complete her quest. *Three.* She thought about the hopelessness she felt when she got the chance to see her sister again, only to be parted from her until now. *Two.* Here they stood, victorious, in a land cleansed of all that had corrupted it, with hope for the new world. *One.* Mara beamed. Finn took the picture.

As Mara flapped the picture to develop it, Aeun held out a hand for the camera. When Mara handed it to her, the goddess pulled her hand back, and the camera disappeared into the folds of her dress. "This is the last of the modern devices in our entire world. It's time it goes home as well," the goddess explained.

Mara, Kara, and Teddy spent some time writing letters to Toren while Finn sat at a distance with Aeun and discussed something with her that made him fling his arms in frustration, snap, and huff. Mara looked at her family as she wrote her letter and tried to tell her dad everything she could. She told him how she understood why he had kept this secret from her, though it hurt to not be able to give him a proper goodbye. She told him about Teddy and about Kara. She told him she loved him and would miss him. A tear dropped down onto the page, and Mara wiped it. She looked up to see her uncle and sister struggling with the same problem.

Soon, they had finished, folded up their letters, and reluctantly handed them to Aeun. "I will take these to Toren on Earth. When I have done so, I will return to my brothers and sisters so we may close this door forever. You should begin your long journey home," the goddess said matter-of-factly.

Teddy nodded. Mara reached out a hand, and the goddess took it and shook it. Then, with a flash of white light, she was gone. A weight lifted from Mara's shoulders. She breathed deeply and glanced across the clearing at her sister. They smiled at each other, and tears filled both their eyes as they closed the distance and finally embraced.

✣

Toren Green sat out in the forest behind his home. He often spent his time thus, closing his eyes as he sat on a stump or in the dirt, and imagining that he was back home in Aeunna. That life on Earth had just been a bad dream. He breathed deeply and thought of the Aeunna trees and the bearkin bustling about. He thought of the trial he had completed to become the Ranger for the brief time that he was.

When he opened his eyes, a figure stood at the edge of the clearing, watching him. He started, standing up and brandishing a stick. "Who are you?" he asked.

"Ever the warrior," she said, slowly stepping forward. "Let me tell you, Toren of Aeunna, your daughters also lack the appropriate respect for someone of my status."

The stick fell to the ground. Toren knelt beside it and bowed his head. "Aeun, I never imagined I would see you again, especially not on Earth."

He looked up to see her lip curled in disgust. "Oh, believe me, I would not be here by choice, Toren. This land is filthy, and the forest is lifeless. Alive, yes, but with no spirit." She sighed and sat on the stump beside Toren. "I've come here at the request of your daughters," she said.

"My daughters?" Toren rose abruptly, nearly knocking the goddess to the ground in his surprise.

He stammered an apology as he helped her to settle herself, but she waved a hand dismissively. She reached into her flowing hair and pulled out a bundle, and when she held it out to Toren, he snatched it away and hungrily searched through the contents. Three letters and a ... picture.

He looked long and lovingly at the polaroid of his family. Teddy and his bald head were just as Toren had remembered. Mara looked like a warrior. Kara looked at peace. And was that really a dragonwolf? Dragonwolves came back? Reluctantly, he set the photo on the ground beside him and opened the first letter—Teddy's.

As Toren made it through each letter, Aeun simply sat and waited patiently. It took him a bit longer to make it through the final letter—Mara's—because he was so overwhelmed with emotion, and the tears were preventing him from seeing his daughter's words. When he finished, he folded up the letter, pressed the collection of letters and photo to his chest, and sobbed.

Aeun leaned forward and rested a hand on his shoulder. "You have sacrificed much for Ambergrove, Toren," she said gently. "When you completed your trial, you were so full of hope for Aeunna. You imagined the bright world you would create for your people, and you took great pains to bring that world to fruition."

Toren nodded miserably.

"Your sacrifice was a steep one. You never wanted to come to this accursed place. You left a home you loved to protect a people you would never see again, knowing that this decision would also mean the loss of at least one of your children. You gave your life for the people of Aeunna. You should know that it was not in vain. Your daughters are together, and Mara has completed her Ranger trial. They will return to Aeunna and live peaceful lives. New heroes will rise to help Ambergrove because your daughter has opened that door ... because you gave her the key."

Toren nodded again, consumed by the tears, so Aeun reached a hand under his chin and raised his face to look at her. "Your sacrifice means that the world you loved can thrive. You have done well, Toren the Badger."

Aeun faded away, leaving Toren alone in the forest once more. He held out the picture to look at it. His daughters would be safe. They would live out their lives under the love and protection of their uncle. Aeunna would grow. He heard a car door slam and angry voices behind him, and he turned to see his house in the distance.

*A house, not a home*, he thought. *My home is in Ambergrove, and it always will be. But I will gladly live out the rest of my days here with the knowledge that my loss meant something. Something great.*

Toren sighed and stood, holding tightly to his final connection to Ambergrove, to the family he had lost. As he strode out of the forest toward the sound of his wife's displeasure, he only smiled.

✦

"It is time."

Aeun stood in front of her brother, Baerk, on his home island. Baerk had lain peacefully in his hammock, but now he stood. "Yes? Time for what?" he boomed.

"You know what," Aeun snapped. She crossed her arms, and butterflies fled her dress. "I am gathering everyone to close the doorway to Earth. Mara has defeated the evil."

"Told you this would happen," Baerk said smugly.

"Yes, you did, and I am not too fond of the way things came about to this just end, but do you really have to rub it in? It has been thousands of years since you have found a loophole in my magic."

"Exactly. Who knows how many years it will be again?" Baerk grinned toothily. "I need to savor this."

"Okay, but savor it quickly. It's time for us to go," Aeun snapped.

"It's time for us to go?" someone asked as they stepped out of Baerk's home.

Aeun glared. "Not yet, you. You can ruin my magic some other time," she spat. "Baerk, can we go now?"

Baerk sighed and rose. He approached the person and rested a hand on their shoulder. "Soon. Not long now." He paused and smirked at his sister. "Now, let's go, Aeun."

✦

Eaogh stood on his island with his hands raised and his eyes closed. He was surrounded by plant life of all seasons. Trees covered in snow melded right into trees just beginning to bloom. He smiled.

"Are you coming, brother?" Aeola asked.

149

The goddess of protection knew better than anyone how emotional Eaogh would be at this time—her island was right next to his.

"Almost. It has been so long since my magic has been potent enough to affect all of Ambergrove. After so long stagnant, it's time for spring."

He stood for another moment, then lowered his hands, grinned, nodded, and followed his sister off the island. Aeun was gathering everyone in the center of the triskele, where she'd had Baerk create a temporary center island with his magic.

Eaogh and Aeola were the last to arrive. Their mother and father, Maonna and Daeda, were there, and all their brothers and sisters were in deep discussion about what they planned to do now that their powers were no longer dampened by Earth's poisons.

"It is time, my children," Maonna said warmly.

The mother goddess was short and stocky. Plain, as the deities go. Her long, brown hair was tied in a simple braid, and her brown eyes were soft and kind. By comparison, Daeda was like a giant next to her. His scraggly brown beard could not fully hide his rosy cheeks, and his blue eyes twinkled while he looked around at his children.

"Neadae, come." Daeda gestured toward the center.

Whenever something needed to be done, Neadae was the one who provided the will to do so. The goddess of skill and determination strode confidently forward. She stopped at the center of the small island, nodded to her parents, and crouched on the ground to draw a symbol. To many, it would just look like scribbles. To the gods, it was the runes that symbolized each of them combined together into one bindrune. When she was done, she stepped back, and so did Maonna and Daeda.

The gods and goddesses created a perfect circle around the symbol, and then they all reached out their hands to clasp the hands of whoever was next to them. Every one of the gods and goddesses stood together united, and if Haeyla and Toren participated only because they were on either side of Uehrae, the god of strength, and he was smashing their hands, so be it. Haeyla's crimson eyes burned with hate, and Toren's darted around madly.

Maonna and Daeda began to chant and sway from side to side. The others all followed suit. An amber light began to emanate from the symbol in the center. It grew and grew, spreading to touch each of the gods and goddesses. Each person began to shine, enveloped by the amber light. The light pulsed, slowly at first, and then faster and faster as they chanted. Then it shot out in all directions like an explosion of stardust. Fine specks of brilliant white light floated in the air and then came to rest on the ground.

"It's done," Aeun said triumphantly. "The doorway to Earth is closed forever."

# Chapter Thirteen

# A New World

Kara squeezed her big sister as tightly as she could. They didn't know how long it would take after Aeun left for the doorway between worlds to be closed forever. It could have already happened. It could have just taken moments.

"I'm so sorry, Mara," Kara sobbed. "I'm so sorry. I got mixed up and taken in, and I almost caused you to fail."

"You didn't, lass." Teddy strode up behind Kara and gave her a small pat. "What happened to you says more about Gaele than about you."

"You wanted to see the best in her. That's not a bad thing," Mara added. "But it's okay now. We're together."

"I'm sorry I tried to hurt you, uh, sir," Kara told Teddy awkwardly.

Teddy held up a hand. "Water under the bridge. And it's Teddy. Uncle Teddy."

Kara looked at her sister. Mara chuckled and nudged her. "Yeah, that's exactly how he introduced himself to me." She straightened and said in her best deep and important voice, "Bond. James Bond."

The girls giggled and hugged each other.

"Great. Now there are two of them," Finn grumbled.

Kara turned to look at him, and he winked. "Thank you for saving me and holding me on solid ground for a minute," she said timidly.

"Ah, no worries. I'm Finn. Just Finn."

Thundering footsteps came their way, and Mara was surprised it took Keena as long as it had to—

Keena crashed into them, knocking all four of them to the ground like bowling pins. She licked each face in turn—Finn, then Teddy, then Mara, then Kara—and then thumped her tail and woofed at Kara.

"And this is Keena," Mara said with a giggle. "Remember how I said dragonwolves were good? Well, this is the goodest girl in all the worlds! Yes, she is!" Mara smooshed Keena's face and scratched her chin. "Alright, Keena Keena. Let us up," she groaned.

They looked at each other and laughed as Keena backed up and let them all stand.

"You did it, Mara. It's done," Teddy said.

Kara looked at Mara and then at Teddy. "But what now?" she asked.

Teddy's eyes began to shine and well with tears as he replied, "Well … now we start our journey home. We have quite a few little stops to make before we get there, but we're going home."

"Where's home?" Kara asked.

Mara smiled. "You'll love it, Kara. Remember the old forest kingdoms we pretended to rule as kids?"

Kara chuckled and nodded.

"Well, it's like that. Only it's real. I can't wait to show it to you." Mara grinned.

"May as well get started, then!" Finn called.

⊕

They began their trek slowly. Kara insisted on going to where Haeyla's Roost had once stood, because she had possessions in the fortress she wanted to look for, and she wanted to get her horse. As they neared the area where the fortress had been, they were met with an eerie sight. The ground was level. No walls, nor buildings, nor even any rubble remained. It was just flat and bare like the city never existed.

"But … what about everyone and everything else that was here?" Kara asked quietly.

"The people and Earth things all went to Earth," Teddy said. "That's what Aeun said anyway."

"But what about the animals?" Kara squeaked. "They weren't here by choice, and those horses were all treated so poorly by so many. My horse, Flintlock, was about the only living creature here I know really cared about me while I was here. Animals can't pretend." Her voice broke. "And I left him here."

"Maybe something else happened with the animals," Mara reasoned. "We saw birds and woodland creatures on the way here. Maybe this only applies to people and things, not animals—or, at least, animals who don't want to stay with their people."

She rested a hand on Kara's shoulder, but her sister shook it off. "You don't understand, Mara. I had a good life here. Or at least I thought I did. And those animals were all innocent. If something bad happened to them, it's my fault. We have to find them." Tears streamed down her face.

"We will," Mara said softly. She rested her hands on Kara's shoulders. "But you have to calm down so you can think, and Teddy too." She raised her head. "Teddy? Have you—"

"Tracks," he said. "Here."

"Here too," Finn added.

They both pointed to the northwest. Kara whistled for Flintlock, but he didn't come. Seeing the desperation on Kara's face, they veered away from their journey back to *Cronecrusher* to follow the trail into the upper forest. They ended up in a secluded grove, where they found dozens of horses from the Roost, identified by the saddles and other gear they still wore.

Some of the horses knew Kara and easily settled. Mara and Teddy tried to explain to them that they were friendly and were trying to help, but Mara knew from talking with Swish, the last horse they'd had, that horses only talk back to creatures they trust. They could have been trying to talk with Kara, but Mara and Teddy had no way of knowing that until—or unless—Kara took the test with the Great Silver Bear to prove herself a forest dwarf. But that was a concern for later.

"Keena, if they won't talk to us, will they talk to you? If Mara or Teddy can tell you what we need to tell them, you can tell the horses, and they would be talking to another animal instead of a person," Kara offered.

"Or you could talk to Keena," Teddy muttered.

Mara nodded. Kara looked back at Keena, and she bobbed her head in agreement.

"Um, okay," Kara began awkwardly.

"It's alright," Finn told her. "You can't make more of a fool of yourself than I have." He winked.

She smiled and cleared her throat. "Dragonwolf Keena, could you please let the horses know that we mean them no harm? The cities have been destroyed, and they are free now. We just want to take away all the straps and things the other people put on them, so they can truly be free. We're here to help."

Keena slowly walked up to the mare who appeared to be the leader of this newfound herd and relayed the message. The horse watched as Keena spoke, and then she snorted and whinnied in response before turning to face the other horses, rearing up, and neighing harshly. The herd slowly made their way toward the group, and Mara laughed and said, "I guess they understood the message."

They slowly approached each horse in the grove and removed whatever tack remained. Many were half-saddled, likely in the panic as the people were trying to escape the city. They left the horses free, and although they didn't find Kara's horse, Flintlock, she was content enough with this small rescue to carry on. Mara vowed to send someone back there now that the land was safe, to ensure that all the horses could be free of their tack without having to wait for it to wear or break off, but that would require more resources and time than they had available just then.

⟐

As the days passed and they walked through what was once Chaosland, they discovered more and more mysterious occurrences with the creatures there. The animals they passed were bolder, seemed more intelligent, and were grateful to them—as if they understood that the disappearance of danger in the area was due to them. One night as they camped, a pack of coyotes came to greet them. The alpha, an exceptionally scarred, lighter coyote, stepped ahead of the pack to speak to them.

*I am Ghost,* he told them. *You are the ones who had dealings with the packless one.*

"Yes," Teddy answered quietly. "Shadow helped us when we needed help. He died bravely, fighting the people who have hurt your kind. You are free of them now and have nothing more to fear."

*All the animals in this land were wrong to refuse you help when you asked for it*, Ghost growled. *They will not do so again. Farewell, coyote-friend.*

The coyotes melted into the darkness as if they'd never been there. Mara turned to Teddy. "Well. I doubt you thought you'd ever be called 'coyote-friend' in your entire life!" she joked.

"Wait, what?" Kara asked.

"Don't worry about it. We won't be eaten by coyotes today. That's all you need to know," Finn told her, laying back to rest by the fire.

"That's the long and short of it," Teddy muttered.

By the morning, they learned what Ghost had meant. Various woodland creatures stopped by their camp throughout the night. Some came just to see them, but many brought gifts of some kind. The owls brought the most gifts.

Each day, as they walked back to the southern tip of the land now freed of Gaele's hold, they saw more and more animals and received more and more gifts. It was a blessing in itself to not have to hunt or forage for food during that trip.

Most interesting, though, was the peacefulness and outright magic of the setting. Glowing plants none of them had ever seen before crawled through the undergrowth. They passed a few creatures that had an aura of magic around them, and they glimpsed some creatures they were sure couldn't have been there. The world was changing around them, and the animals they saw all seemed peaceful.

One evening, when they stopped to make camp, Finn straightened and looked around them like a child who'd lost his mother in the grocery store.

"What is it, Finn?" Kara asked. "Timmy fall down the well?"

He gave her a look of mock annoyance. "No," he said. "Timmy is probably at home in his bed, and if he isn't, he should know how to behave around wells."

Mara smacked her own forehead and laughed. "Okay, what's really going on?" she asked.

"This here is where Fear used to be," he said quietly.

"What? How do you know?" Teddy asked. "There's n—"

"There's nothing here?" Finn finished, turning to Teddy. He crossed his arms. "Now, I know that we didn't have much use of my labors for very long, after we went to Darkness and got ourselves a *real* map, but I would know that silly hill there. I drew it, remember?"

"Yeah! Remember, Teddy? That was when you scolded him for shouting at us down the hill. And me and—" Mara stopped.

"And you and Kip raced," Teddy finished quietly. "Yeah, I remember." He cleared his throat awkwardly. "It's funny how even this city is gone. Wasn't it supposed to be the one good one?"

"I mean, probably," Kara began, "but didn't that goddess say that everything had to go, even the camera? This was still an Earthlike city."

"There's something else different, though, isn't there?" Mara asked.

"What's that, lass?" Teddy replied.

"Are there seasons in Ambergrove?" she asked.

"How do you mean?"

"Winter, spring, summer, fall. Seasons. Is that a no?"

"I have heard of those, but no, we haven't since well before I was born," Teddy said. "Why?"

Mara pointed at the surrounding trees. Everything was just so green. Pink buds were already beginning to bloom. There was an air of new life around them, and not just because the land had been so desolate before.

"I knew I wasn't just that oblivious," Mara said.

Kara put a finger up. "Actually, you were still oblivious if it took you this long to realize there *weren't* seasons either."

Finn clapped for Kara and then turned to Teddy. "What does it mean to be having them now?"

Teddy looked at the blooming around them. "I knew the gods were powerless to deal with the science, but maybe it lessened their magic too. The seasons stopped because Eaogh didn't have the power to bring the seasons."

"And now he does?" Kara asked.

"Seems so."

"What else has changed?" Mara wondered, looking around.

"I guess we'll find out. Come on," Teddy said.

As they made their way through where Fear had been, it really sank in that all the modernities were truly gone. The land had been cleansed, and only animals and plant life were left to see it.

"Is this just what Ambergrove is really like?" Kara asked one day.

"Hmm …" Teddy rubbed his beard. "Well, sort of."

"The magic part is new, as we said. Some of the creatures we're seeing are new. But, yes, Ambergrove as a whole is very different from this place as you came to know it. Aeunna is quite similar to what we've seen the past few days. It's green and beautiful and full of life. And the people live in harmony with the animals," Mara said wistfully.

"And there's family there," Teddy added. "It's a wonderous place, and your family is there for you. You will love it, Kara. I have no doubt."

*I will love it too?* Keena asked.

Mara chuckled. "Yes, you too, Keena."

Kara opened her mouth to speak, but Finn said, "It's not everyone who can understand the animals. I can't. It's just the forest dwarves who can."

Keena bowed her neck in a nod.

"If you choose to undergo our trial, you may one day be able to speak to them too," Teddy said severely. "But more on that later. Now that we have our bearings, we can make the final trek to our dinghy in the morning."

"It'll be fine, Kara," Mara assured her sister as *Cronecrusher* sped through the water near Questhaven. "Ashroot is more person than creature. You won't need to have the gift of the forest dwarves to talk with her. And she's nice."

"Much nicer than the giant wolf pack!" Finn interjected. "Giant, fanged—ow."

Mara looked to see Teddy leering at a properly chastised Finn. Kara giggled. Mara added, "What Finn meant is that one of them is *named* Fang. They are fearsome to creatures who wish them harm, but they will be kind to you. You just won't be able to understand what they say when they are kind."

"Ah."

"Now's the time, if you want to do the honors, Finn."

Finn drew his signal horn and blew. Mara gave Kara a side hug as Questhaven came into view, and they could see the large forms of the wolves approaching the beach. Keena flew to land as soon as she saw the wolves' approach, but that didn't stop Mara shouting to Ashroot when she saw her, "We did it, Ash! We're going home!"

Ashroot hooted from the beach. When they reached it with *Cronecrusher*, Mara jumped off the dinghy, hand in Kara's, and pulled her sister over to meet Ashroot.

"Nice. To. Meet. You," Kara said slowly.

"Wh-what's she doing?" Ashroot asked.

"Oh, I'm so sorry! I thought Mara was just messing with me. I thought—"

Ashroot chuckled. "It's okay! It's a common thing for humans, but we'll make you forest dwarf soon enough. Family of Mara's is family of mine," Ashroot said warmly. "Call me Ash."

"Uh, thanks ... Ash," Kara said with a timid smile.

The bearkin poked at Kara and said, "Oh, you're all skin and bone! Come with me, and I'll fix you something to eat."

Kara turned to Mara for help, but her sister just ushered her on with Ashroot. As Kara was led away, Mara faced Fang and Moon, who stood regally as their pups skittered around them. She nodded gravely to Fang.

*You were successful, then?* he asked.

"Yes, Fang. The leader has been defeated. All the bad there has been wiped clean. At least where those people are concerned, you and your family are safe," she replied.

*Good.*

Howl stopped licking Keena and whined. *Does this mean you all are leaving now?* he asked.

Mara nodded.

*Keena ... stay?* he asked.

Mara's heart sank. "Well ... I'd hoped Keena would come home with me to Aeunna ..."

Keena bolted over to where Mara stood and placed herself firmly behind her. *I'm staying with Mama,* she said.

*Good,* Mara thought. She couldn't imagine saying goodbye to her beloved pup, but the wolf was so crestfallen. She cleared her throat. "Perhaps, since Keena is bigger now, she can come visit you or something."

The wolf nodded once before yipeing and running off into the forest. These goodbyes would be harder than before.

Kara stayed in Kip's tent for their last night at Questhaven. Mara knew she should explain about Kip, but she wasn't sure how, and she really didn't want to broach the topic with her sister so soon after they got her back. So, she just told Kara not to mess with any of the things in there. It was a bed and a room of her own, at least, until the bunks were all loaded back on *Harrgalti*.

On the first night, Kara met Ashroot and the wolves, they had a nice dinner, and they planned how they would get up bright and early the next morning to pack up the entire camp, with the hope that they might set sail for Gylden Grotto by lunchtime. When the plan was set, they all went to bed—except Mara.

In the dead of night, while everyone else slept, Mara found herself at the spring. Her wounds from the duel with Gaele had healed well enough, so she just slipped into the water and sat looking at the stars and feeling the water as she ran her hands back and forth across the surface.

She pulled the picture of herself with Kip out of its safe pocket and held it up one final time. "We did it, Kip," she whispered. She gently kissed the photo and slid it back in her pocket before looking around her. "Thank you for sheltering us all this time," Mara told the island. "We have survived over a year in the shadow of the darkness itself, and we would not have done that without you."

Mara sighed and looked for the constellations Kip had shown her. The water around her began to ripple, so she sat up in alarm and looked around her. From the center of the pool, a shape emerged.

"You're welcome," came a feminine voice.

Mara squinted at the shape in front of her and saw that it was a woman—a woman made out of water. She gasped. "Who are you? What are you?" she asked.

The woman smiled and sat at the edge of the pool. When she sat, her body became solid, with blue skin like Finn's, dark blue hair that rippled down her back, and a blue dress that faded into water below her torso.

"I am Laeghu, goddess of the water," she said simply.

"You're the one who has gifted the animals here with water?" Mara asked.

Laeghu nodded. "I used to help the whole world, but when the magic faded, I was forced to reserve my powers. I focused them here, on these islands, so the animals here might be surrounded by wildlife and plenty."

"So, all the islands are like this? With a magic spring that's the source of all the water?"

"That was my goal, though as my power waned, so did the water."

"What did you do with Kip's hammer?" Mara asked, a little too loudly.

"What?"

"Kip's hammer. I cast it into this spring, and it disappeared. I would like it back," she said.

"I don't have it, Mara," Laeghu said simply. "I haven't been to this island in centuries. The source of the water on this island is here, yes, but I am not the only one who can do magic."

Mara's face fell.

"But not to fear, young Ranger," Laeghu said pleasantly. "I did come for a reason. I wanted to give you a warning. To create something new, you have to leave something old, and the earth is one with the water as well as the trees. Sometimes the water needs it more."

"What is that even supposed to mean?" Mara asked.

"You will know in time," the goddess told her. Then Laeghu sank into the water and disappeared.

❖

It took no time at all to pack up the camp the following morning. Mara considered telling Fang and Moon who provided the island's bounties to them from the spring, but she decided as soon as she saw the wolves lumbering out of the forest that it wasn't her place.

Keena and Howl shared a tender moment Mara chose to ignore, and

Fang hauled *Cronecrusher* up to the deck for them. Then they said their goodbyes. The pups all whimpered and Ashroot sobbed when she said goodbye to them. They had been her constant companions for over a year, and it was tough to finally be letting go. Moon thanked them one final time for saving her life when they first arrived, and Fang shared a stoic and approving head nod with Teddy. Then, tears shed, camp gone, they set sail for the south.

They reached Gylden Grotto just as the sun was setting over the mountain. Finn, Ashroot, and Keena all stayed on *Harrgalti*. Keena had grown far too large to make her way through the tunnels of the grotto—which was part of the reason Hodd had stayed with her the previous visit. They did all help the dock men to unload *Cronecrusher* before Teddy, Mara, and Kara made their way through the docks with bags of supplies.

As they had grown to expect, the mountain's leader came to greet them. "Brother! Sister!" Hodd called. "Ah—Dragonwolf, I see you have saved your little sister." Hodd strode straight to Kara and reached out a hand for her to take. She shook it. He continued, "I am Hodd, leader of the Gylden Grotto mining dwarves. You are kin to us, though you are not officially a forest dwarf ... yet." Hodd guffawed before turning to Mara. "Now, what is it you need, Dragonwolf?"

Mara smiled and held out the load she bore. "We're here to return the remaining supplies you and your people gifted to us. We have been successful. The forbidden lands will plague your people no more."

Hodd whooped and gave Mara a fierce hug, lifting her up in the air despite being half her height, and spinning her around before letting go. Then Hodd's face tightened as he gave Mara a serious look. "Our people will not forget what the forest dwarves have done. You are welcome in our halls whenever you need, and keeping our supplies is the least we can offer you."

"No, it isn't. These will get better use by your people now that we are on our way home. Please allow us to rest here for the night one more time and enjoy your people's company. We will be on our way in the morning."

Hodd nodded. "You know the way."

He beckoned to a few dwarves to take their supplies and they headed off toward the tavern.

The next morning, after sleeping sprawled on the floor of the one room above the tavern, they were abruptly awoken by knocking on the door. Teddy opened it to receive the message master.

"Good morning, brother," Teddy greeted him. "Do you have a letter for me from Freya?"

"Not exactly," the dwarf began awkwardly. "It's—uh—it's for one of your party."

Mara stood and stepped toward the door. "Who's it for?"

"Uh ..." the dwarf rubbed his neck nervously. "It's for Kip, your gnome."

The color drained from Mara's face. Teddy glanced at her and back to the message master. He held out a hand to accept the letter, thanked the messenger, and closed the door.

"Um ... who's Kip?" Kara asked.

Mara didn't hear her. She took the letter from Teddy and sank back to the floor. She dimly heard Teddy explaining that Kip was the one Gaele had killed and was taunting Mara about during their fight—a man that Mara had loved. She sighed and opened the letter. Her eyes immediately filled with tears.

"What does it say, lass?" Teddy asked.

Mara's voice cracked as she read, "Dearest brother, it is so good to hear from you. It has been so long. I am glad to hear you have found a lifemate. Just a little bit of time without us underfoot, and you've made your own life. I'm so happy for you."

"Lifemate?" Kara asked. She gasped. "Like life partner? Were you two married?"

Mara choked and cleared her throat. "No. No, uh, we were going to be when this was all over, but we didn't get the chance. He gave me his ring the day before we left Questhaven on the journey he ... didn't come back from. This letter must be that old."

163

"What else does it say, Mara?" Teddy asked gently.

"I won't give you all the details now, but Loli and I are not at the Big Hill anymore. We have taken up residence in a little cottage off the southern coast near the mouth of the long river. I hope your letter didn't take too long to get to us," Mara read.

Teddy swore.

"Loli is more excited every day waiting for you to come back here and tell him the story of your adventure. He's getting bigger, but he still carries at least one of your carvings around with him everywhere. I know you're busy, and if you are going to fight the big bad, that means I'll see you soon. So, I'll cut my letter off here. I love you brother. Kisses from Loli," Mara finished. She slowly folded the letter, staring at nothing and trying to remain calm.

"So, it took so long for his letter to get to her because she's not where he thought she would be. Where is this place?" Kara asked.

"I remember it from my travels as a younger man," Teddy said quietly. "I can get us there."

"We have to go there?" Kara asked. "Why?"

Mara's hand balled into a fist around the letter. "Because. There's something I have to do."

# CHAPTER FOURTEEN

# LOLI

Hodd pulled Mara into a final tight hug as she stood on the dock. She supposed she should have expected the man to get emotional, given all that had happened in the time they had been coming to Gylden Grotto, but the tears were a surprise. When he released her to embrace Teddy, it looked to Mara to be the most uncomfortable hug her uncle had ever received, and she wished she still had a camera to take a picture. She stifled a giggle.

Hodd went with them out onto the dock and whistled for Keena. Without hesitation, the dragonwolf appeared, landed, and rolled over next to Hodd. He scratched her belly as if she were a small puppy and not a beast ten times his size. Then, he procured an entire rump roast from a pouch at his hip. He presented it to the dragonwolf with a grin, and she licked his face before gingerly taking the meat out of his hands with her teeth and prancing back to the ship.

Hodd turned back to Mara, wiped his tears, and sighed deeply. "Any of you are welcome here whenever you need. And I mean any of you. I know that you have a sea elf hiding aboard." Mara tried to hide her shock, but Hodd waved a hand and handed her a small, wrapped object. "Give him this—a small token of our gratitude for all he has done."

Mara nodded and gave the dwarf one final hug before she, Teddy, and Kara boarded *Harrgalti* and set sail for the Gnome Lands.

As Kara stood at the helm of *Harrgalti*, she was just happy to have a useful job. In the months that she had been with her grandmother, not once had she felt useful. On this voyage the past week or so, she'd periodically taken the watch. It helped her to learn more about the people she was with. Tonight, she was on watch with Finn.

He was the one she'd learned the least about. She wanted to know why he always wore headbands. She wanted to learn more about who his people were and why they were the way they were. The only sea elves she had met were the few Gaele had in her command—all soldiers who scared her—and Finn seemed nothing like them.

*For one,* she thought as she turned around to where he sat at the stern, *something seems to be eating at him, and he hasn't said a thing about it.* She made a face. *I guess that part is like them.*

Kara cautiously walked to the rear of the ship. When Finn didn't look up, she cleared her throat. His emerald eyes met her grey ones. "What's eating at you, sea elf?" she asked. "Do you want to talk about it? I know you don't really know me, but ..."

Finn sat back and looked at her for a moment. Then he nodded. "You know, an outsider's perspective may just be the thing I need," he admitted. "Tell me, what do you know of sea elves? Be honest."

Kara looked at the deck for a moment, wondering if there was any right answer. Really, there was. He'd told her. She gulped. "Sea elves are barbarians. They seem to delight in torture and killing, and they don't have any feelings at all—total apathy for what goes on around them," she said. Seeing how Finn's brows furrowed, she added, "Sorry. You told me to be honest."

He nodded slowly. "Yes, I did." He cleared his throat. "Now, I want you to answer quickly without thinking. Alright?" She nodded. He asked, "From what you know of me in the few weeks since you've met me, would you classify me as a sea elf?"

"No," she said quietly.

"No," he repeated. "And why not? You can think first this time."

She looked out across the water before answering slowly. "You're kinder than the sea elves are. You didn't jump in and fight me that first day when I saw Mara in the park. You comforted me when I almost fell into that chasm without telling me that I was weak for being afraid. You get along with other people because of who they are and not what they can do for you."

Finn nodded speculatively. "Thank you, Kara, for your honesty. Now tell me—are you excited to be going to your new home?"

That was it. He would say no more on the subject. She would have to ask Mara later why Finn would ask her such questions and think only she would give him an honest answer. As their watch wore on, she told him of her own fears instead. How nervous she was about meeting more family and having them turn out to be the same as Gaele. How she worried they would shun her because she served someone like Gaele. Her fear of not fitting in.

By the time Teddy had appeared on the deck to take over the first watch of the morning, Kara felt like she had told the kind sea elf her entire life story, but she still knew nothing about him.

⊕

A few nights later, Finn took the first night watch alone. Knowing quickly that they were on course, he set the pin in the wheel and sat cross-legged in the middle of the deck. He pulled a small item out of his pocket and peered at it.

His gift from the mining dwarves had only given him more cause for confusion about who he really was and who he was meant to be. He traced the features of the little, ruby creature. It was a sculpted red dragon that would fit in his palm. It was beautifully carved, and he did like it, but it wasn't really the gift for a sea elf. A sea elf would have a sea serpent, not a clearly fire-breathing dragon.

He sighed and lay back on the deck to look at the stars. He always thought it was silly when someone looked for the constellations in the sky, but he'd become desperate for answers. He didn't know who to look for. He'd ignored all his lessons about the gods as a child. He settled for Uehrae, the god of strength.

He closed his eyes. "Please help me to find the strength to move forward and to embrace my own destiny, whatever that may be. I need guidance now more than ever. Uh ... thanks," he finished awkwardly.

When Finn opened his eyes and looked back at the sky, the stars in

Uehrae's constellation seemed to swell and contract, as if the god were giving someone a hug. *Surely not,* Finn told himself.

He shook his head and spent the rest of his watch pacing the deck. Before long, Mara had come to relieve him, and he was left to lay in his bunk and wonder until sleep overtook him.

⊕

During one of Finn's day watches with Ashroot, he spotted something in the distance and sent the bearkin down below deck to get Mara. When she got to the top of the stairs, she quickly asked, "What? What is it?"

"We're here," Finn replied softly.

Mara turned to see the Gnome Lands come into view, and she suddenly realized she was not ready. Forget talking to Kip's sister. What in the world was she going to say to little Loli? She ran back below deck and rifled through the chest at the foot of her bed.

"What are you doing, Mara?" Kara asked. Teddy stood beside her, apparently broken out of a conversation.

"We're here," she told her sister flatly.

Teddy gave Kara a curt nod and strode up the stairs to the deck, but Kara still stared at Mara. "What's wrong Mara?" she asked quietly.

"Aunt Freya was upset about the Ranger trial because she knew that Teddy would be coming with me," Mara began. She pulled a shirt from the chest and flung it on the bed. "When she warmed up to it, she made me this dress with a bunch of stuff embroidered on it—ah." Mara pulled the dress out of the chest and stood to shake it out.

"You're going to wear a dress?" Kara asked.

"Yeah, well the people didn't take too kindly to our bringing weapons last time. I don't think there will be any danger here, and this dress is meant to be a symbol of my trial. I've only worn it a few times before." Mara grimaced, remembering that most of those times had not been pleasant.

Since Finn and Teddy were on the deck, Mara quickly shucked off shirt and pants to slip on the deep blue dress and underclothes. She would still wear her dragonwolf bracer, and she slipped her father's dagger into its place in her boot. As she laced up her bracer, she looked at the amber Mark on her left arm. Both were symbols of her duty, identity, and success. She traced the flow of the triskele and marveled at how it still had raised lines like a fresh tattoo, even though it was magically imprinted by a goddess. She hoped it would earn her respect in certain circles—but the sister of her one dead companion was not likely to care.

"Here, sit." Kara gestured to Mara's bunk as she picked up a hairbrush.

To take her mind off the more important dilemma, as Kara began to brush her hair, Mara asked, "How should I wear it, do you think?"

"Just wild and free would be perfect."

Mara nodded, causing Kara to rip through a knotted spot in her hair. She winced. Kara giggled. When Finn came down to tell Mara they'd reached the shore, she stood and breathed deeply.

"Alone? Really?" Teddy asked, crossing his arms.

"Yes—well, just me and Keena," Mara replied. "I don't think it's necessary for anyone else to go, at least not at this point."

"If that's what you think is best, Mara, we'll just wait for you here. We trust your judgment," Finn said. He patted Teddy on the shoulder and the old man grunted in agreement.

Mara nodded and turned. "Are you ready, Keena Keena?"

Keena spread her wings and wagged her tail in response. "I guess that's a signal we can all understand!" Kara said, laughing.

"I guess it is." Teddy chuckled.

"Right." Mara hopped up on Keena's back. "I'll be back before you know it. Let's go, Keena."

Keena took to the sky and flew over the Gnome Lands in search of Kina's cottage. They spotted it quickly—too quickly. Mara saw smoke rising from the cottage chimney and suddenly found it hard to breathe. She patted Keena's neck in a signal that meant she needed to land. The dragonwolf lowered to a cliff by the sea that still allowed Mara to see the cottage in the distance. As soon as Mara's feet touched the ground, she dry-heaved.

It took her a few moments to compose herself. She breathed deeply, in the nose and out the mouth, as she looked out at the challenge ahead. Then she turned, crossed her arms, and stared out over the water beyond.

"I have to make sure I don't do the wrong thing again," she muttered to herself, remembering her last time in the Gnome Lands.

Chief Sokti had been cordial with Teddy, even friendly. But the moment Mara shook his hand like a man, she was no longer welcome. She learned later that he forbade his people from going after their families—those she was then instructed to save as part of her trial. Two of the survivors had been Kip's sister and her son, Loli. Saving her life and that of her son should have endeared Kina to Mara, but trading their lives for her brother's had never been the plan. Had she not saved them, he wouldn't have come along. He never would have met her. There was no way to know how Kina would act until Mara saw her.

"I guess there's nothing for it but to just do it," Mara grumbled. "Right, Keena?"

*Hi, friends! What are you— Hey! Ow!*

Mara turned in alarm to see Keena surrounded by a flock of birds. They were flitting down onto her back and pulling tufts of hair and scales where they could reach. Crows. The clever birds did have a nasty way of annoying other creatures, particularly when they decided to pull nest materials from a living source.

Keena roared. *That's it, you birds!*

She spread her wings, and the birds scattered. She rose into the air and chased them up into the sky and around nearby trees. Mara shook her head and turned back to the cottage. She sighed and steeled herself. *Nothing for it. Time to go.* With one last deep breath, she started walking.

⊕

The gnomish cottage was not what Mara would have expected. The Big Hill was exactly as it sounded. The towns in the Gnome Lands were made up of networks of underground homes tunneled into the hills—one of which was big. It seemed all homes in the Gnome Lands were built into hills. The chimney poked out of the top of the hill, and at its face, Mara could see two arched windows and an arched door, but the home itself was otherwise hidden by the hill. A small fenced-in garden surrounded the entrance.

Mara rested a hand on the garden gate, took a deep breath, and opened it. She stood in front of the door for a few moments trying to bring herself to knock. She could hear talking and laughing coming from inside. Mara held her breath and knocked on the door.

The laughter stopped. "Who's there?" came a female voice.

"It's Mara, the one who brought you and your son out of the chittering darkness almost two years ago," Mara said quietly.

"Oh, it's the nice lady!" she heard Kina say, presumably to Loli.

"Uhkel Tip?" came a child's voice. "Uhkel Tip!"

There was a clatter from within, and the door swung open to reveal a haggard but smiling woman and a small boy who peered around Mara and hopped up on his tiptoes as he searched. Mara avoided Kina's gaze for a moment before looking miserably into her eyes. The woman's face fell. Her eyes darkened.

"He's not with you?" she whispered.

Mara shook her head slowly and mouthed, *No.*

"Wh-where's …?" Loli asked. "Uhkel Tip pay hide an' seek?"

Mara's breath caught in her chest as she shared a look with Kina. Kip's sister wiped her face and put on a smile as she went to her son. "Loli. Loli my boy, Uncle Kip can't be here with us right now. Why don't you go inside while I talk to the nice lady, okay?" Loli stuck out his lower lip for a moment before nodding. "Okay," Kina repeated. She kissed her son on the forehead and patted his back as he turned and headed back into the cottage. Mara watched him go, and only felt she could breathe again when the door shut behind him.

"He's dead, isn't he?" Kina asked quietly.

Mara didn't turn. "He is."

"When did it happen?"

"About six months ago. Uh, six moons," she corrected quietly.

A hand gripped her arm and yanked her around with surprising force. "Six moons?" she hissed. "*Six moons?* How could it take you so long to tell me about it? Couldn't you have sent a letter or—"

"We couldn't!" Mara protested. "Kip didn't know you were here. His

letter went to the Big Hill. We didn't receive your reply until the last visit
we made to Gylden Grotto right as we were about to sail here. We couldn't
have gotten a message here any faster."

Kina released Mara's hand and turned away, shaking her head.
"Unbelievable."

"We did everything we could, Kina."

*"Well, it wasn't good enough!"* Kina hissed.

Silence.

"I ... I know that. I know, Kina. But please trust that I did everything
I could for him. Just like I did everything I could for you when you were in
the cave." Kina flinched. "I'm sorry," Mara added hastily.

"Yeah, I'm sure you are."

No use. Mara knew that feeling. The feeling of hatred and disgust with
what you know and what you are. Nothing she could say now would do
anything for this pain. She flipped up the edge of her dress and pulled a
small carving out of her pocket. She stepped forward and slipped the thing
into Kina's hand.

"I know you don't believe me now, and I know there's nothing you want
to do with me, but I'm here to fulfill a promise. Kip promised that he would
bring this carving home to Loli and tell him the story of this adventure. I'm
here to tell it ... when you're ready."

A playful bark came from the edge of the trees, and Keena bounded
forth. She skidded to a stop when she saw the look on the gnome's face.
Kina looked back and forth between the carving and the creature. Then she
turned to Mara. "I'm ready now," she said shakily.

❖

Kina grudgingly agreed to allow Teddy, Finn, and Ashroot into her
home as well. Mara informed her that they all had stories to tell about Kip,
and that Teddy and Finn would bring a chest full of Kip's final possessions.
Kina didn't want all those people in her home, and once Loli saw a giant
fluffy animal outside his home, he refused to leave the dragonwolf's side.

Kara, having not been told that the others were only allowed because
they had a reason to be there, came along. Once everyone had been

introduced and Loli settled himself against Keena—who was handling her first experience with a toddler quite well—they built a fire just outside the garden. As the sun began to sink in the sky, Mara began her tale.

"The last day you saw your uncle, he got on a boat with me to sail to a magical land. A few magical lands. Our first adventure involved magical water. You see, this water was icy, because the thing in it was a kraken!" She tried to use a spooky and suspenseful voice. Loli jumped, but he stayed silent. Mara went on, "Now, you see, your uncle Kip was ready to tell you this story as soon as we got to the magic water. He spent all his free time making a carving for you. Then, when we least expected it, the ice kraken came!"

Loli buried his face in Keena's fur. Mara chuckled. "No, it's okay, it's okay. He got a big stick, and Teddy there got a big stick." She pointed to Teddy, then to Ashroot. "Then Ash had daggers and I had axes. We fought and fought and fought. And you know how we won?"

"How?" Loli squeaked.

"Well, your uncle Kip walked right up to that kraken and *poked* him in the eye!" she said, poking Loli's belly as she did.

Loli giggled and cried, "Den what? Den what?"

Mara turned to her companions. They looked at each other for a moment, and then Ashroot stood. Mara sat down next to Loli as Ashroot began. "Well, then there was a lot of time when he was helping. We, uh, fixed the boat and sailed up to pick up this guy," she pointed to Finn, "and we sailed all the way around the world to where the gods live. Then we went to a special island that had animals on it like Keena."

"Teena! Yay!" Loli said, patting on Keena's chest.

"Yes! But these big wolves didn't fly like Keena. And some of them were little, like you. Goblins came! Yellow, scary goblins. They tried to take the puppies and hurt their mama. But your uncle Kip said no. Mara and Finn and Teddy fought the goblins, and Kip went out to make sure they would never ever come back again. There's a bunch of wolfies running free on an island because of your uncle Kip. He was very brave whenever he needed to be, and he made sure that the puppies were safe like you."

Keena licked Loli's head as he nuzzled into her fur and smiled. Ashroot turned back to the men, who looked at her briefly before Teddy stood and

Ashroot returned to her seat. Teddy strode over near Loli and knelt on the ground.

"Now, son, what you need to know about your uncle Kip is that his first goal in this entire world was to finish his mission so he could get back to you," he told the boy, tousling his hair. "Uncles don't care about anything more than keeping their Lolis safe. But to do that, he had to keep all the rest of us safe while we were in a dangerous land. And he did. We had to fight people with scary metal sticks that spit fire. There were giants! There were goblins! There were humans! And they can be just as scary sometimes," Teddy said dramatically.

He glanced at Mara before continuing, "Now, you see Loli, I'm a very big man, and I was very proud and didn't think I needed to be protected. Your uncle Kip protected all of us by fighting alongside us, but he also protected me by convincing me to stay safe by wearing a metal shirt. Us uncles have to look out for each other, you know?"

Teddy reached out and tapped a finger under Loli's chin, and then he stood and tousled the boy's hair once more before returning to Ashroot and sitting. Then Finn took a deep breath and stood. As he walked over to Loli, he slipped his necklace out from under his shirt. When he reached the boy, he knelt and showed the carved bullet to Loli.

"You know how your uncle Kip liked to carve things for you when he told a story? Well, he did that for me too," Finn said.

"Weally?" Loli asked.

Finn nodded. "Really. You see, there were a lot of scary things where we were. Really scary things. I didn't know what to do, because I kept getting scared. Do you get scared sometimes, Loli?"

Loli nodded slowly.

"Of course, you do. Everyone does. That's what your uncle Kip was trying to show me. He lit me a candle so I could see when it was scary, and he told me a story all about being afraid, and how it's okay to be afraid, especially when you think you're alone. You're never alone, and even when you feel like you are you can always stand up and face the thing that's scary. Then he gave me this."

Finn held the bullet up for a moment and then put it back in his shirt. "After your uncle Kip gave me such really good advice, we went and faced scary people, and I was really scared. But I thought about what your uncle Kip said, and it got me through it all. The things he told you will last forever, and they will help you all the time, because he was really wise and just wanted to make things better for the people he cared about."

Finn's voice broke at the end, and he returned to his seat without another glance at Loli. Loli began to fuss, and Mara put an arm around him. "It's okay, Loli. There's one more piece of the story to tell. Are you ready?"

Loli looked at Mara with wide eyes. Keena licked his face again, and he laughed, hiccupped, and then nodded slowly.

"Okay." Mara took a deep breath. "Your uncle Kip came with us when we first went to fight the most terrible, bad person in all the forbidden lands. He knew before he went that there was a chance he might not come back. But it was really important that we stop this bad person, so he went anyway. He got hurt, the kind of hurt you can't come back from. It wasn't because he did anything wrong. He protected me. He cared a lot about me, little Loli. Not near as much as he cared about you, but a lot. And when I was threatened, he put himself between the danger and me. That's what a hero does, Loli. We were able to do what we set out to do because he put himself between the danger and me, and he came with me on that trip so he could put himself between the danger and you."

"He did?" Loli whispered.

"He did, little Loli," Mara said. She gave the boy a squeeze. "So, you see, Loli, your uncle Kip is a hero, and so, so loved. He helped rid the world of the deepest evil so you could have a better life ... and he wanted you to have this." Mara held out the dragonwolf carving for Loli to take. Keena fidgeted as Loli looked up at her and back to the carving, and then he gently grabbed it in his little hands. "I promised that I would make sure this got home to you. Your uncle Kip is here with you now, in this, and he will be forever in you," she finished quietly. Her voice cracked, but she willed the tears away.

Loli looked at the little carving and squeezed it tight. The light had all but disappeared from the sky, but as the child held the carving, a new light appeared. The carving began to glow green. The glow brightened and brightened as they all watched in shock. Then, with a flash, the carving disappeared from Loli's grip, and the child began to wail.

# Chapter Fifteen

# The Green Glow

Kina's garden fell into a stunned silence but for Loli's cries. Why had this happened? *What* had actually happened?

"It will all be well, child," came a booming voice.

They all turned toward the forest as a hulking figure stepped out in dirty, brown clothes.

Mara stepped forward. "Wait, I know you!" she cried. "You're—"

"Baerk, the god of the gnomes," Kina breathed.

Baerk beamed at Kina and lumbered forward to kneel beside Loli. "It will all be well," he repeated.

"Did you take it?" Mara snapped. "Why?"

Baerk stood. The smile did not vanish from his face, although he had never been spoken to in such a way. Mara had a way of disrespecting deities. He straightened. "There was a deep magic to this world long before our world was linked with Earth, before it was corrupted."

"Yes, I know that," Mara said. "Aeun told me that when she gave me this!" She stretched out her arm palm up to reveal her Mark from Aeun.

Baerk chuckled. "Yes, my sister told true to a certain extent. The corruption of Earth and the complications of science caused magic to go away, and eliminating that corruption allowed magic to return." He paused. "There's an older magic, a magic that's stronger than Ambergrove itself. You called upon this magic long ago, and only this would allow the other deep magics to return as well."

"What is that even supposed to mean?" Mara asked, irritated.

"It means this is not the first time there has been a green glow due directly to you." Baerk turned his gaze to Ashroot. "Has it, bearkin?"

They all turned to look at Ashroot, who shrunk herself as small as she could. "What does he mean, Ashroot?" Teddy asked quietly.

"Well ... I wasn't sure if what I saw was real. And it was so long ago," she mumbled.

"Tell us, Ash," Mara urged.

Baerk gestured to Ashroot, who began, "Uh ... well it was soon after Kip joined us. He was carving the ... thing ... and you two went below deck to rest while Teddy and I kept watch. When I came down to get you, I saw you glaring over in his direction before rolling over, and when I looked over at him, the carving was glowing green."

Baerk grinned and cleared his throat. Then he rubbed his hands together and opened them again, palms up. The carving rested there in his hands, aglow as before. "And that was the first time you called on the deep magic, Mara."

She stared at the glowing figure and the gears began to turn in her mind. *Was that what I thought I saw in the tent . . .?* She was jostled, and she looked over to see Teddy's concerned eyes.

"What deep magic?" she squeaked.

Baerk waved a hand and a stump appeared beneath him as he sat in it. Mara's eyes widened. Keena growled and Baerk silenced her with a look before turning back to Mara. "I mean, Mara, that this green glow happens when ancient magic is called upon. It is a magic that cannot be conquered or controlled by any other magic in the world, and it is the mother of earth magic."

"When has this glow happened, great chief?" Kina asked quietly.

Baerk smiled. "Well, my child, it has only happened when Mara here has had a strong feeling about your big brother—well, and one other time. More accurately, when she made a vow. The kind of vow that must come to pass. A vow that is spoken with such power and strength that it calls on the ancient magic as an ultimate truth. It's not a promise. It is something that will happen. That must happen. The very foundation of this land demands it."

Kina looked at Mara in awe, and the others did the same, but Mara just shook her head miserably. "It didn't though, Baerk," she muttered.

"What was that?" he asked.

"It didn't," she repeated. "Nothing that I promised to him came to pass."

Baerk held up a hand. "Not *yet.*"

"What is that supposed to mean?" Teddy snapped. Perhaps remembering to whom he spoke, he added, "Great Baerk, I'm sorry, but what is that supposed to mean? Kip is …" Teddy looked over at Loli. "A sacrifice was made to ensure the success of the Ranger trial."

Baerk waved a hand and looked back to Mara. "Mara, you called on the ancient magic when young Ashroot saw you do it, as you sailed through the Ice Mountains and prepared to face the kraken. You looked across the ship at this man you hardly knew, at the carving he had made, and you said that you would make sure he got back here to give his carving to little Loli. Aeun didn't realize what was happening at that time, but I did. My deep connection to the earth has been strained for as long as the science has been here. But as soon as you said those words, something stirred and began to wake."

"Okay, but clearly I wasn't able to—" Mara protested.

"Dragonwolf, just sit and let me explain," Baerk said impatiently. "Man, Aeun wasn't kidding," he muttered.

Teddy laughed despite himself.

Baerk continued, "Next, also with young Kip, you talked of being lifemates. You had your little date to the spring, and it went so well. You were going to go home and be lifemates. So, when you went to your tent that night, you touched his token to you, and you said again that you would bring him back to young Loli. You vowed that you would be lifemates and build a life together, and you would make sure it came to pass."

Baerk paused and looked at Loli. The god held up a hand to count. "That's two."

Loli nodded.

Baerk went on, "Next—and my personal favorite—young Kip had died. Someone has to die for a Ranger trial to be completed, after all. My sister, Easha, goddess of death, was on her way to pick him up. Then you looked out over the sea at the raft that was now aflame, and you vowed that it would not be the end." Baerk shook his hands in the air. "Then, green light. Kip was on the raft ... and then he wasn't."

"What do you mean he wasn't?" Mara snapped.

Baerk grinned. "Kip had died, and you just refused it. You'd said you would do these other things. You said. This vow sent out a pulse throughout Ambergrove. Easha felt it. I felt it. Aeun felt it. And then Kip disappeared. Oh, how marvelous."

Baerk clapped his hands together and sighed. Mara glared at him and cleared her throat pointedly. He continued, "Ah, right. So, next, you were crazy with grief, hammering left and right. You came to your senses—with help—and then you went to the spring that is blessed by Laeghu. You said you would always be his, and you said you would defeat Gaele the way he would have wanted you to. You let the hammer go. Then, again, green light. Then, again, it disappeared. Poof."

Baerk grinned. "And now we are at the crescendo of the whole thing. You see, your task from Aeun was not to bring the magic back. Your task was to defeat Gaele. Had you just killed or imprisoned her, you still would have completed your Ranger trial, and Ambergrove still would have been without magic. But you spared her, and when she returned your mercy with treachery, the magic that was brewing in you boiled over."

"Wait, *I* did that?" Mara asked incredulously.

"You buried your hands in the dirt, and you told Gaele that you would make sure Ambergrove was free of her forever. You said you would wipe the whole continent clean. And then—shaking. Cracking. You removed Gaele from this world and sent her to another, along with all of the corruption in the land. You pressed your hands into the earth and said no."

Mara looked at her hands. They had been hot and sore when that had all happened, but surely that wasn't because *she* had done it.

"With that act, you stripped this world of its bonds. The gods' powers returned in full force, and worldly magic that has lain dormant for centuries came alive again all over Ambergrove. Seasons returned. Magical creatures may be seen roaming the wilds. Magic itself has been granted to those who would have had it without the bonds in the first place. All over the world, it is born again. You did that."

He paused for effect and watched as Mara tried to process the information. When she looked at him, wide eyed, he continued, "You set the wheel in motion by one simple vow. You told a man you hardly knew that you would bring him back to his family. Or rather, you told the carving. Then, as you progressed on your journey, time and time again, you called on the magic. Finally, you returned to do the thing you first vowed to do. And when you handed the carving to Loli, the wheel came full circle, and the other things you vowed finally had to come to pass." He threw his head back and cackled. "Believe me, I have never seen my sister so angry as she was when she realized that your power broke a magic as strong as hers. But you could not have brought the magic back without it."

"What do you mean by that? No one can overpower a god," Finn said.

Baerk grinned. "Aeun's power is binding. Someone must die for a Ranger trial to be completed. And so he did." Baerk paused. "But his story doesn't end there. *You* made sure of that."

Baerk held out the carving, and the green glow grew. It rose and floated over to the edge of the trees, where it expanded and became a flash. When the glow dimmed, the dragonwolf carving remained, held in the outstretched palm of a smiling gnomish man.

Mara blinked to bring her eyes into focus. Kina cried out and Loli clapped his hands. As Mara blinked more rapidly, she blinked away tears, and her vision cleared. There Kip stood, as if he'd been there all along. He was exactly as she'd last seen him when the raft floated into the sea ... and a green flash appeared on the horizon.

Clad in worn, black pants and shirt stood a man who'd barely reach her shoulder. His black hair had grown shaggy, and his earthen skin was free of its former scars. Behind the scraggly beard, the gnome smiled, and when she looked in his eyes, they twinkled—with tears and with love.

"Kip!" Mara cried.

She moved to run to him, but Baerk snapped his fingers and a vine shot out of the ground and held her back. "Now, you have waited six moons, you can wait a little more," he told her.

But she didn't think she could wait more. Neither did Loli or Kina, who stood and also had to be held back by vines. Keena leapt forward, and roots came up to hold her down. Baerk peered around the fire. Finn and Teddy both held their hands up in surrender.

Baerk cleared his throat. "Now then." He turned back to Mara. "You and Kip are bonded to each other. You were bonded to each other from the moment you met, from the moment you first called on the ancient magic. Once you used the ancient magic, nothing would ever be able to keep you apart. No person. No magic. You only strengthened that bond over time. You promised that you would see each other again. You vowed that you would be lifemates. You must be lifemates, for your magic is so strong it can conquer gods. It can conquer death. In the early years of Ambergrove, the ancient magic was the mother of earth magic, and so the product of your bond with each other will be a child of earth magic."

"Wh—"

"You and Kip are destined to be together. You called upon the ancient magic to rid the land of chaos, and you allowed all magics to return to Ambergrove. Earth magic will return, led by a child of yours and Kip's. It is woven into the very fabric of this world," Baerk said firmly.

Mara looked disbelievingly at Kip, who smiled back at her with tears streaming down his face.

"Now, then!" the god said loudly. "I do believe we've talked enough." He looked at Kip. "Dear boy, I enjoyed our time together on my island, even if you did everything in your power to leave it and come back to this family of yours." He gestured to everyone in the clearing. "It's a nice family you have here."

"I know," Kip said with a smile.

"Until next we meet then, Kip." Baerk turned. "Mara. Family."

He tipped his head and snapped his fingers, and then the god vanished. With him vanished the stump chair he'd conjured and the roots and vines holding everyone back. They began to run—all of them—but Mara crossed the distance first, crashing into Kip and squeezing him in the tightest hug she could manage.

He fell to the ground and rolled to keep from tumbling into her. Mara sat on top of him, caressing his face, feeling his beard and his chest and looking into the deep brown eyes, then she threw herself down on his chest and hugged him while he stroked her hair. When she looked up, and their eyes met, they shone with great emotion. He pulled her back into his arms and held her tight, whispering into her hair. "I love you, Dragonwolf."

Just then, Loli crashed unceremoniously into his uncle, knocking Mara to the ground. She laughed and wiped away tears as Kip sat up and hugged Loli.

"Oh, I missed you, little man!" he cried. He grabbed the child's hands. "Still got all your fingers and toes? . . . Yep! You been eating your vegetables, even the nasty, green ones?"

"Kip!" Kina scolded, crossing her arms as she stood by her brother. The grin and the light in her eyes told a different story.

"Oh, sorry. *Especially* the nasty green ones?" Kip corrected.

Loli smiled and nodded.

"Now then, I hear you already got the story from Auntie Mara here, but would you like this?" Kip asked, picking the carving off the ground and handing it to the boy.

Loli squeaked and grabbed the carving, inspecting it, squeezing it, and shaking it before sticking out his lip.

"I don't think it's going to glow anymore, honey," his mother said gently as she knelt down to rest a reassuring hand on his head. She laid the other on her brother's arm and whispered, "It's so good to see you. I missed you so much. You have no idea how things have been."

Kip covered her hand with his as her tears began to flow again. "Hey, it's alright. We'll talk about it all soon."

Just then, a whooshing and flapping sound caught them all by surprise. None had watched Keena as she ran; all were making their own way back to Kip. Keena now landed in the clearing from the opposite direction. Kina stood and pulled Loli back as she approached, and Mara rolled out of the way before turning to look. The dragonwolf walked slowly toward Kip, who stood and waited. When Keena reached him, she sat, tucked her ears back, and dropped a small, chewed-up, slobbery, wooden ball at his feet.

*You were gone so long, I got too big for my toys*, Keena whined.

Teddy threw his head back and laughed, Ashroot grinned, and Mara hung her head and snorted. Kara turned to Finn, who said, "Well, I don't know what the dragonwolf actually said that made them all laugh, but Kip made that disgusting thing for her when she was little. I think that's funny." He smiled.

Kara turned instead to Teddy, who translated for her, making her and Kina laugh with them. Kip smiled as he picked up the slobbery mess. "I think I can make you some bigger ones, Keena."

Keena licked him, and when he threw the ball out into the woods, she chased after it. Kip turned and strode over to Teddy. He reached out his arm and the two clasped arms. "It's good to see you again, son," Teddy said with a nod.

"It's good to be here," Kip replied. Kip gave Teddy a pat on the arm and turned to Finn, reaching his arm out and shaking it as well. "Have you been the hill lion?" he asked.

Finn nodded. "As much as I can, friend."

"Good."

When Kip reached Ashroot, she was crying. She flung her arms around him and squeezed. He returned the gesture. There was no need for words with them. They hugged tightly for a moment before Kip released her and smiled at her. She nodded at him as he turned to the final person in the clearing.

"H-hi," Kara managed.

"Why you look familiar!" Kip said. "You look just like my Mara! You can't be." He turned to glance at Mara and back around. "You're little Kara, aren't you? Mara's sister who made her the little pink thing?" Kip tapped his wrist to demonstrate what he meant.

"I am," she said nervously.

Kip pulled her into a warm hug. "Welcome to Ambergrove. I've heard so many good things about you. I'm sure you'll love it here." Kara's face reddened, but she only nodded. "Now then," Kip began, turning around to survey the people—and Keena, who'd retrieved her ball. "I don't know about you, but I'm *hungry*. The gods have surprisingly little food on their islands. People food anyway."

"I think we can rustle up something," Kina said.

"No gweenies!" Loli cried.

"Okay, no greenies." Kina tousled her son's hair before heading back into the house, Ashroot trailing behind her.

✤

As they ate, they told Kip what had happened in his absence. Teddy explained how Mara had acted a fool for months after he was killed. Kara tried to explain her involvement in everything, but when she began to tell him she started out working for Gaele and appeared in Ambergrove right when he had died—and it was then that she fully realized the blood was Kip's, not Gaele's—Kip held up a hand.

"It doesn't matter what you did then. You were scared and alone. No one can fault you for what happened after. What matters now is that you're here with us."

Mara told him about the final battle, that the one time the green glow happened when it wasn't about Kip was when the earth ripped open to consume Gaele and all her followers and things. "I knew somehow that it must have been because of what was just happening, but I had no idea that I could cause something like that. And then Aeun appeared, told me that I completed my trial, and gave me this."

Mara showed him the triskele Mark on her arm. Kip cackled. "And Aeun was saying how you did such a wonderful job and did everything you needed to do. Meanwhile Baerk and I were sitting back and *laughing*. She was not happy at all. No one has ever thwarted the Ranger trial death rule, and I'm sure no one will again."

"How do you know all this when you were with Baerk?" Finn asked.

"Uh, I didn't," Kip said awkwardly. "Aeun told us about it afterward. But, oh, to have been able to see it!"

Kip stuffed his mouth with food. Although he would tell them some of what happened while he was with Baerk, he would not tell them that he had been livid in the early days on Baerk's island. He'd demanded that the god show him what was going on in his absence. He spent a lot of his time sitting in front of a pool and watching things unfold. He knew what Kara had done because he watched her do it. He also watched her struggle with the turmoil and fear.

He'd watched Teddy go out into the woods and rage on his own, smashing his fists into trees until he had no more energy left. He saw Mara's descent, but he also saw her efforts to save Kara. Saw her lay into that foolish mining dwarf and saw her wear a layer-cake dress. He'd seen Aeun's proclamation of victory to Mara and been so proud of her, and he was shocked out of his reverie when an excited Baerk had told him just how mad Aeun was going to be when her little trial was thwarted by the same ancient magic.

"What's happened to you, Kina?" Kip asked, hoping they wouldn't pick up on his intentional change of subject.

Kina looked around the clearing before answering. Loli was fast asleep on Keena's fur. When she spoke, she kept her voice low anyway. "I told him we were going on an adventure like Uncle Kip," she said.

"And why did you really leave the Big Hill?" he asked.

She sighed and stood. "Chief Sokti was not happy to find his citizens rescued. He turned the people on us, saying that we only survived because we, too, were the darkness and that no one should be made to endure our chittering. So, he cast us out."

Teddy swore. "The Sokti I knew—"

"I know," Kina said. "He used to be good. Something happened to him. He isn't anymore. It's like we were a daily reminder that Mara had proven him wrong. We left, but I had never been anywhere else. I've never fit in with anyone else. So, we wandered a bit until we came here. The place was abandoned, so I cleaned it up and we've been living here."

"What about the others?" Mara asked. She'd saved seven people from the spiders. Had they all been cast out?

"They scattered. Some are in other hills, and some are in their own cottages. Turm and Jyla stayed here with us for a while, and we still send each other supplies and things. Not sure what we'll do now."

Kip glanced at Mara, who was already reaching out to pat Kina on the shoulder. "I don't know what all being the Ranger truly entails, but if Kip will be my lifemate, you will be my sister. The sisters of the Ranger should always be welcome in Aeunna."

"That is, unless she's a homicidal manic who wants to watch the forests burn," Finn quipped, patting Teddy on the shoulder. The old man glared at him, but Kara giggled.

"Well, *my* sisters are always welcome," Mara said. "How about it?"

Kina looked around her for a moment and then down to where little Loli slept peacefully against Keena. "Let's do it," she said.

## CHAPTER SIXTEEN

# FINAL VOYAGE

After well over a year in that cottage, Kina figured there would be more there to take. She was packing up her entire life—hers and Kip's, since she'd brought his belongings with her when she fled the Big Hill. Sure, she would be leaving things for Turm and Jyla, but she was really taking most of her belongings besides the garden.

Thankful that the visitors, her new family she supposed, were outside with Loli and not underfoot trying to help her pack, she surveyed the place that had been her home. Behind her, she heard the door open and close.

"I'm sorry to have left you in the dark for so long," her brother said from the door. "You seem to have done well for yourself while I was gone."

"Yes, Kina who can't do anything right finally did something right on her own this time," she snapped. "And now I'm leaving."

"You know that's not what I meant," Kip said quietly.

"Really? When in my life have you not come to bail me out of my messes?" she asked, wheeling around. "Even when Loli and I were captured, I'm sure you thought it was somehow my fault, because things usually are."

"Kina, I—"

"Don't tell me you didn't."

"Kina."

"What?" she snapped.

He sighed. "I don't know if you heard all the things the actual god of our people was saying out by your garden last night, but I was dead and now am not. I just do not care about certain things that happened in the

187

past. Dying and spending months stuck on an island watching my life go on without me has a way of putting things into perspective."

Kina reddened. "Sorry, brother."

"Hey, no, no, no," he said, pulling his sister into a hug. "No, no. I don't want sadness or pity. I'm here, and you're here. We're going to a new home. A good one. And we're going to have a family for the first time since we were young."

Kina nodded into his shoulder and squeezed into the hug. She took a deep breath. "There is one more thing I want to do here besides just pack up my things."

"Name it."

"Another family lives nearby. One that helped me when I needed it. One that also fled the Big Hill. I want to tell them that I am leaving and I will be safe. My home will be open for the next family that needs it."

"I'll make it happen," Kip said.

He went outside, and when he returned, he informed her that she had an express ride to wherever she needed to go. She was grateful for the solution, but she was not excited to fly a dragonwolf *anywhere*.

They took a few days to pack up Kina's belongings and take them to *Harrgalti*. After their initial outburst of affection, Mara and Kip refrained from public displays. However, when Kip carried a chest below deck and saw his hammer sitting on his old bunk, Teddy came below to find Kip holding Mara consolingly, and they didn't stop when he came down.

"What's this here?" Kip had asked her, holding up the hammer and pointing to a nick on the head.

"I ... boulder ... broke it," Mara mumbled into his hair as he held her.

Kip chuckled. "Well, that's okay, isn't it? It's a weapon. Now, it has character. I'm glad you kept it for me, at least for a while."

In truth, it had appeared on Baerk's island months before, and Baerk told him he would get it back when he resumed his voyage, probably because the god expected a frustrated Kip to turn the weapon on him after so long trying to leave that island.

"What is it, Teddy?" Kip asked, looking up at where Teddy stood by the stairs.

Mara turned as Teddy replied, "You're needed up on deck, Uncle Kip."

Kip loosened his hold on Mara and handed her the hammer, and she gently kissed his forehead before letting go and watching him go up the stairs and onto the deck. Then Mara sank onto his bunk and looked at the hammer in her hands.

"What is it, Mara?" Teddy asked.

"I don't understand, Teddy."

"What don't you understand?" he asked.

"How is this here?" she asked, holding up the hammer. "How is Kip here? How did I call on some ancient magic and why was I worthy of it? Or even worthy of you or Kip or being the Ranger?"

Teddy stepped over and sank onto the bed beside her. "What is this really about?"

"What? That's not enough?"

"It's well more than enough, but I don't think any of those things are what's putting that dead look in your eye when they're all good things."

Mara glanced at Teddy and then rubbed her thumb on the nicked part of Kip's hammer. "I didn't take care of this, Teddy. I should have taken better care of it. Even though I didn't, Kip came back, but . . ."

"But what?"

"But we're finally about to set sail for Port Albatross. This entire time I've been saying that I need to do these things to prove I'm worthy of being the Ranger, but that doesn't prove I know how to take care of thousands of people. What if I do something wrong and they get nicked? What if I'm not good enough?" she asked quietly.

"You are. You know how I know?"

Mara looked up. "How?"

"Because no good leader has ever sat up in a tower and thought that they were perfect at the job. You worry about not being perfect. You worry about how your choices will affect the people you lead. Every day for the rest of your days, you will worry about them. You'll make mistakes—everyone does—but a good leader puts the people first and keeps trying to make their lives better, and I know that's what you will do," Teddy told her. He nudged her playfully. "Besides, if they do get nicked, Freya will be there to patch them up."

"I bet you're ready to see her," Mara said with a smile.

"I have been ready to see her since ... hmm ... right before we fought the goblin raiding party," he told her.

"Really? You got all the way to Questhaven bef—"

"No, no, when we fought the raiding party on the way to Darach," he corrected.

"Oh! ... Yeah, a few days after we left Aeunna sounds about right." She chuckled.

"Just you wait. We'll get to Aeunna, you and Kip will become lifemates, and we'll see how many days you're happy to be away from each other."

"He was dead and now he isn't. I already don't want to be away from him," she muttered. "I feel like if I blink, he'll disappear."

Teddy wrapped an arm around her and squeezed. "That feeling will pass with time," he said quietly. "Peace is on the horizon, and we are going home."

⊕

Kip could hear the child's cries way before he could see him. Kara was crouched next to Loli on the deck, and when she tried to comfort him, he squalled and cried harder. Kara looked up as Kip approached and mouthed an apology. He waved a hand dismissively.

"Hey, what happened, little man?" he asked as he knelt in front of Loli.

"HRBNEE!" he cried.

"You hurt your knee?" Kip asked. Loli nodded miserably and Kip added, "How did you do that? Can you tell me quietly?"

"Tipped onna for paying."

"You tripped on the floor while you were playing?"

"Yeah."

Kip rolled up Loli's pants and examined the knee. There was a little redness, but no scrapes or bruises. "Oh, I see," he told Loli. "You've got a boo-boo here that is going to take special Uncle Kip power to fix. Are you ready?"

190

Loli nodded and sniffled. Kip grinned and winked at Kara before gently pushing Loli to lie back on the floor. He pulled up Loli's shirt to reveal his belly button. Taking a deep breath, Kip bent down and blew a raspberry on the child's belly. Once, twice, thrice. Loli began to laugh, so Kip did it one more time, and then he looked at the knee again.

"Yep! That fixed it! Good as new!" he told the boy.

Loli jumped up and hugged Kip.

"Why don't you come with me and Auntie Kara back to your mama's house so we can get some more of your things to put on the ship? How does that sound?" Kip asked.

Loli nodded and ran down the plank and off the ship. As soon as he was out of sight, they heard a thud.

"Are you okay, buddy?" Kip hollered.

"Tay!" Loli responded in the distance.

"Okay, good!" Kip laughed and shook his head as he turned to Kara. "Thank you for your help with him. I'm sure you didn't do anything wrong. He's always been a dramatic and needy child."

"How did you do that?" she asked awkwardly as she stood.

"Do what?"

"Figure out what he was saying! I mean, I knew what he did because I saw it happen, but I couldn't understand what he told me besides that he wanted you," Kara said.

"Oh. Yeah. Well, it took some time. Boy was quick to start babbling, but he apparently hasn't learned to turn that babble into words, so it's about the same as I remember it. I suppose there wasn't a great opportunity for him to talk to anyone besides Kina since then, so it would make sense for there to be little difference. But anyway—you pick it up the more you hear it. You'll figure him out by the time we get to the mainland. Maybe he'll be using real words by then!" Kip replied.

"Maybe," she said quietly. "I liked that you called me Auntie Kara."

"Well, that's what you are, aren't you?" Kip said with a grin. "Come on, let's go make sure he makes it to the house in one piece."

They didn't have far to go, because Kina and Keena flew over just as they were stepping off the ship. Loli came running back toward the dragonwolf, and as she tried to land, she had to dodge the giggling child.

Kina slid off Keena's back and turned a sour look to her brother. "Kip, if you ever suggest to me to ride any animal other than a well-trained, very, very, *very* old horse, I will send you back to Baerk's island myself!"

"What? Did you not have fun?" he asked innocently.

Keena barked and yipped.

"No dice, Keena," Kara told her. "None of us get it. You're talking to literally everyone who doesn't understand you."

"Well, besides Finn," Kip noted.

The dragonwolf huffed and turned her attentions to Loli, who was wrapping his arms and legs around one of her legs.

"How did you fare otherwise?" Kip asked his sister.

"It went well," she replied. "I told them about where I was going, and they were so happy for us. There's two families that have been living in that house for the past few months, so one of them will move their family here instead. We're going to leave a lot more than we planned, so we should be about ready to go."

"Well, let's go see," Kip said. "I, for one, do not want to see how grumpy the old man gets the longer we wait."

As suspected, their remaining belongings were packed up in no time. Once everything had been loaded onto the ship, they set sail from the Gnome Lands on the final leg of their voyage back to Port Albatross.

⊕

Finn swung his sword, and it met Kip's with a clang. The two men panted and wiped their sweating faces as they circled each other. Teddy, Mara, and Kara all came onto the deck to see the battle well underway. Keena, Ashroot, Kina, and a giggling Loli were sitting on the sidelines to watch.

"What's this then?" Mara asked.

"We need to get Kip back in shape," Finn said.

"What do you mean? I'm in shape. Look," Kip taunted before tucking and rolling to Finn's other side and slapping his thigh with the flat of the blade.

Before Kip could stand back up, he'd been rapped in the back with the flat of Finn's blade. "Yes, I see what you mean. I guess all shapes are relative," Finn retorted.

"Round is a shape," Kara said.

Mara grinned at her sister and made a gesture to show she understood the reference—something from their childhood no one here would get. Kip stood and gasped theatrically in Kara's direction before ducking a swing from Finn at the last minute.

"Alright, then. That's enough, lads. Let's call it a draw. Finn, you're needed for some supper preparation," Teddy said.

The men stopped and lowered their swords. Finn gestured to Teddy with his. "You know, it is just a hurtful stereotype that elves are good fishermen. Just because I grew up on the water does not mean I can commune with the beasts that are in it."

"If you don't want us to assume you're the great fish whisperer, perhaps just once you should do a merely passable job when you're fishing," Kara quipped.

Everyone laughed but Finn, who scowled at Kara. "Perhaps you would like to spar with Kip, then, while I go and whisper to the fishes, eh?"

"Sure, if you can handle it, I'm sure I can too," she retorted as she jumped up and took his practice sword.

Finn grumbled as he stalked off in search of his fishing pole. Kip grinned in Finn's direction before turning to Kara. "Have you sparred before?" he asked.

She made sure Finn wasn't looking, and then she shook her head.

"That's okay. Basically, you start by tapping swords together to indicate you are ready to begin. Then, it's the same as any other swordfight, just with one condition—you aren't trying to hurt me. You're trying to tap the flat of your blade somewhere on my body, and each hit is a point. Good?"

"Yeah, I've got that," Kara replied with a nod.

"Okay, we'll go slow to start with and speed up as you're ready."

Kip raised his practice sword in the ready position, and Kara raised her sword to tap his. He swung slowly, and she blocked. He swung again, and she blocked. Then, he held his sword up and gestured for her to come at him. She swung timidly, and he blocked. She swung again, a little more forcefully, and he dodged.

"Good, Kara," Mara said. "Now, really give it to him!"

"Whose side are you on?" Kip asked.

"Hey, I'm with the underdog."

"That would be him, then," Kara said. Kip raised a brow. She raised her hand waist height and added awkwardly, "because of the ..."

Kip gasped dramatically and lowered his sword as he looked at Mara. "Are you sure she's your sister? She really needs to work on the sparring talk bec—ow."

While he wasn't looking, Kara had rapped the flat of her blade on his stomach. "At least I know not to turn your back on your opponent," she said playfully.

"Oh, that's how it is? Mhmm. Okay," Kip replied.

"Maybe you are out of shape, Kip, if a sixteen-year-old unpracticed youth can get the first blow in," Teddy said with a grin.

They got back to it, more determinedly this time. Kip went easy on her, and they all knew it. There really wasn't a need for a winner or loser—but that didn't mean they weren't going to keep score. Once they both started breathing heavily with the effort, Teddy called for them to finish up. Kip pressed forward and knocked Kara to the ground, reaching his free hand out to grasp her shirt so she would fall down easily.

"Valiant effort, sister, but you—"

Kara spun and swung a leg around, taking both of his out from under him. When he fell unceremoniously to the ground next to her, she tapped her practice sword on his chest.

"Winner!" Teddy boomed. "Well done, my girl!"

"No, wait, that's another draw, isn't it?" Mara asked.

Kip sat up and turned to Mara. "No, actually, I knocked her down, but there's no point for that because I didn't get a hit in." He looked down at Kara and tousled her hair.

"Hey!" she protested.

"Get used to it," Kina called. "That's what brothers are like."

Loli was excited to be at sea, and after a little seasickness, and few days to get his sea legs—which, for a small child, was not much better—he spent a lot of the voyage pinballing from one side of the ship to another, looking at all the creatures in the water.

Teddy stood at the helm, and Kara watched Loli while his mother helped Ashroot with lunch below deck. She soon discovered that babysitting Loli required all hands on deck—literally and figuratively. The boy was full of questions, and she was still trying to learn the things he said.

As Loli stood on his tippy toes to look out over the water, he heard snippets of their conversation.

"... I don't know, Teddy. Really, I just hope she doesn't hate me," Kara said quietly.

"She won't hate you. She likes Mara, and Mara's the one who pulled me away on this dangerous trip," Teddy replied.

"Auntie Tawa, was da?" Loli cried, looking out over the water and pointing as something that looked like a ball came to the surface.

"He said—"

"I know what he said, Teddy. He says that one a lot," Kara told her uncle. She came over to the bulwark and leaned to see what he saw. "What is it, buddy?"

"Dare!" he said, pointing.

"Ah! That's a turtle, Loli. Can you say tur-tle?" Kara asked.

"Tuhtle," Loli said.

"Close enough. Turtles are really old. They live in big shells, and they swim all over the water," Kara explained.

"Nite?" Loli asked.

Kara turned to Teddy, who said, "Yes, they're nice, buddy."

"Tay."

Loli ran over to the other side of the ship and looked over again at the water as Kara straightened and turned back to Teddy. "Anyway, that's different, Teddy. She had a really important mission, and you were on the same side. You protected each other."

"Hey, look at us," Teddy replied. "Same side. Same—"

"Auntie Tara, was da?"

Kara walked to the edge of the ship just as a dolphin burst up out of the water, sending a spray onto the deck as it splashed back below. Loli giggled and clapped his hands joyfully.

"That's a dolphin, Loli," Kara told him. "Can you say doll-fin?"

"Dahfin."

"That's right! Dolphins are big fishes that like to play in the water by jumping up and down."

Loli ran along the bulwark around the deck, jumping up and down and shouting, "Dahfin! Dahfin!"

As he ran around, he heard Teddy and Kara talking.

"…and you can … don't worry about …"

"…but what if … I don't want to … if I could just …"

Loli stopped jumping. "Auntie Tara, was da?"

It looked like a horse. He'd seen horses before. One of his mama's friends had one. But this also looked like a fish. Kara came up behind him and peered into the water. "Uh … I don't actually know what it is, buddy. Teddy?"

"Uhkel Teddy, was da?"

Teddy sighed and put the pin in the wheel to keep it sailing true. When he looked over into the water, he swore. Kara clapped her hands over Loli's ears and kicked Teddy in the shin. He hardly moved.

"What is it, Uncle Teddy?" she repeated.

"The horse's head, the fin-like mane, the giant tail of a whale … that's a hippocamp," he muttered.

"Hip tamp! Hip tamp!" Loli cried, stamping his feet and running around the deck again.

"But those are make-believe!"

"Have you ever seen one here before?"

"No one has seen one for generations."

"But what does that mean?"

"Hip tamp! Hip tamp!" Loli cried.

"We'll have to talk about it later," Teddy said wryly.

The hippocamp was just the first magical sea creature they saw on the way to Port Albatross. As the days wore on, they spotted a sea serpent and a morgawr, which Mara and Kara both referred to as a Nessie. At night, the water seemed to glisten with an unidentifiable light, like magic was flowing through the sea itself. As they neared Port Albatross, it became a game to count the hippocampi they saw swimming alongside them.

Teddy said that the signs they saw in the forest when they left what was formerly known as Chaosland, and all the new creatures they were seeing in the sea, were signs that magic was seeping back through Ambergrove. How exactly, none of them knew, but what they did know is that there was new life all around them.

"You know what this voyage needs?" Mara asked one night after supper.

"More daring swordfights with Kara?" Finn joked.

"More of Finn's delightful cooking?" Kara retorted.

"Some peace and quiet from fussy children?" Kina interjected, glaring at them both.

"No, but we do have a child here with us now. I think we should play Teddy's favorite children's game," Mara said, grinning at her uncle.

"Game! Game!" Loli cried.

"Yes, I'd like to know what this game is," his mother said.

"Did my dad play it?" Kara asked.

Mara and Teddy shared a glance, and Teddy said, "Yes, lass. Yes, he did."

"How do we play?" Kina asked.

Quick directions were given, and then they cleaned up the table together and went up to the deck to play Bullfrog's Hunt. Loli was given an advantage, since it was a game with no winners—and they wanted to avoid Loli getting hurt or someone else getting kicked in the head—so when it was Loli's turn to jump, Kip picked him up and sprung him over his mother.

Kip himself missed the first jump, and the game began. They played until Loli was ready for bed. When his mother was walking him down the stairs, he began to rub his eyes and cry.

Teddy said, "Don't worry, little man. We'll play it every day when we get home to Aeunna."

"Every day?" Mara murmured.

"Pomise?" Loli asked.

"I promise. Now, you get on to bed," Teddy replied.

"You sure you won't get tired of playing it every single day?" Mara asked when Loli was out of sight.

Teddy's eyes began to shine and water. "You know, there came a time when I got tired of playing it with your da," he croaked. "I will never tire of it again."

Mara wrapped an arm around him and squeezed, and Kara hugged the other side. After a moment, Teddy sniffed and shook them gently off, saying, "Now it's time for those of you who don't have first watch to head to sleep."

Kip, Ashroot, Finn, and Kara headed down to the bunks. They were short one bunk since they'd picked up three people in the Gnome Lands, so Kina and Loli bunked together in the bunk that was once Kip's, and Kara took the one that had previously been unoccupied. Since there was always at least one person on watch at all times, Kip placed his trunk next to Mara's and slept in whichever bed was free at the time. This time, he slept in Mara's.

As Kip drifted off to sleep, he closed his hand around the trinket he wore. Baerk had shown him what had happened after his death, and the god seemed to relish in the pain that unfolded as Kip's body was prepared and he was pushed out to sea. Watching as Mara snapped off the necklace he'd made for her on the eve of the Serpent's Gauntlet, he could almost feel her delicately tie the thing around his own neck. That was the first time he'd tried to attack Baerk, and it wouldn't be the last.

The necklace had been a treasure, a comfort in those months alone on the island. He would hold it in his hand every night when he went to sleep and imagine that he was back with Mara. It had become a habit, and nothing changed when he was finally reunited with his family—past and future. He still held the necklace. He still dreamed of her. Only, this night, he dreamed of a village in the trees and a miserly old gnome sitting in a rocking chair beside a white-haired forest dwarf.

The smiles he saw on their faces shone like beacons, and the warmth of them seeped through Kip as he was nestled under his blanket in Mara's bunk. He looked in the old gnome's eyes and saw only contentment.

*Soon,* he told his elderly self. *Soon we will be to Port Albatross, and from there . . .* *Aeunna.*

# CHAPTER SEVENTEEN

# PORT ALBATROSS

As they say, time flies when you're having fun—and the expanded crew of *Harrgalti* enjoyed each other's company. Ashroot insisted on switching out the plain, blue sail for her special one before they reached their destination. A few days out from Port Albatross, Teddy and Finn dug out the blue kraken sail with the colored chevron background—a sign of their might that hadn't seen the light of day in over a year. Before long, the mainland was in view, and the sun had just set when Finn steered *Harrgalti* to the docks of Port Albatross. Lanterns were lit down the streets and on buildings.

"We can leave *Harrgalti* at the dock for the night. There's sure to be rooms for us at The Pleasant Mariner," Teddy said.

They took only what they needed for the night and walked up the cobbled streets to the familiar inn. Whereas the port was settling down for sleep, they could hear the bustle of the inn well before they reached the doors. Mara stepped to the front of the group and pushed them open. The sound and smells hit them like a slap. An impossibly stronger hit immediately followed Bowen the innkeeper's booming cry. The large human had a bearlike grip.

"Tederen! Young Mara! Bearkin!" Smashing hug, smashing hug, smashing hug. "And you look almost like young Mara. Are you also a forest dwarf?" Bowen asked Kara.

"This is my little sister, Bowen," Mara said, resting a hand on Kara's shoulder.

"Sister! How marvelous! Welcome, Mara's sister!" Bowen boomed, doling out another smashing hug to Kara.

"Kara," she squeaked.

"Welcome, Kara! And who are these new ones?" Bowen bent down to pat Loli on the head, but the child tucked himself protectively behind his mother.

Kina chuckled. "This is Loli. He's a little shy around … big people. I'm Kina, his mother."

"Loli and Kina! Welcome to my inn. I am Bowen." He looked at Kip. "And you must be the lucky husband and father."

Kina and Kip glanced at each other before bursting into a fit of laughter. Seeing Bowen's bewildered expression, Kip said, "Ah, it's a common mistake. This here's my little sister. Loli is my nephew. I'm Kip. And before you get started, this guy is Finn. No relation." Kip stuck a thumb behind him to gesture to Finn.

"Ah, well. Welcome *Brother* Kip and No Relation Finn!" Bowen reached out a hand to each man, and they shook it before Bowen turned back to Teddy and Mara. "Is that all of your company now?"

"No, actually, we've got one more, but I'm not sure if you'll be able to accommodate her," Teddy said, winking at Mara.

"Come on, then. Let's see!" Bowen boomed.

Mara beckoned Bowen to step just outside the inn and then called, "Keena Keena!"

Keena flew down and landed on the ground in front of Bowen. The portly man stumbled backward into Teddy's waiting arms, and Teddy steadied him.

"That's a …" Bowen began slowly. He turned to Mara. "You really are a dragonwolf!"

"More than you know," she replied with a smile. "You can pet her. She doesn't bite."

Bowen reached out a hand to pat Keena's nose. Emboldened, he then scritched behind her ear and down her neck. She wagged her tail.

"Well, Bowen, do you think you have accommodations for her?" Teddy asked.

Bowen stammered a moment before whistling sharply to call a few of his hands to him. A human man and woman emerged from the inn at his call. "Move the horses to the northern stable and lay out thick, fresh bedding for this one in the western stable. She is to be the only one in it and be given anything she needs." The hands nodded and headed off in the direction of the stable. "Now," Bowen spun to face Mara and Teddy. "You *must* tell us your story."

Mara and Teddy exchanged a glance. They had just docked after weeks at sea. None of them were in the mood to tell a story. "Is Salali around?" Mara asked. "I'm sure she has a story she could tell tonight."

Bowen shook his head. "Nah. She did stop in a few days ago, but she left yesterday. Something about a red dress."

"Oh," Mara replied quietly.

Kip stepped forward. "Tell you what, Bowen. Why don't I tell you the story of Mara's trials leading to the Dragon's Teeth tonight, and Mara and Teddy can tell you the rest of the story tomorrow? To tell you the truth, I've done more playing than working." He tousled Loli's hair.

"Wonderful!" Bowen boomed. "Come in and eat, and then you can tell us your tale!"

Bowen turned and headed back into the inn as Kip asked, "Wait, what do you mean by 'us?'"

Teddy clapped Kip on the shoulder and chuckled as they all headed inside for a warm meal. Kip consulted briefly with Mara beforehand so she could fill in some holes for him from before he joined them. Then, they sat around a table together and ate while Kip sat by the fire and told the tale of Mara's trials to excited children, including Loli. Unable to tell a story without whittling, Kip made some hasty animals as he told the story of Mara and the Dragon's Teeth.

"Not too far from here, in the land of the forest dwarves, there was a girl named Mara. Mara wasn't like other girls. She was special. Really special. I mean, she—"

Teddy cleared his throat.

"Anyway!" Kip went on, "Mara was the person who was supposed to be the great Ranger of the forest dwarves, but to do that, she had to prove herself first. The first thing she had to do was prove that she was one of the forest dwarves. Forest dwarves, you see, can talk to animals. So, they sent her out into the forest to the lair of the Great Silver Bear.

"She took weapons with her, as anyone should do when they go out into the forest alone, but she didn't want to fight the bear. Her best friend was a bear, you see." He gestured to Ashroot, who waved. He went on, "So, she talked to the bear, told him what she was there for, and you know what he did?"

There were scattered shouts of, "What?" and "What did he do?"

Kip grinned. "He talked back. And then he gave her two presents. He let her take a book from his treasure and in return took something from her, and then he gave her a cut here," Kip drew a hand across his chest, "to show her people that she'd seen him and he'd blessed her. So, then, she went back to her people, and they gave her a big forest dwarf to go on her trip with her. Then her forest trial was complete."

The children ogled Mara, peering at her chest in search of the scar. Kip made one final cut to the little piece of wood in his hand, blew on it, and then reached down to hand it to a small girl in the front. She peered at the crude little bear and grinned toothily. Kip pulled out another piece of wood as he began again.

"Next, she, the big man, and the little bear came here to this inn! They stayed here for a little while to make final preparations, and then they got in the boat and sailed to their next destination, the Gnome Lands—my lands—for her hill trial. For her hill trial, the chief of the gnomes had her go outside the village to the scariest place nearby: the Cave of Chittering Darkness!"

The tone had the desired effect. The kids gasped and squeaked. Kina cleared her throat this time, and when Kip looked at her, she made a pointed glance toward where Loli sat, clearly distressed, listening to the tale. Kip nodded to her and went on.

"You see, there were really brave people in there. Kids, and mamas and dadas, who were able to live in that cave with the scary things because they were brave. But they didn't need to stay there and be brave. Instead, they deserved to be safe in a home. So, Mara went into the caves to get them. Guess what she found?" Kip looked around at the kids.

"Goblins!" one shouted.

"Bats!" shouted another.

"'Piders," Loli whispered.

"Correct!" Kip said brightly. He patted Loli's shoulder. "There were spiders. Not little spiders, though. These were big, giant spiders, and this trial did mean she had to fight. Mara went through the whole network of caves, defeating the spiders until she came to the lair where the people were. She brought them outside, and they were safe, never to have to live through anything so scary again. Never ever. ... And then *I* decided to come along with Mara, and the hill trial was won," he finished.

Kip sat in silence for a few moments as he finished the carving he was working on, and then he blew on it and handed it down to a young boy in the middle of the group of children. The kid squawked and dropped the little spider before realizing it wasn't real. Laughter rang through the inn. Kip grinned, picked up another piece of wood, and went on.

"Then, she had to go get her last person, a fearsome sea elf! To do that, Mara had to go to the sea elves' lands, taking us along with her, and complete something known as the Serpent's Gauntlet. During this gauntlet, Mara had to go through ten rooms, fight the queen's champion, and win. First, she had to fight a shark! Then, she had to fight jellyfish and get some gems to make a key. *Then*, she had to fight spiky, wood men and get to the other side of the room. Then, she went to a room with a kraken in it!"

The kids all gasped, and Kip laughed. "Well, she'd defeated krakens before, so this time was easy for her. Then she had to climb up a mountain and back down, across a sea of brown, and to another intelligent creature. This creature was a giant turtle. She talked to the turtle just as she'd talked to the Great Silver Bear, and the turtle told her how to move forward. She got through the last trap, got herself bandaged up, and went for a final duel with the sea elf champion. When she won, a sea elf came along with us. *That* one." Kip gestured to Finn, who made a face he thought was scary. The kids laughed.

This carving had been an easier shape to complete quickly, so he simply tossed the little sea turtle into the crowd of children, and one near the back caught it. Kip smiled, and then he picked up a collection of small pieces of wood.

"Finally, Mara sailed across the sea to the Dragon's Teeth, and she did something no one else had been able to do. She sailed through it! We all celebrated, and then Mara went to see the goddess Aeun. A little while later, we sailed back through the Dragon's Teeth again and began our next adventure ... which you will hear tomorrow, children."

The kids all groaned. Kip chuckled and passed out his final carvings, passing one to each of the kids who didn't already have one of the bigger ones. They were just carved to look like pointy teeth. That was the end of his part of the story. When the tale was done, children and adults alike cheered for Kip and for Mara. Bowen said his customary closing for the night, and they all headed up to their rooms.

✦

When Mara awoke to the sound of waves and seagulls the following morning, she was reminded of her first morning at Port Albatross and how excited she'd been to see the sea. She'd had more than enough of the sea after a two-year voyage, but she still rose early and dressed, heading down to the dining area for a bit of breakfast.

She ate a hash brown casserole provided by the morning cook. There weren't many others in the hall when she arrived, and most were weary adventurers with no mind to pester her—for that, she was grateful. She had her breakfast in silence and headed out the door down to the market with the early morning light.

She knew right where she wanted to go. She weaved through the shops until she could see the rising smoke of a blacksmith's forge. She saw Gryffyth before he saw her. "Excuse me, sir, I'm looking for a Welshman to make me a cage for my hair. Know anyone like that?" she asked. Gryffyth turned and Mara threw her hands up in mock surprise and cried, "Oh, I see you do!"

"Hey there!" Gryffyth greeted her. "You're Teddy's kid, right? Clara?"

"Mara. Niece. Close," she replied.

"Been quite a while, hasn't it?" he asked.

She nodded. "How are things?"

"Business is good. Did you really want another bun cage or were you just getting my attention?"

"No, I would like another one," she replied, "with this symbol in the dome and the head of the stick." She stuck out her left arm and turned it over so he could see the leafy triskele Mark.

His eyes widened. "Is that—"

"Yes, from Aeun. I did what I set out to do, and I'm going home to Aeunna."

"I guess congratulations are in order, then. Ranger." Gryffyth tipped his head respectfully.

"My thanks, Gryffyth," Mara replied. "Now I really must be on my way. I'm looking for Lir."

"Ah, Lir's not at port right now," Gryffyth told her.

"He's not? But I thought he was always here."

"Normally he is, but he goes out to test the ships on the waters and he goes out to get more wood to bring back to the shipyard. Lir doesn't build a ship unless he harvests the wood himself," Gryffyth explained.

"So, where is he now?"

"He's doing a bit of both. He sailed around to Nimeda to get some sgiath wood for some rowboats for a large cargo ship. He's due back in about a week."

"Marvelous," Mara muttered. The last thing any of them would want would be to hang around in the port to wait for Lir's return, but they had to be there to give him *Harrgalti*. "Thanks, Gryffyth. I'll need to go tell the others. Thanks for your help, Welshman."

Gryffyth grinned at Mara and winked as she waved and turned away to head back to The Pleasant Mariner.

❖

"Well ... that's unfortunate," Kara said.

"Unfortunate?" Teddy snapped. He rubbed his bald head and angrily scratched his beard. "Yeah, it's a little unfortunate," he added more calmly.

Kara and Mara shared a glance, Kara's sheepish. Mara couldn't explain to her sister now that it wasn't her fault he responded the way he did. Teddy had been away from Freya for so long, and it was finally almost time to see her again. Now, he would have to wait longer.

"Teddy, why don't you show everyone around the port this week?" Mara said gently. "It will make the time go by faster and you'll be able to help Kina and Loli see things."

"And maybe Finn and Kip," Kip said, winking at Mara. "We can make a big family event out of it before we start spending less time with each other."

Teddy turned to look at the apprehensive glances from the others. "Aye." He sat at the table in The Pleasant Mariner as breakfast was brought out, and he ripped open a biscuit and stuffed it in his mouth before asking, "Wha blyu be doin?"

"Didn't your mother teach you not to talk with your mouth full?" Kina asked scathingly.

Teddy gulped. "Sorry, lass." To Mara, he repeated, "What will you be doing?"

"There's a few places I wanted to look at last time we were here. I've been keeping them in mind for whenever we came back. But I'm sure you can entertain yourselves, right?" Mara asked before ripping off a piece of another biscuit and stuffing it into her mouth.

❖

When Mara walked into the colossal library at Port Albatross, she was amazed to find a collection of books that would rival the Library of Congress. Shelves lined the walls from floor to ceiling, and to the same height all throughout what she could see besides what appeared to be the librarian's table. Each shelf had its own rolling ladder. It was a reader's paradise.

Mara walked up to the counter, where an ancient man sat writing. When she approached, he looked up, grumbling about preparing a catalogue of fire books a week in advance, and pressed his glasses up on his nose. "How may I help you, my dear?" the man asked.

"Hi! I was wondering if you have any books on ancient history or ancient magic I could look at," she replied pleasantly.

"Certainly. Right this way, my dear."

Mara thought she could hear the creaking and cracking as the old man stood. His body was so hunched there was barely a change to his height. He picked up a walking stick that was nearly twice his size and shuffled out from behind the counter. Three of his slow, shuffling steps amounted to one of Mara's steps, but she patiently walked beside him as he led her into a side room that had a table in the center and was lined with shorter shelves.

"This here is our ancient history," he said, pointing to the shelves to the left. "It covers the oldest things we know of our world." He pointed to the right. "This here is about the magics we once had, before the forbidden lands became forbidden and science corrupted magic." He patted Mara gently on the arm. "I am pulling materials for a mining dwarf patron, so I may not be at the front desk, but please do let me know if you need anything else."

She thanked him, and he left her alone in the room. She started on the left, pulling books out and stacking the ones she thought would be helpful on the table. Then she went to the right. When she had a tall stack piled up, she went to the table, sat, and opened the first book.

The first thing she learned was that the Ambergrove she'd come to was very different from how it had been before. So many customs of this world had fallen by the wayside over the millennia, and as a result, the age she was living in was referred to as the Lost Age. Seasons stopped, and most thought of time stopped. Years, months, and days had not been catalogued since the start of the age.

Before science came and magic was lost, the people went by a calendar system similar to the Vikings. As with the runes, there was really no telling which came first. The year started with the first full moon of spring, and each month was exactly twenty-eight days, or a full turning of the moon.

The First Age was the age of the dragons. That was the time before people were created and the evil dragons had to be imprisoned in Fengel. Once people were born, the Second Age began, and it was known as the age of man until the magic was lost.

She found so much about magic itself. The ancient magic used to be known and revered. It was said that only a small few could call upon the ancient magic. It was said that in the core of Ambergrove, deep underneath the earth, the first dragon lay dormant. This dragon created the world as it was, created the first dragons, and even created the gods before it went dormant. When someone calls upon the ancient magic, they are calling upon the world dragon and channeling the power of the dragon itself.

Mara looked down at her hands. She'd been channeling the power of a dragon? She shook her head. *Nah.*

It was said that the dragon gifted magic to the gods so that they could care for Ambergrove after it was gone. Some magic of mortals is gifted by the gods, but there are still always a chosen few whose power comes directly from the world dragon. People used to be able to harness the elements, and magical creatures walked the earth, swam the seas, and soared in the skies. It sounded like a paradise.

She didn't realize how long she had been reading until the librarian returned to the small room with a lantern for her use. Her stomach grumbled. She returned all her books to the shelves, thanked the librarian, and headed down the street back to the inn for supper. When she returned to The Pleasant Mariner, an audience sat ready for her and Teddy to continue their tale. And so they began.

❖

After a few days of touring with an increasingly grumpier Teddy, everyone decided to branch out on their own—or, at least away from Teddy. Ashroot didn't feel the need to do much of anything else in Port Albatross, so she spent her time in the kitchens of The Pleasant Mariner, assisting the cooks and teaching them some bearkin methods of cooking. Kara, Kip, Kina, and Loli went to find fun places together. Finn hung around the shipyard.

It was Finn's hovering and reflection that allowed him to be the first to see Lir's return. He had seen other sea elves in the port the past few days. Some had tried to engage with him, but none seemed to realize that he was their prince—or at least he used to be. They were just travelers with the intent of going back home, but he was intrigued by Lir, half sea elf and half forest dwarf. A man of his own.

Lir steered the cargo ship into the dock as if it were no more than a small sailboat. When the blue-skinned, ginger-haired, bearded man strode off the docks, Finn was there to meet him. He stood squarely in front of Lir with his arm outstretched.

Lir stopped and did not reach out his own hand. "You are?" he asked suspiciously.

Finn reached up a hand and slid off the bandana that covered his rounded ears before reaching his hand out again. "I am Finn, and I'd like to talk with you."

Lir glanced at Finn's ears only briefly before taking his outstretched arm. "Lir."

⊕

That evening, when Finn returned to The Pleasant Mariner, he sat down for dinner and told the group that Lir had returned. Early the following morning, Teddy was beating on doors to wake them all up. Mara and Finn were the only ones who would come along at that hour. Breakfast was barely-cooked muffins as they walked down the street.

Lir was standing on the deck of *Harrgalti* when they approached the docks just before sunup. He greeted Finn with a nod, Teddy with a clap on the shoulder, and Mara with a brief hug before making a show of resting his hands on his hips and looking sternly at Mara.

"She's pretty banged-up there, lass," he said disapprovingly.

"We slew an ice kraken while on this ship, Lir! A kraken!" Mara replied. "Tentacles and icicles and … stuff." She raised a hand. "Oh! Then, *then* it was fixed up by Isi in Nimeda. You know her. And uh … then we went through the Dragons Teeth. But I only bumped her a few times, I swear."

"It's true." Finn added. "Sailed like a proper sea elf she did."

Lir leered at him and then at Mara. "Very well, then. I'll be taking her back off your hands then."

Mara nodded. "We'll just get all our stuff out and loaded into a wagon then."

Lir held up a hand. "Not all of it."

"What do you mean?" Teddy asked.

"I've come to an arrangement with the prince here," Lir said, gesturing needlessly toward Finn.

"Finn?" Mara asked quietly.

Finn met her gaze. "Mara, we have all become a family over the time

209

we've been together, but I cannot go to Aeunna with you. I assume you thought I would. But I have a duty to my people, just as you have to yours. Lir has graciously agreed to give me *Harrgalti* so I can do just that."

"But what if they want to kill you like they wanted to kill me? What if you need help?" Mara asked.

Finn shrugged. "It's my duty." He pulled the bullet necklace out of his shirt. "I have to live despite my fear, even when that fear is my own people. I have to face them and see if I can change them as I have changed."

Teddy stood in front of Finn. His eyes watered. "You're a good man, son." He held out an arm and shook Finn's, but he held on tight. "But you had better march your blue butt back up to The Pleasant Mariner with us and say goodbye to the one who gave you that," he pointed at the necklace, "and the lass who fed you all this time, and the pup who flew across the sea to bring help for you on our darkest night." He pointed at Finn's covered ears.

"Yes, sir." Finn nodded respectfully to Teddy, who pulled the young man into a firm hug.

"Right then." Teddy cleared his throat. "Best unload the rest of our belongings from the ship, and you can help us take it back before you head back out to sea."

As they hitched horses to one of the loaded wagons and prepared to ride in another, Finn said his goodbyes.

Kip stood nearest to Finn, so he gave his friend a hug first. "Remember, if the darkness comes and you cannot live despite it, live *to* spite it," Kip said. Finn nodded seriously, gave his friend a pat on the back, and released him.

Mara was next. She smiled at Finn. "I know you are going on a journey to find yourself, to a certain extent, but just remember you are a good man, and we would not have made it here without you." Mara gave him a tight hug and sniffled.

When Mara stepped back, Kara stepped forward and said, "Ditto," and hugged Finn quickly as well. Keena opened her mouth to speak, then closed it, shook her head, and gave him a few big licks to the face before whining and trotting away. Last was Teddy.

Teddy chuckled and said, "Well, I guess that needs no translation." Then his face fell, and he cleared his throat. The two men faced each other stoically for a moment, and then Teddy reached out his arm to shake Finn's. "Toren is still my boy, even though he is another world away, and we will never see each other again. No matter where you go, you are my boy, and you will always have a place with me. I am honored to have fought by your side."

Teddy blinked back the tears, and Kip gave Mara a little side hug as tears began to stream down her face. Finn's eyes were watery. He bit his lip, and then he pulled Teddy into a firm hug. After a moment, they released each other, and Teddy patted Finn's shoulder once more before stepping back. Then, the time had come, and they piled into the wagons and parted ways.

When Teddy and Mara drove the wagons eastward out of Port Albatross, Finn turned heel and headed back to the docks, ready to begin his own adventure.

# CHAPTER EIGHTEEN

# THE RETURN JOURNEY

Mara insisted on stopping at Brynmor before they went home to ensure that the forest dwarves she had met in Questhaven had made it back home and were following her charge. The road back to Aeunna would be a little twisted, so they led the wagons across the plains to the southeast of Port Albatross, Teddy somewhat grumpily.

Ashroot, Kina, Kara, and Mara took turns driving one wagon while Loli played in the back of the wagon with the ones who weren't driving. Sometimes he would throw the ball for Keena. It wouldn't go far with his weak, little arms, so Keena made a show of flying around searching for the ball before landing to get it and bringing it back to him.

Teddy and Kip rode in the other wagon, which was also full of supplies. With the concentrated time alone together, Kip took the opportunity to speak with Teddy about some things that had concerned him about his new home.

"No, it's not all giant," Teddy reassured him. "If you handled the size of *Harrgalti* well enough, you'll do just fine in Aeunna."

"What is it like, though?" Kip asked.

"Well, you're coming in with Mara. If you were just an outsider coming into Aeunna, I can't say you'd exactly be welcomed. But you are going as Mara's lifemate. You and your family will be welcomed into our community with open arms."

"And, uh ... you'll be okay with me leading them, after Toren was—"

Teddy guffawed. "You won't be leading them! We don't have the male-leaders-only nonsense you gnomes have. You may have died for the Ranger trial, but you weren't the one *on* trial. Mara is our Ranger, and she's the one who will be leading. Though I'm sure she'll be taking your advice from time to time. Lead the people. Ha!"

Kip's face flushed. "Well, then what will I be doing?" he asked.

Teddy made a face and pondered for a moment. "Well, that's up to you, I guess. Everyone pulls their weight in Aeunna, but we have soldiers and hunters aplenty, and the lifemate of the Ranger shouldn't be in undue danger all the time. If you know a trade or have always wanted to learn one, now would be the time for that," Teddy explained. "But no need to worry about taking Toren's place. You are already like my own son, and I support Mara's decision," he added awkwardly.

Kip smiled. "Good. I can't wait."

⊕

With the wagons, they were able to cross the plains quickly, and they entered the forest of Brynmor only a couple days after leaving Port Albatross. Just on the edge of the forest, they met a disturbing sight. A strange woman ran from two men who shouted and jeered at her.

"Come on, demon!"

"You're going to burn, demon!"

Mara picked up her axe and launched herself off the side of the wagon and onto Keena's back. Kina grabbed the reins before they fell.

"Come on, Keena," Mara urged.

Keena charged directly toward the men, knocking one of them over as she forced herself between the men and woman. She stretched out her wings and roared, sending a burst of fire into the sky. The men stumbled over themselves and stopped. The woman stopped, too, safe on the other side of Keena.

"What is the meaning of this?" Mara demanded, brandishing her axe for the men to see.

The man who had been knocked over cowered some, but the other made himself tall and announced, "That creature is a demon, and we are sending it back to Hell where it belongs."

213

"Hell does not exist here, buddy. Try again," Mara said.

"She does the devil's work. We saw her. She touched plants, and they grew. She went into trees, and they moved."

"Oh, yes, that sounds really evil," Mara remarked sarcastically.

The other man realized the sarcasm a little too late, replying, "It do— Oh."

Mara hopped down from Keena's back and gave her pup a pat before striding forward, axe in hand. "I take it you both are from Earth?"

"Yes," one spat. The other nodded.

"You came to a fantastical world when you were sixteen, and that was jarring enough, but the world you came into did not have magic. Now, it does. Magic has just returned to all of Ambergrove for the first time in many lifetimes. I know, because I'm the one who brought it back. You're going to see magic and magical beings and creatures everywhere from now on. If you go around trying to kill them, I will come for you personally, do you understand?" She gestured back to Keena who roared a great burst of fire. "And when I come, I'll be bringing this magical creature with me. Is that what you want?"

The man on the ground glanced at Keena and shook his head. The other man shifted his weight as he looked at Keena and shifted his sword and torch in his hands. "Think carefully before you choose," Teddy warned. The others had caught up with their wagons and had drawn the horses to a halt a short distance away.

The man charged at Mara, swinging his sword. He was clearly unpracticed with the weapon. Mara brought her axe up and around and twisted the blade from his grip, flinging it far away in the same motion. She pushed the man with her shoulder and he fell, but he quickly scrambled to stand back up. "Keena, rough him up a bit, will you? But don't hurt him ... much."

Keena wagged her tail and was on top of the man in two bounds. She snatched the man in her mouth and rose high into the air. They watched and listened as the man screamed. She flung him up into the air, then let him drop before catching him by the leg and soaring upward. She did this a few times. He dropped the torch and it fell down onto the other man, making him squeal. Finally, Keena flew down and let the man drop to the ground from a few feet in the air.

He lay there on the ground, panting and groaning. "Wh-what ..." he whimpered.

"That is a dragonwolf. An endangered species of loyal creatures who will not stand idly by while you attack peaceful magical creatures just for having magic. Every time you push at someone like her," Mara pointed at the woman, "someone like this dragonwolf will push back."

"D-d-dem—"

"They are *not* demons. They are creatures of magic you will have to get used to living with if you're going to be in a magical world for the rest of your life," Mara snapped.

Teddy jumped down off his wagon, sword in hand. "Now, I suggest you fellows leave this area before the dragonwolf or any of the rest of us have anything more to say to you. This forest is under the protection of the Ranger of Aeunna." He gestured at Mara with his sword. "If you harm any peaceful creature in her forests you will answer to her, to her dragonwolf, and to all forest dwarves. Now, *git!*"

The men scrambled to stand and ran off without looking back. Mara turned to the woman. "Now, what exactly are you?"

⊕

"I am Brynna, a dryad of Brynmor forest," the woman said. "I and my brothers and sisters are the shepherds of the forest. We have lain dormant for hundreds of years."

Mara peered at the woman. Her skin looked like bark and her hair was made of long, twiggy branches with leaves. She wore a dress of moss that cascaded down to trail on the ground.

"You were awoken when magic returned," Teddy said.

The dryad nodded. "The forest has been neglected for far too long. It will be a difficult task to restore it to its former life."

"Please let us know if the forest dwarves can help you with that in any way, Brynna," Mara said kindly.

"I will pass your tidings along to the lord of the dryads, though he may already wait for you in Aeunna," the dryad replied. "In the meantime, you have helped by preventing the humans from harming me, and that is all that need be done."

Mara nodded.

The dryad tipped her head in Mara's direction, and then she laid a hand on Keena's snout. "May I have your swift assistance, friend?" she asked the dragonwolf.

Keena bowed her head and crouched down in response, allowing the dryad to climb up onto her back. Keena soared high up into the sky and flew swiftly over Brynmor forest. As she flitted over, they could see the dryad fall into the embrace of the forest.

Keena flew back to them, and they continued on their own path to Brynmor village.

A familiar face came riding out to greet Mara as Brynmor village came into view.

"Willem!" Mara called. She jumped down from the wagon and stood, arms outstretched. "Here I am."

"That you are!" the young man said. "I guess I shouldn't have doubted you."

"No, you shouldn't!" Mara replied with a smile. "Now, I have completed my Ranger trial. The poison in the forbidden lands is no more. I am here on my way home to Aeunna to keep my promise and see what it is you need."

Willem smiled and nodded. "Follow me."

They followed Willem to the borders of the village, where they were stopped by an old, green-skinned man with an air of authority. He looked to be on guard, but when he saw Teddy, his grip on the spear he held slackened.

"Tederen! How goes it, young man?" he asked. "What brings you here to Brynmor?"

Willem rode his horse forward and said, "With respect, Cormac, this is the Ranger of Aeunna." He gestured to Mara, who stepped forward.

The old man sized her up. She positioned her arms that both her bracer and her Mark were visible. "Very well," he said finally. "Ranger, what brings you to Brynmor?"

Mara glanced at Willem. "I met Willem here while I was out completing my Ranger trial."

Cormac glared at Willem. "What were you doing out in the forbidden lands?" he snapped.

Before Willem could answer, Mara held up a hand. "He did not go to the forbidden lands. I met him on an island south of there. It is not his fault, nor is it the fault of anyone who sailed with him and his captain."

"Captain? Boy, what did you—" Cormac began.

"With respect, sir," Mara said loudly, "I am telling the way of it." Cormac quieted, and she continued. "The leader of chaos in the forbidden lands was none other than Gaele, my grandmother, and Teddy's sister. She poisoned many people with false promises and imagined familiarity. She was crafty and cunning in her control, and none who fell under her schemes can be held responsible for believing them."

"But— What— But they should be punished!" Cormac said finally, aghast.

"If we punished everyone who has ever been misled, how many people do you think there would be left in Ambergrove?" Mara said sternly. "It was a simple mistake."

Cormac eyeballed Willem for a moment and then nodded grudgingly.

"Great!" Mara said. "Now, when I met Willem before, he indicated that Brynmor has faced hard times and could use more support from the Ranger of Aeunna. I would like to sit down with you and discuss what it is you need."

Cormac's brows raised. "Y-yes!" he stammered. "Yes, please come into Brynmor."

The village reminded Mara of Robin Hood's camps in Sherwood Forest. They led their wagons past the gates and left them with a hostler who would take care of the horses—and Keena—and then they followed Cormac up into the town.

At the ground level were all the buildings they couldn't have higher up. There were stables and kitchens, a guardhouse, and some other warehouses. The rest of the village was in the trees. Mara felt a pang of homesickness when she saw the rope bridges connecting the network of trees, and she was sure Teddy felt the same itch to leave and go straight back to Aeunna.

217

However, where Aeunna was entirely Aeunna trees—trees gifted by Aeun that were hollowed out for use as homes—Brynmor did not have Aeunna trees. The trees were tall and sturdy, but there was not one type of tree that dominated the town. The homes just looked like simple treehouses. It seemed to be a village made in the image of Aeunna.

Cormac had a meeting area in the center of the network of trees. While he had Willem take the others to get some food, Cormac and Mara sat down to discuss Brynmor's needs and wants. Truthfully, they weren't as bad off as Willem had made it seem, though Willem was prone to exaggeration. However, there were still areas in need of improvement.

Mara sat with Cormac and made a list of his grievances, telling him that she would make sure once she got home to Aeunna some Aeunnans were dispatched to Brynmor with the necessary resources, and she would go to the other villages to see what else they needed as well. At the end of the meeting, Cormac asked her if there was anything she needed.

"Actually, there is something you could do for me," Mara said.

"Name it, Ranger."

"Have you noticed that magic is returning to Ambergrove, and with it magical beings?"

"I can't say that I have," he replied. "Where did you see them?"

"Just outside Brynmor forest, actually. A dryad was being attacked by some humans who were formerly from Earth. They thought her to be evil and tried to harm her. We stopped them, but there are surely more dryads out there in the forests who are in need."

Cormac nodded. "Where there is one, there are many. How can we help?"

"I am going home after this, and while I intend to make my stance known as soon as possible, the dryads are in danger now. Someone needs to inform the surrounding villages," she explained.

Cormac nodded seriously. When they left Brynmor a little while later, riders on all the available horses in the village left as well in all directions. They carried a message from Mara to all: The dryads and other magical beings in the area were under her protection. Harm would invite harm.

As Mara, Teddy, and Ashroot had done on their trip from Darach, she and her companions stopped by the river to eat and rest on their way to Darach this time. Kina let Loli roam a little bit, checking every few minutes to make sure he'd obeyed her command to stay out of the water.

Loli took that command to heart, keeping his body out of the water, but throwing other things into it. What he didn't see at first was all those things coming right back. As he walked down the river, a trail of wet items lined up behind him—the rock he threw, the bread, the shoe. The last thing he threw in came back a little close to him, and the splash of water drew his attention.

He saw the line of wet things behind him, and he picked up the closest thing and threw it back in. The water immediately spit it back out. He giggled and threw it back. The water spit it back out. He giggled and screamed like children do when they're highly entertained, and that drew the attention of the adults—who all turned at the noise just in time to see his shoe get spit back out at him another time.

"Wait, what?" Mara asked. She turned to Teddy.

"Hey, don't look at me. My age no longer means anything now that we're living in a world of magic," he said grumpily.

Mara stood and walked over to Loli, who was still throwing the shoe back into the water. She held his hand when he picked it up again to throw, and then she looked around her at the other wet things. "Loli, how about you don't throw things in the river," she said gently. "It seems like the water doesn't like it when you do."

"You've got that right!" came a voice from the water.

A form rose up out of the water, and Mara half expected Laeghu to appear, but this was a manly form. "What are you?" Mara asked without thinking. "Oh, sorry."

"No, no, I expect the 'what' and not 'who' for at least the first few centuries," he said. "I am Hydr, and I am the naiad of this river."

His form rippled in what Mara suspected was a respectful bow. She returned the gesture. "I am Mara, the Ranger of Aeunna. I am sorry that Loli was throwing things into your river."

"No, *I* am sorry," his mother said, stepping forward toward the naiad.

"I did not think about what he could do to the things around him. I only thought for his own safety."

"Yes, much of the world would be more pleasant if individuals thought about the damage they could do and how to protect what is around them," the naiad said bitterly. "But no matter. It is done now."

"Do the naiads have a lord or lady like the dryads do?" Mara asked.

"We do not. We follow the orders of Laeghu herself. Nor do we require protection as the dryads do," Hydr replied.

"Oh, you heard? From a dryad I guess," Mara said. "Why don't you need help when they do?"

"Come to the edge of the water," he commanded. She stepped forward and he held out a hand. "Now, touch me."

Mara reached out to grab his arm, and her hand passed right through. "Again," he said.

She reached for his chest and again went straight through. She waved her arm around inside his chest before pulling it back.

"Now, one more time," he said. "Gently."

She glanced at her companions and reached out a palm to his chest. It was solid. She pressed her hand a little bit and then laughed. Suddenly, it was liquid again, and she hadn't been expecting it. She'd leaned forward a bit too much, so she tripped and fell through him and into the river. She spat and sputtered, and she heard the naiad chortling as arms tucked under hers and hefted her onto the bank.

As he set her down on the ground, the naiad said, "You see, we cannot be touched without our consent, so outsiders don't present any danger for us."

Mara glared at him. "Do you think there was maybe another way you might have explained it without dunking me in the river?" she asked.

"This is funnier," Kip said.

Mara turned. All her companions were laughing with Hydr. Loli rolled on the ground in his mirth. Even Kina cracked a smile. Mara smiled too, as she wiped herself off.

"Okay, point taken," she told the naiad. "Just let us know if you do need help, unlikely as that may be."

The naiad bowed his head and disappeared into the water with a splash.

✦

As they reached the willows lining the outskirts of Darach, they were greeted by a familiar face.

A young, grey dog, hackles raised, stood at the edge of the village. When she saw the dog, Ashroot jumped out of the wagon and came forward. "Hey, there, Pepper. Are you still my friend?"

The dog wagged her tail and yipped, jumping on Ashroot and covering her with kisses.

"Some guard dog you are."

Mara recognized young Iona, not by her voice, but by the authoritative way the child approached them. The green-skinned girl looked disapprovingly at them, but more so at Pepper, who trotted obediently back over to her.

"Iona! My, you've grown," Mara said.

"You haven't," the girl snapped. "Come on, Pepper."

The girl beckoned her pup and they left, without even giving poor Keena the chance to say hello.

"She's … nice," Kip muttered.

"Believe it or not, that's nicer than she was the first time," Mara said. "Let's go."

Iona may not have stuck around, but she sure spread the word. The villagers gathered to greet them. Callum, the village leader, a reddish man with long, green hair, stepped to the front of the crowd. They brought their wagons to a halt, and Mara and Teddy jumped out. Callum strode up to them and gave them each a firm shake.

"Teddy. Mara. What brings you back here to Darach? Have you been successful?" he asked.

Mara beamed. "Yes, we have." She showed him the Mark on her forearm.

"Excellent!" he cried. "We'll have a feast for you in celebration! Come and tell us all about your journey!"

After introducing the rest of their group to Callum, preparations were made, a feast was had, and a story regaled yet again. When it was time for bed, they stayed once more with old Brana at her boardinghouse. Teddy, Kip, and Loli took one room, and Mara, Kara, Ashroot, and Kina took the other.

The following morning, after a bracing breakfast from Brana, they prepared to head out again, this time with two additional companions. Rona and Tilly, two of Darach's good hunters, would accompany them to Aeunna so they could bring the wagons back to Darach and on to Port Albatross. Mara, Teddy, and Ashroot said their goodbyes and they all loaded up in the wagons, finally on the last road to Aeunna.

✦

Teddy became more and more impatient as they neared Aeunna. He pressed them to push the horses as much as they could without hurting them. They rode until they could ride no more, rested the bare minimum, and got started again as soon as possible.

The trip should take two days by wagon, and Teddy shaved off as much time as he could, but not even he could plan for everything. Just a few hours away from Aeunna, they heard crashing and squealing in the trees around them.

"Boars!" Rona shouted.

"Protect the horses!" Tilly shouted, jumping out of the wagon.

"Keena! To the skies!" Teddy commanded. "No fire!"

Keena flew up in the air as she was told. *There's a lot of them,* she howled. *Four, coming from all sides.*

Teddy released a string of curses. "I am not going to go away for my home for years just to die right before I get back to it!" he shouted.

"Are boars that bad?" Kina asked as she clutched onto Loli.

Kip and Mara shared a glance. "Just stay in the wagon, and stay away from the sides," he told his sister.

Ashroot fished her bow out of the supply store and handed Mara's to her. Mara passed her bow to Kara. "Do you remember how to use this?" she asked.

"I'll manage well enough with our lives on the line," Kara replied.

They readied their bows and stood up in the wagons, ready. Rona stood with a boar spear in front of one wagon, and Tilly stood in front of the other with a matching spear. Teddy and Kip took the rear—Teddy with his sword and Kip with his hammer. Mara stood in the front with the spearwomen, axe in hand.

"What about you, Kip?" Teddy asked.

Kip hefted the hammer, testing its weight. "I'll be fine."

"Keena! Let us know where they are from up there!" Teddy called. "Ashroot, translate for Kara. Kip, I'll translate for you."

*One coming from the front. Left side,* Keena said.

Mara stepped up next to Tilly as a large boar crashed out into the clearing. Its tusks were almost the size of her forearm. Boar hunts were dangerous for a reason, and none of them but the spearwomen should be even attempting this feat. Mara took a deep breath and hefted her axe. Teddy'd had a point. One wrong step and they would be lost only a few hours from home.

An arrow whizzed past Mara's ear and into the boar's shoulder, making it turn away from her for a second, distracted by the wound. *Perfect.* Mara charged forward and raised her axe, grunting with the effort as she brought it down with all her might. It sunk deep into the boar's neck. She quickly pulled it back and dodged as the creature thrashed madly, trying to prevent the inevitable. With one harsh squeal, it collapsed, dead.

Tilly and Rona whooped, but there was no time to rest.

*Rear right!* Keena growled. Mara returned to the center front just as Keena added, *Front left!*

Teddy stood fast. There was no telling when a boar would appear on that side. For now, Kip was on his own. Ashroot fired as the boar came into view, and the arrow shattered on the beast's head. Kara fired right after and barely missed. Kip stood at the ready as the boar pawed at the ground and charged.

He stood still until the last second and then stepped to the side and swung his hammer. It hit the beast's shoulder. It stumbled and fell, and then it squealed and snorted, turning angrily back toward Kip. At the front of the wagon, another, smaller boar had appeared. Kara shot as soon as she saw it, nicking Mara's arm as the arrow whizzed by, piercing the boar through the eye. It collapsed. Mara cheered, patting her arm to make sure there wasn't too much blood.

"Keena! Any more on this side?" Mara cried.

*No, Mama! The last one is coming in the rear.*

"Good!"

Mara, Rona, and Tilly ran in between the wagons to help Kip and Teddy. Kip's boar charged him again just before they reached the rear, and he tried the same move again. The tusk connected with the hammer and broke off, but the beast also trampled over Kip on its way through. Rona charged forward with her spear and thrusted clean through the boar, using the length of the spear to pull the creature back away from Kip as far as she could before the spear sliced back out. Mara ran to him as the spearwomen backed Teddy.

"I'm fine," Kip panted. "Just winded and banged up. I'll be fine."

Mara stood over him with her axe raised as the final boar charged toward Teddy. As Teddy stood at the ready, Tilly and Rona thrusted their spears from either side of him, dealing death blows to the boar and holding it in place at the same time. It fell.

Mara dropped her axe and turned once more to Kip. He smiled and patted her arm. "I'm alright," he insisted.

Mara helped him to stand, and he checked her arm. It was just a scratch, thankfully, though when the boars were down, Kara dropped the bow, lunged out of the wagon, and ran to Mara, her face white with fear. Kip gave Mara a pat and then went to the wagon to check on Kina and Loli. It took them a few moments to notice Teddy's glowering.

"What's wrong, Teddy?" Mara asked.

He sheathed his sword and grumbled, "Didn't even get one swing in."

"There's just no pleasing you, is there?" Kip called.

Victorious, they paused long enough to butcher the boars so they could bring the meat with them to Aeunna, and Rona and Tilly could take some on to Darach, and then they continued on their way in a tense silence. Finally, in the late hours of the morning, the borders of Aeunna came into view. They were home.

# CHAPTER NINETEEN

# RANGER OF AEUNNA

A stout woman with her hair tied back in a long braid sat in the healer's hut in Aeunna. She was making her way through the inventory when a commotion filtered in from outside. Cries of "They're back! They're back!" grew louder and louder. As Freya poked her head out the door, a young boy skidded to a stop outside her hut and panted, "They're back, Mistress Freya." He gulped. "Tederen ... Mara ... Ashroot ... back."

Freya's knees buckled, and for a moment she collapsed on the door frame to steady herself. Then she hiked her skirts and broke into a run.

⬦

When the wagons reached the outskirts of Aeunna, Teddy sprang out and charged into the village to search for his beloved lifemate. He passed dozens of people he knew—old friends, pupils, even his protégé Cora—but there was only one person he needed to see. Cora nodded to him as he passed, and she pointed in the direction of the healer's hut where Teddy saw the most beautiful sight of his life. There she was, with her grey locks in a braid and her usual pocketed dress and stained apron on.

"Freya," Teddy whispered.

He closed the distance in three bounds and reached her just as her knees buckled. He took her into his arms and held her tight. Her hands were pressed up against her body and her face was buried in his chest. He pressed his own face into her hair and breathed deeply, taking in the familiar

225

scent of herbs. He petted her hair as she sobbed into his chest, just grateful to have her in his arms again.

Teddy kissed the top of her head and held her silently. Once her sobs had faltered and faded to a contented sigh, she pulled back and looked up into his eyes. She reached a hand up to his cheek and smiled.

"Are you alright?" she asked him seriously.

He nodded. "I'm missing a few fingers, as you know, but otherwise I'm in one piece," he managed.

"And Mara?"

Teddy grinned and slipped his hand into Freya's. "Come on."

He led Freya determinedly back through the crowd to the edge of the village, where the wagons had just come to a stop. Mara spotted them immediately and jumped out of her wagon, turning and beckoning to a nervous Kara to do the same. When Kara's feet hit the ground, Mara grabbed her arm and pulled her toward Teddy, releasing Kara just in time to be pulled into a tight hug from Freya.

"Oh, Mara!" Freya cried. "You did it! I'm so proud of you!"

"Thanks, Aunt Freya," Mara whispered. "I missed you."

"I missed you, too, my dear."

Mara pulled out of the hug and reached a hand out toward her sister. "This is my sister," she told the woman.

"*You're* Kara," Freya said. She reached out and pulled the girl into a warm hug.

"You know me?" Kara asked timidly.

"Of course, I do. Mara talked about you all the time when she was here with us," Freya replied, pulling out of the hug and cupping Kara's face in her hands. "I'm your auntie, and Aeunna is your home, for as long as you want it to be."

"I told you there wouldn't be a problem," Teddy told Kara with a wink.

"What was that?" Freya asked, peering at Teddy with a disapproving eye.

"That's my girl!" Teddy said, opening his arms and hugging Freya and Kara at once.

He looked up to beckon to Mara, for his first beloved niece to join in the hug, but when he saw her smiling, he also saw her turn back in the direction they came. Keena sat uncertainly, her tail tucked between her legs,

Kina and Loli stayed huddled in the wagon, unsure, and Kip stood, bold as brass, unwavering under Aengar's disapproving glare.

⊕

Ashroot skittered through the streets of Aeunna. Most of the forest dwarves herding excitedly toward the edge of the village were looking for Mara, but she knew where the bearkin would be—the one bearkin she wanted most to see. She gingerly stepped into the kitchens and grinned when she saw the dark brown bearkin giving out orders. Specks of grey spotted his coat where they hadn't before. Someone patted him on the shoulder and pointed in her direction.

"Hello, Da," Ashroot said quietly.

Mapleleaf dropped the plate of food he was holding. "Daughter!" he cried.

"Mara brought me back," she said, "and I have this for you."

As bearkin scurried around to clean up the mess from the dropped plate, Mapleleaf slowly, disbelievingly, walked over to his daughter. Ashroot pulled out a rolled-up piece of paper from her pack and offered it to him. Mapleleaf took Aeun's recipe out of Ashroot's outstretched hand and dropped it to the ground before pulling his daughter into a tight hug.

"I'm so glad to have you home with me," Mapleleaf said. "I missed you so much, my daughter."

"But what about the …"

"I could have lived my life happily without the blessing you earned from the goddess, but I couldn't live my life at all with you lost somewhere out in the world," Mapleleaf said awkwardly.

Ashroot smiled and squeezed her father more tightly. A young bearkin who was helping clean up Mapleleaf's mess bent to pick up the paper and said, "Here's the thing you dropped, sir."

Mapleleaf loosened the hug and glared at the young bearkin. Ashroot grabbed the paper with a subtle nod to the bearkin as Mapleleaf snapped, "Tuliptwig, get back to work. The rest of you too."

As the other bearkin hurried about their business, Ashroot offered the paper to her father again. It was a greenish-brown paper with a vine tying

227

it closed and a triskele seal holding the ties. Mapleleaf accepted the paper, took a deep breath, and broke the seal. Tiny butterflies fluttered out of it and disappeared. He unrolled the scroll and found nothing but a blank page. However, as he looked at it, gold letters began to write themselves on the paper. Astonished, Mapleleaf read aloud.

"Mapleleaf the bearkin, your daughter has come to me with a request from you. Though that request would have been better put to Paeor, who created the anamberries, this is quite a spectacular situation. Before you stands your daughter, victorious. She has done what no other bearkin has ever been able to do. She left the safety of her home to go on an adventure. She traveled all over Ambergrove and fought beasts—even so far as to take part in the slaying of a kraken and to lead a dragonwolf in battle."

Mapleleaf looked up at his daughter in awe, and some of the other bearkin murmured and nudged each other behind him. He went on, "When Ashroot left to attempt this impossible task, you set her with another task more impossible still. However, of her own volition, she was able to complete it. She does not have anamberry secrets for you as you had requested. You will not be handed anything from me or from any of my kin. Mastery comes not from me, or from Paeor, or even from Ambergrove itself. Before you stands the most accomplished of all bearkin. The greatest recipes your kind will ever know are not given by the gods. Ashroot earned them, and she will be the key for the rest of your people to learn all that she has learned in her time away from Aeunna and all she will learn throughout her days. Before you is Ashroot, and she is the gift. Do not forget it."

Mapleleaf watched as the goddess's signature appeared on the paper, and then with a slight popping sound, the paper turned into a cluster of tiny, green butterflies who fluttered high above Ashroot's head and then disappeared. When Ashroot looked again at her father, he simply stared. Every eye in the kitchen bore into her for one brief moment, and then the bearkin knelt and bowed around her.

❖

Keena cowered by the wagon while Kip pet her neck and Kina reassured a frightened Loli. A lot of loud people bustled around Teddy and Mara, and now Kara. Mara gestured back to the wagons only briefly, seeing the fear on the other's faces. She accepted a twig from Rhodi and used the microphone-like device to speak to the entire forest floor.

"Hello, all! Thank you for your warm welcome back to Aeunna. I have missed this place and you, and it is good to be home. We will tell our story in time and introduce the new friends and family we've brought along. I can smell the evening meal cooking. For now, please prepare for the evening meal and leave us in peace to settle in and unpack. We'll reveal all in time."

Teddy and Freya beamed at her as they hugged each other. Those nearby heard, "You heard her. Clear off! Don't make me use my training voice!" as Cora successfully herded the others away.

Mara stopped in front of the fiery-haired, heavily-tattooed training master on her way back to the wagons. "You're definitely a more formidable commander than the previous training master," Mara joked.

Cora turned and gave Mara a quick squeeze. "Well, someone has to keep the people in shape, don't they?" she said, and winked. "Now, did you get some Marks on you during your travels?"

"Just one," Mara told the woman, upturning her arm and pulling her sleeve back to reveal the amber triskele on her forearm.

Cora pulled back her own sleeve to reveal the dragon's breath triskele on her own arm.

"Well done, Ranger!" Cora exclaimed.

Mara grinned and nodded. "We can talk more later," she said happily before turning and heading back to where the others stood at the wagons, passing Aengar as he strode away from the wagons in a huff.

As Mara approached the wagon, Rona was passing Loli down to Kina, Kip was comforting Keena, and Tilly was passing supplies to Kara and Teddy on the ground. As Kina tucked Loli at her hip, she glanced at Kara and then at Teddy and Freya.

"Where do we go?" she asked.

Kara grimaced. *Where would they go? Where did they all belong?*

"With me," Mara said. "The Ranger house has more than enough rooms for all of you. My home is yours."

"Nonsense, Mara," Freya said.

Kara looked apprehensively at her. "Why?"

"Oh, nothing you did, dear," Freya reassured Kara with a pat. "No, but from what Teddy told me about this one," she gestured to Kip, "he and Mara will be lifemates. Take it from an old woman—no new couple starting out wants to have a house full of people."

"I beg to differ, mistress Freya," Kip said. "I would like nothing more than to have my family close for a while."

Freya looked Kip up and down and smiled. "That may be, but for now, I, too, have a nest that needs filling."

"What do you mean, Aunt Freya?" Kara asked.

Freya smiled warmly at Kara and then reached a hand out for Loli to grasp as she smiled at his mother. "I mean that Teddy and I have enough room in our home for both you young women and the little man too."

Teddy took a chest out of the wagon and hollered over Freya's shoulder, "How about it? Once you settle in, if you'd like to move to your own homes, you can do that as well."

Kara and Kina exchanged a glance, and then they both nodded.

"That settles it," Freya said. "Seoc and Moire, please bring their things to Tederen's and my home."

Two forest dwarves—Mara's good friends during her first six months in Ambergrove—nodded obediently, and supplies were fully unloaded and carted through the village and up to either Mara's home or Teddy and Freya's. Rona and Tilly, anxious to return home to Darach, said their goodbyes as soon as the wagons were unloaded and led the horses back into the forest in the direction of home.

As the rest of them prepared to head to one home or the other, Aengar appeared once more in Mara's path.

"Rangerling—" he began.

"Uh, Ranger, you'll find, Aengar," Teddy snapped.

"Not quite yet, Tederen, as I'm sure you are aware," Aengar retorted. He gestured to Mara. "You must go visit the Oracle."

"Now?" Mara asked exasperatedly.

"Yes, now," Aengar repeated. "Fly your dragonwolf up there to see her before you return to your home to prepare for the evening meal."

"Don't worry," Kip told her as he lay a reassuring hand on her shoulder. "I'll go with Teddy to his and Freya's home and wait for you there."

Mara nodded, and he squeezed her shoulder before joining the others. As they walked away, Mara got on Keena's back and grumbled, "Been gone for two years and saved the world, but no, can't rest for five minutes first. Why would we do that?"

Keena huffed and then launched herself into the sky toward the top of the tallest tree in Ambergrove.

&#x2747;

There was no way Keena would be fitting into the Oracle's house, but to Mara's surprise, there was an elephant-sized stable now next to the Oracle's hut, and inside were freshly grilled meats. Mara ushered her pup to the food before taking a deep breath herself and walking toward the Oracle's hut.

It was just as she remembered. Various tapestries covered the otherwise bare walls. A lone chair sat in the main room with a small table in front of it with prepared tea already on the surface. Nearly disappearing in the cushioning of the armchair was the oldest-looking person Mara had ever seen. Her long, grey braid trailed to the ground and across the floor.

Mara remembered the first time she came to the house and had been so shocked to see the ancient woman. The Mara of then was much more timid and fearful than the Mara of now. She steeled herself and walked right over to where the Oracle sat in her giant chair. "Oracle, I—"

"Well, hello to you, too, Ranger," the Oracle said in her ancient voice.

"Uh ... hello, Oracle, I—"

"Yes, yes, I know. You have places to be. Things to do. This is one of them, dear Mara. Now, would you just sit a moment?" the Oracle pleaded with a hint of amusement in her voice.

Properly chastised, Mara walked forward and sat on the floor by the Oracle. "Sorry, Oracle," she said quietly.

"Ah, yes. Well, youth does demand a certain level of urgency that old age does not, hmm? Now, then. There are a few matters at hand. Foremost, you cannot expect your dragonwolf to live in your home."

"What?" Mara kicked the table as she jumped, startled.

"You heard me, Mara. She is a dragonwolf. She cannot be with other dragonwolves, but she needs to be able to touch the sky. I learned of her in a vision some time ago and had the stable prepared for her arrival. She will be well taken care of, but we will get to that later."

"But—"

"Don't 'but' me, Dragonwolf," the Oracle said sternly.

Mara opened her mouth and silently closed it.

"Now then, I will be present when you are officially named. Keena will bring you down today, and she will bring me down at that time, and for the ceremony, but after the ceremony, you will not see me again until you are ready for further advice," the Oracle explained.

"Okay," Mara said quietly, though it hardly cleared anything up.

"I have a small, metal whistle you will be able to use to call her to you when you need her, and you may certainly seek her companionship whenever you please, but her home will be here. Understood?"

"Yes, Oracle," Mara said.

"Very well. Then, Kernunos, please make yourself known and give Mara the whistle," the Oracle said.

A wooden wall in the Oracle's hut wobbled a bit, and then a man materialized out of it. His whole body was made of bark, his hair and beard canopies of Aeunna tree leaves. A robe of pure gold settled on his shoulders as he leaned forward and handed Mara the whistle.

"You're the lord of the dryads, aren't you?" Mara asked.

The man tipped his head, a regal nod. "I am Kernunos, lord of the dryads and voice of the trees."

"A dryad told me that you were waiting for me in Aeunna," Mara said.

"Yes, in addition to being the lord of the dryads, I am the dryad of the Aeunna forest," he explained. "I wanted to speak with you about my return to this place, what the trees want, what I want for them, and what the Ranger's partnership with the dryads would be."

Mara nodded.

"Well, if you two are ready to crack at it, I am just going to doze off here. I don't have the energy you young ones do," the Oracle said sleepily.

"I'm centuries older than you," Kernunos quipped, but the Oracle had already fallen into gentle snores.

⊕

Mara had far less time than she'd hoped to give Kip a tour of his new home before the evening meal, but, as she had done when she first stayed in it, he only needed to see a little bit on that first day. As soon as she opened the door, it was apparent that her house had been kept up in her absence. She couldn't see a single speck of dust on the long unused countertops or bookshelves.

"This is your home?" Kip asked as she showed him the first area—kitchen and sitting room—with two long, curved hallways along the back wall going back as far as he could see.

"Yes, it is. There's a lot, but there's meeting rooms and spare bedrooms and stuff all down there," she said awkwardly. "How about my room first?"

She took one of Kip's hands in hers and steered him toward her bedroom. As soon as she opened the door, however, the smile faded. There, in the doorway, she spotted the very thing Teddy had pointed out to her when she first came into the house—a carved name.

"This was your da's room?" Kip asked.

Mara nodded as she let her fingers trace the name. "Yeah, Teddy said my dad and I had the same idea when it came to choosing a room. We both picked the first one."

Kip chuckled. "Yeah, that sounds like you."

"I hope ... I hope he's alright," Mara said quietly. "I hope he got our messages before the door closed."

Kip laced an arm around Mara's waist and whispered, "I'm sure he did."

A single tear streamed down Mara's face. "Yeah, me too," she croaked.

"Now, what say you and I get dressed for this fancy meal, then, eh?" he asked, smiling reassuringly.

Mara nodded.

Kip's belongings had been taken to the second room down. Apparently, the movers didn't realize the nature of their relationship. No matter. While Kip hunted in his trunk in the other room and dressed, Mara pulled her trial dress out of her trunk, smoothed out as many of the wrinkles as she could, and put it on. As a final touch, she switched out the plain bun cage she got from Gryffyth for the wolf and dragon bun cage Teddy'd commissioned their first trip through Port Albatross. Her new one she'd save for later.

When they'd descended the village tree and arrived at the tables on the forest floor for supper, Mara groaned. Gone were the days of everyone eating around a campfire or all around one table. Of all the things in Ambergrove, the thing she least missed—besides Aengar—was standing up on that accursed dais *with* Aengar and giving some sort of speech or being ogled at while she ate.

There was a difference to the table on the dais, however. Another table had been brought up and five seats were added. With a sharp sting of horror, Mara realized they were the last to arrive. Keena sat at the edge of the dais, and the Oracle sat in the seat closest to her. Next to the Oracle was Freya, then Rhodi, then Cora and Aengar. At the other end was Teddy, Kara, Kina and Loli, and two empty seats near the center for Kip and Mara.

Thankfully, she was able to settle into her seat without incident, surprised and grateful that Aengar hadn't required a speech before supper. However, as soon as the meal was over, Aengar stood with the microphone stick and announced, "The rangerling will now tell us the story of her trial so the Oracle may decide if she be worthy as the Ranger."

*Oh, so that's why the Oracle is here,* Mara thought. *Like I haven't told this story enough.*

Kip gently squeezed her hand as she stood to move to the center of the dais. She looked out over all the people in the village, took a deep breath, and then told her story. As each of her companions entered the story, she pointed them out where they sat on the dais. When she told of Finn, she sent out a silent word for his safety, unsure of his fate after weeks apart. When she told of Gaele and her banishment to Earth, there was a collective gasp. When she finished the story, she held up her left arm to show the Mark given to her by Aeun.

Roaring cheers echoed through the forest. Aengar took the microphone stick back from Mara and handed it to the Oracle. The forest floor went immediately silent. The Oracle smiled and said quietly, "It is pretty clear that young Mara has far exceeded the bonds of her trial. By Aeun's blessing, she has earned the title of Ranger." There were muffled cheers, but great pains were taken to remain quiet in respect of the Oracle.

She continued, "As Aeun told our Ranger, the world has changed. The wheel of fate is ever turning, and it is up to us to face what it brings."

She handed the stick across Freya to Rhodi, who said, "Forest dwarves, it is time for two special events. Foremost, the Ceremony of the Forest will commence tomorrow before the evening meal. Mara will take up the mantle of Ranger. Secondly, as she told us in her tale of her trial, she and the gnome, Kip, have decided to become lifemates. Out of respect for master Kip, we will hold both the Earthfasting and Rootfasting ceremonies tomorrow at midday."

Before Mara had the chance to ask what any of those ceremonies were, the forest erupted into cheers and tables began filing out as the villagers returned to their homes.

⊕

It was customary that couples be separated the night before a fasting, just as it was customary for the groom not to see the bride before the wedding on Earth. Kip spent the night in the second room while Mara stayed in her own, but that was the only way they would be parted for many days to come.

They were awoken by the smell of sausage gravy—Mara's favorite. She jumped out of bed and rushed out of her room to find Kip already sitting at the counter talking to Ashroot.

"Ash! Where have you been? Did you talk to your dad?" Mara asked excitedly, giving her friend a brief hug before sitting down for her own breakfast.

Ashroot told them what had happened with her father while they ate, and Mara peppered her with questions. Finally, Ashroot reminded Mara that it was about time for the morning exercise on the training grounds, and

Mara dragged Kip down there with her. She was excited to see that Teddy had done the same with Kara and Kina.

When the exercise was over, Mara found herself bodily steered by a gaggle of women to the showerhouse and then away to a lower room in the village tree. To her relief, most of the women then filtered back out, so only Freya, Kina, Kara, and Cora remained.

Cora steered Mara to a chair and pressed her into it.

"What is this?" Mara asked.

Behind her, Freya explained, "I came from Earth, Mara, just like you. At my fasting, I wanted to follow the Earth traditions as well as those of Ambergrove." Freya stepped around the chair and held out a beautiful, white dress. "One of those things is the dress, and a common thing is wearing the dress your mother wore. Well ... this is the dress I wore."

The dress itself was white, but embroidered on it were many different colors. Mara suspected the woman had sewn it herself. An intricate Celtic knot of red, orange, green, brown, blue, and light blue bordered the hem, the wide neck, and the bell sleeves. Small symbols in red, orange, and blues cascaded up the dress from the hem, and a belt of vines and green leaves was settled at the waist. It was just beautiful.

The women helped her dress, and Freya refitted the dress for Mara's figure, and then Kara brushed Mara's hair. When she was ready, Freya gave her a kiss on the cheek and led her out the door, where Teddy stood ready to offer his arm. As Mara approached the village center and saw Kip standing up on the dais, she realized he'd been kidnapped and dressed as well.

Kip beamed at her as Teddy walked her up to the dais. When she stepped up beside Kip, Aengar led Rhodi to the center to officiate the ceremony.

The Earthfasting was the gnomish ceremony of bonding, and it was the easiest of all the other ceremonies to incorporate into the Rootfasting. Rhodi began by having Mara and Kip join hands and explaining the ceremonies to them. Mara could feel Kip reassuringly rubbing her hands with his thumbs as Rhodi began.

"We are gathered here this midday to join not only two people, but two people of vastly different worlds. Young Mara and young Kip have been on quite the journey together. They have become bonded together so strongly that not even Easha could tear them apart. In reverence to the gods, they will be joined as lifemates in the ceremonies of both our people."

Teddy stepped up onto the dais with a small table. He placed it between Mara and Kip and placed a pot, a cup of dirt, a seed, and a small knife on top of it. As Mara looked over the items in confusion, Teddy retreated, and Rhodi began again, picking up the cup of dirt and the knife.

"An Earthfasting is a bond sealed by the earth itself. To be joined in the earth, Kip and Mara will join themselves with it," she said.

Kip flipped Mara's hands palms up and placed his right hand above her left and her right hand above his left. Before she could so much as gasp, Rhodi had sliced across her palm with the knife. It wasn't deep, but it was deep enough to hurt and deep enough that blood immediately dripped from it. Rhodi did the same with Kip's, and then she held both their hands over the pot as she poured the dirt into it, mixing it with their blood. Next, Rhodi picked up the seed and handed it to Mara and the remaining dirt to Kip.

"Do as I explain," Rhodi whispered.

Mara nodded.

Kip nodded.

They looked into each other's eyes as Rhodi went on. "Rootfasting requires a couple to take root together. They are beginning a new life as one, so must one new life begin. One puts a seed into a pot," Mara placed the seed in, "and that seed will begin to grow as the other provides it with the safety in which it must grow." Kip put the remaining dirt in the pot, and then Rhodi grabbed both their right hands and placed them palm down on top of the mound of dirt. "In the Ranger's case, this is an Aeunna tree. If the couple's fasting has the approval of our goddess, Aeun, then—"

A sprout forced its way between Kip and Mara's fingers, stretched itself up until it was a few feet high, and then butterflies burst out of its leaves and fluttered through the clearing.

"Then, well, that," Rhodi said. Laughter rippled through the crowd. "These two have been fasted. They are now lifemates in the eyes of the gods and are joined forever."

Mara had no idea how long she had been crying, but as she looked into Kip's eyes—her Kip, her lifemate, who would be hers forever—she saw his were red from crying as well. He smiled as she bent down and kissed him. The gasps and murmuring around her told her the kiss was not an Ambergrove custom, but she didn't care, and she hoped she'd never have to let go.

⊕

Shortly after the ceremony, Mara returned the dress to Freya and spent the day hand-in-hand with Kip, giving him a tour of Aeunna. But, to her chagrin, before long, the light was beginning to fade into the trees, and it was time to prepare for the evening meal—and another dress.

This one, she had seen before. The ceremonial dress she'd worn on her second day, the one she had so shamefully hitched up, was the dress she was meant to wear for the Ceremony of the Forest. It was a soft, green dress with embroidered accents of light and dark green—vines, leaves, and woodland creatures. She donned the dress, tied her hair back in her new, triskele bun cage, and then walked down to the evening meal with Kip. This time Kip was the one to escort her up to the dais and pass her over to Aengar, who stood with Cora and Rhodi beside him.

As soon as she stopped beside him, Aengar raised the stick and called for silence. He procured a little, metal whistle from his robes and blew it, and then Keena came gliding down from above. People moved needlessly to make room for the dragonwolf, but she settled herself delicately by the dais and lowered her head so Aengar could help the Oracle to step down.

He guided the Oracle to stand in front of Mara and then handed her the stick, kneeling and holding her arm to support her as he did. The Oracle smiled sweetly and peered around at the villagers before she spoke.

"Your rangerling came to you a frightened child from Earth. A child whose heart and roots were here in Ambergrove. She went on a journey, proving herself a true forest dwarf, a protector of others, and a true servant of Aeunna. Kneel, Mara," the Oracle commanded.

As Mara knelt, Cora stepped forward with a small pillow. On the pillow lay circlet made entirely of one emerald, carved to look like leaves and vines. The Oracle took the circlet and held it above Mara's head. "Mara,

Dragonwolf of Aeunna, do you swear to serve, protect, and lead the people of Aeunna justly and with love for as long as you are the Ranger?"

"I do," Mara declared.

"Do you swear to protect the forests, and the animals within them, from harm from outsiders or otherwise?"

"I do."

"Do you swear to take care of the forest dwarves as a mother would her children?"

"I do."

The Oracle set the circlet on Mara's head and commanded her to stand and face the people. "The vow of the forest has been given. To the people of Aeunna, I present Mara, the Dragonwolf, daughter of the Badger, and the new Ranger of Aeunna!"

Mara knew that around her everyone was cheering. She heard their muffled voices, but in that moment, she ran a hand along the silver bracelet she'd worn since her sixteenth birthday, and she looked up to the sky.

*Mara, Ranger of Aeunna, like my father.*

✥

It had been many centuries since Oesha, goddess of wisdom, had sent her wisdom out to all of Ambergrove. From the moment her magic had returned and the doorway to Earth had been closed, she'd used all her effort to prepare herself for what would be needed the night Mara became the Ranger of Aeunna. The night she told the world.

The old crone leaned over the pool on her island and felt a ripple in the earth as the decree was made. It had come. Mara was the Ranger. She took a deep breath, and her violet eyes clouded as she extended herself to every corner of the world, appearing in dreams and visions to every single person at one time.

*I am Oesha, goddess of wisdom,* the goddess said in the vision. *I have appeared to you with news that affects all of Ambergrove. Just now, the Ranger of Aeunna has completed the Ceremony of the Forest.* The image flashed of Mara kneeling, receiving the circlet, and then standing and smiling.

*The Ranger earned this title by banishing the corruptions of Earth from Ambergrove*

239

*forever. The doorway has been sealed, and that time is over. In ridding the world of the plague in the forbidden lands, Mara has done something better still. Magic has come back to Ambergrove.* She showed images of dryads and naiads, shapeshifting creatures, and a woman shooting fire from her hands.

*The Lost Age is over. When the magic returned, so too did the regularities of Ambergrove. Seasons will change, and with them, lives. The fourth age of Ambergrove has begun. When the sun rises tomorrow, it will be 2 Eoure, of the first year of the fourth age. Be prepared for new magic and new life.*

# 23 TUIFE, OF THE FIFTH YEAR

Mara had long since stopped counting her birthdays, but this one was important for another reason. It marked seven years since she'd left Earth never to return. Seven years since her father had written a letter to her, to be given to the Oracle when Mara arrived in Ambergrove and returned to Mara when she was ready to read it.

At last, the Oracle had decided she was ready.

It was a shame that coincided with Keena's absence, as the dragonwolf had flown to Questhaven to visit Howl and would likely not be returning for a while. It would be such a slog to go all the way up all those stairs in her condition, especially after being able to just fly Keena up there for so long.

"What are you thinking about?"

Mara was awoken from her reverie by her lifemate. They were lying in bed, having not yet found the gumption to get up and begin the climb. He snaked a hand over her belly and gave her a gentle squeeze.

"I think you know," Mara told him.

"Ah, well. I'll be coming with you, so I'll help you up there. Though I don't see how, if she could get you a message to tell you to come get your da's letter, she couldn't just send the letter down to you," Kip said sleepily.

"I told you, the Oracle plays by rules no one else does. She does what she wants."

"That's silly."

"Are you going to be the one to tell her that?" Mara asked, peering over at him.

"Yep. Sure will," he said as he snuggled against her.

"Right, then. Let's go," she said, tapping on his arm.

"What?" he asked pitifully. "But ... oh, fine."

Kip pouted as he stood, shuffled around to Mara's side of the bed, and grasped at her elbows to help her stand. They dressed and went out to the kitchen to have their breakfast. Ashroot had gone back to bringing Mara her meals, like she had before they left Aeunna, but she had taken on her own duties in recent years, finally following in her father's footsteps, and Mara had done a lot of sleeping in. So, she and Kip ate the fruit and muffins that were sitting on the counter for them, and then they headed out onto the pegs of the village tree.

The Oracle needed some supplies from the village, which they were supposed to pick up on the way so Kip could haul them up to her, but they were meant to be delivered to the village tree by then. They weren't to see the Oracle without them, so they had to go on a hunt first.

"Loli!" Kip hollered. "Loli! Where is that boy?"

"Relax. We'll find him. I'm sure he hasn't gone far," Mara said. "He's probably out training."

"Young 'in is old enough to have the all-day trains, but he's not out there," came a voice from behind them.

Cora approached, with Rhodi and Aengar at her heels. The three forest dwarves, who had before been the village council, became Mara's official advisers after she'd become the Ranger. Their approach couldn't mean anything good. More delays before she made it up to the Oracle.

"What is it? What do you need?" she asked them.

Aengar stepped forward. "The dwarves at Faolan are reporting attacks on the dryads, likely from Marauder's Cove."

"They are counting on us here in Aeunna to protect them," Rhodi breathed.

Mara sighed and rubbed her temples before replying.

"As they should. For now, send supplies to Faolan and have Faolan send an emissary to Marauder's Cove. I will confer with Kernunos later today to see how he would like the dryads to be helped," she told them.

Aengar and Rhodi nodded. "I will pass it along, Ranger," Aengar said.

Mara turned to Cora. "You said Loli wasn't out training. How do you know? Do you know where he is?"

Cora chuckled and shook her head. "Boy was determined to do a good job. He said his uncle Kip shouldn't have to bear the weight while also carrying you. Took those things all the way up to the Oracle himself," she said.

"Himself?" Kip snapped. "The wee fool! How could you let him, Cora?"

"Because the lad has an air of the adventurer in him, and he can handle it. Plus—he's not my son. And he's grown, Kip. He's not the wee boy you left in the Gnome Lands when you first went off with Mara. The lad's nearly ten years old now. He can handle a walk up the village tree," Cora explained defensively.

Kip opened his mouth to retort, but Mara stuck a hand out in front of his face and said, "Anyway, Cora! Have you seen Freya this morning? How is she doing with Korena?"

"The lass has been just fine. Don't you fret," Cora said, giving Mara a pat on the shoulder. "And Kara arrived safely in Nimeda to visit your grandmother. She sent word. Anyhow, you two need to start your way up to the Oracle if you're going to make it back down before the evening meal!" Cora said with a wink.

Mara glared at her, but with a sigh, she and Kip began the long ascent to the Oracle's home.

⊕

They met Loli at the very top, sitting on the platform and waiting for them to arrive. As soon as he saw them, he sprang into action, jumping forward and helping Kip get Mara up to the top.

"Sorry, Uncle Kip," Loli said quickly. "I thought it would be helpful for me to just come up here myself, but then after I got up here I thought that maybe you would have looked for me and wouldn't know where to go."

He took a deep, gasping breath and turned to Mara. "And I came all the way up here because I thought maybe I would be able to see the Oracle. I haven't seen her since I was really little, you know, but then I got up here and I ... panicked."

"You didn't panic on the way up here, boy?" Kip asked somewhat sternly.

"All you have to do is look up instead of down, Uncle Teddy," Loli joked.

Kip glared at him. At near ten years old, the boy was just independent enough to make trouble. Kip opened his mouth to speak, but Mara, rested a hand in his. "I think what Uncle Teddy is trying to say is that it was dangerous, and we were concerned for you. You'll have another chance to see the Oracle."

"You'd better get in there, though, hadn't you, Auntie Mara?" Loli said.

"Yes, and you'd better get your hide safely back down this tree and to Teddy and Freya's house to help your mother," Kip said. "Go on, go on."

Loli grinned and stuck out his tongue before scurrying down the stairs.

Mara walked up to the door, took a deep breath, and went right in. The Oracle sat in her large chair as she always did. This time, when Mara entered, she immediately made the sort of tea the Oracle liked—an Aeunnan oolong, which was sweet and almost floral with a hint of toastiness—only sitting down and speaking to the woman when the cup was ready.

"You are learning, aren't you, Ranger? Something is gained with a little age," the old woman said with a grin. "How do you fare?"

"I'm a little worse for wear, but not much could keep me from coming up here with the news you gave," Mara replied pointedly.

"Ah, yes." The Oracle held up a sealed letter, yellowed with age.

Mara reached out for it, but the Oracle pulled her hand back. "What?" Mara asked.

"You need to know something first. Your father is a man. Nothing more. Just as anyone can grow up to be a villain, anyone can grow up to be a hero. You decide which way you go, and you decide what being the hero means," the Oracle said.

"Uh ... okay. Thanks, Oracle," Mara replied.

The old woman chuckled. "Alright. You're not open to a talk right now.

I get it." The Oracle handed Mara the letter. "Just go out onto the landing and read this in the fresh air."

Mara nodded vigorously and stood, heading out and away from the Oracle's home without another word. As she stepped out into the sun, she saw Kip standing on the landing, looking out across the forest. She walked over to him and held up the letter as he turned. He snaked an arm around her waist.

"Are you ready for this?" he asked gently.

"No, but it's time anyway," she said.

With a long sigh, she broke the seal, slipped out the letter, and began to read:

> *Dearest Mara,*
>
> *I wish I could have told you about Ambergrove before now. About Aeunna. I wish I could have comforted you when you woke up there without us, but you had family there. You had Teddy and Freya.*
>
> *I know by now you have completed your Ranger trial. I have no doubt in my mind that you'll do it and do it well. I told the Oracle to give this to you when you were ready. When you would understand. You see, Mara, I did care for your mother when I was younger, and I wanted Teddy to think that I followed her solely out of love, but that wasn't it. The Oracle told me that Ambergrove would be plunged into darkness by someone from Aeunna unless a prophecy was fulfilled. Unless the child of a Ranger, born on Earth, returned to Ambergrove to become the Ranger.*
>
> *The only way for me to save my home and all the people in it, people I loved who depended on me, was to leave them. You know Teddy well by now. How well would he have taken that? So, I told him I wanted to be with Kenda. I told him I wanted to go. I came here, and I built a life with her, had children, and watched you grow, knowing that one day, I would have to lose at least one of you. It broke my heart. It's breaking now just thinking about never seeing you again, never telling you anything except what's in this letter.*
>
> *Just know that everything I have done since becoming the Ranger, I have done for the people I love. I only wanted to protect you and to give you a good life. But you've been the Ranger for a while by know, and*

*you should understand the bond and responsibility there is to the people. I hope you understand why I had to give up what I loved.*

*Mara, life in Aeunna is a good one. If what the Oracle has told me is true, your actions will affect all of Ambergrove. There's a bright future ahead for you, and future generations will come to turn the wheel of fate further and further still. My heart soars to think of it. Even still, you have a responsibility to all your children, to all the people of Ambergrove. One day, you will have to do what's best for them, even if it rips your heart out to do it. Such is life. Such is love.*

*I love you, my dear child, with everything that's in me. Know that while you are gone from my sight, you will never be gone from my heart. I will think of you every single day until the end of my days. Above all, I will think of the wonderful person you have become. There is a strength in you that can move mountains. That will move mountains.*

*Believe in yourself. Believe in your family. Believe in your people. Know that I am so, so proud of you.*

*Dad*

Mara pressed the letter to her chest and looked out over Aeunna. She could see the people bustling about below. Her people. She felt Kip's reassuring hands around her waist, and she slid her other hand down to rest on her full belly. This was her home, her family, and her children would be born into a world of magic and wonder. Mara smiled and leaned into Kip's embrace, content.

TALES OF AMBERGROVE

# FAMILY GREEN

## A WHEEL OF FATE BOARD GAME

A playable version of Toren's family exercise and board game is available for free download. Scan the above QR code with your phone or tablet or visit www.talesofambergrove.com/tales/wheel-of-fate/ to access game files.

Thank you for being part of the adventure.

—H. T. Martineau

CPSIA information can be obtained
at www.ICGtesting.com
Printed in the USA
BVHW080928010323
659432BV00001B/6

9 781665 560412